Pra
Cole Alpaugh

THE SPY'S LITTLE ZONBI

Finalist, 2014 ForeWord Magazine Book of the Year Award

"Forget James Bond. I'd much rather spend my time with Chase Allen, the idealistic journalist-turned-government spook at the center of Cole Alpaugh's outlandishly entertaining new novel, *The Spy's Little Zonbi*."
—Josh McAuliffe, *The Scranton Times-Tribune*

"Imaginative. Funny. 3D Characters that come to life on the page and leave you wanting more. *The Spy's Little Zonbi* is Cole Alpaugh's best work to date!"
—Michelle Hessling, Publisher, *The Wayne Independent*

"*The Spy's Little Zonbi* defied my expectations. It is at times gruesome. It is at times heartless. Cole Alpaugh's use of dark humor and timing is impeccable .... Part *The Girl with the Dragon Tattoo* and part *The World According to Garp*, Alpaugh's latest offering is an exhilarating read that I highly recommend."
—Ann Schmidt, MLS, The Public Library of Cincinnati and Hamilton County

"*The Spy's Little Zonbi* is a clever and sometimes sad novel about the lunacy of the modern world. It is a vivid, emotional, and imaginative read."
—Olivia Patel, Redbridge Central Library, London

THE TURTLE-GIRL FROM EAST PUKAPUKA

Finalist, 2013 Next Generation Indie Book Awards
Finalist, 2013 ForeWord Magazine Book of the Year Award

"The book is playful and comic in its creation of... misunderstandings and coincidences. As their stories unfold and intersect, one comes to believe the island is indeed paradise, as Jesus plays a heroic role and the cannibal, Albino Paul, the shark god, and the birds play out a finale resounding with echoes of myth."
—ForeWord Magazine

"*Doctor Dolittle* meets *Lost*.... interesting and colorful cast of zany characters on a crash course with fate."
—Michelle Hessling, Publisher, *The Wayne Independent*

"Teeming with outlandish scenarios and bizarre yet deeply compelling characters, *The Turtle-Girl from East Pukapuka* is a veritable feast for lovers of playfully absurd fiction. Who knew cannibalism could be this much fun?"
—Josh McAuliffe, *The Scranton Times-Tribune*

"Would a god really eat his own boogers? He might in this wonderful, crazy, non-linear novel filled with a cast of characters floating in and out of a literary universe peopled with pirates, South Sea Islanders named Dante, Jesus, and Butter, and a Loggerhead turtle with cosmic consciousness. Controlled craziness at its best, this novel dazzles with its stylistic inventiveness. "
—Jack Remick, author of *Blood* and The California Quartet series

"Lyrical and yet wonderfully warped, if *The Lord of the Flies* had been written by Kurt Vonnegut, you would have some

idea of what to expect from Alpaugh's second novel. Heavily outfitted with wry humor and cutting sarcasm, this unique tale doesn't pause for a breath. You are swept into *The Turtle-Girl from East Pukapuka* with the same energy as the tsunami that sparks the critical events leading the reader across the vast South Pacific and at breakneck speeds along a downhill race course, all headed to a place in the afterlife known as Happa Now .... A highly entertaining read."
—Hua Lin, MLS, Los Angeles Public Library

"Butter is a six-year-old Pacific Islander who cares for wounded creatures; Dante is a hot-shot downhill racer; Jesus Dobby runs a scavenging barge; Ratu & Jope are pirates and Abilone is a cannibal. All these characters meet and while it is not always pretty, it is pretty entertaining. I quite enjoyed the ride. Alpaugh reminds me of James Morrow with more gore and explosions. He has created a fairy tale with mythic figures and classic characters; and an assumptive logic to the cosmos that allows him to end the story without tying everything up with a bow. *The Turtle-Girl from East Pukapuka* made me laugh and made me cringe, but most importantly it made me think about the world order and how to spend the time we are here."
—Uncle Barb's Blog

"Alpaugh's words dance in the mind and tug on the heart."
—Regan Leigh, writer/blogger

THE BEAR IN A MUDDY TUTU

"There's a story inside, both charming and heartbreaking."
—Alex Adams, author of *White Horse* (Atria Books/Simon & Schuster)

"If you enjoy fast-paced, quirky reads filled with offbeat, colorful characters and a touch of sorrow draped in the

colorful striping of a circus tent, I think you'll enjoy *The Bear in a Muddy Tutu*."
—Damien Walters Grintalis, author of *Ink*

"Pick up *The Bear in a Muddy Tutu* if you enjoy taking a literary journey that is twisted, peopled by characters who are social misfits, caught up in events that range from bizarrely tragic to merely sad. Reminded me in a way of *A Confederacy of Dunces*."
—Molly Rodgers, Library Director, Wayne County Public Library

"I'd recommend it if you want a charming, bizarre tale with a satisfying, fate-driven ending. It reads a little like Christopher Moore but with more heart. It's fanciful, beautiful, and escapist to the core."
—Mercedes M. Yardley, author of *Beautiful Sorrows*

"A delightful read full of wonderfully twisted characters trying to muddle through this thing we call life ... a must-read."
—LK Gardner-Griffie, author of the two-time Pearson Prize Teen Choice Award-winning Misfit McCabe series

"If you are looking for a 'big top' read with lots of heart and laughs, and characters you can sit down with to listen to their story for a spell, magic, whimsy, and dancing bears, then look no further than Cole Alpaugh's *The Bear in a Muddy Tutu*."
—Shannon Yarbrough, author of *Stealing Wishes*

"From the first page to the last Cole Alpaugh had my attention. His zany and colorful characters and style of writing puts me in mind of one of my favorite authors, John Irving. I suspect that I have now found my next new favorite author."
—Michelle Hessling, Publisher, *The Wayne Independent*

DASH
IN THE
BLUE PACIFIC

DASH
IN THE
BLUE PACIFIC

—

Cole Alpaugh

cp

coffeetownpress

Seattle, WA

9077371794

coffeetownpress

Coffeetown Press
PO Box 70515
Seattle, WA 98127

For more information go to: www.coffeetownpress.com
www.colealpaugh.com

Cover design by Sabrina Sun

Dash in the Blue Pacific
Copyright © 2015 by Cole Alpaugh

ISBN: 978-1-60381-252-8 (Trade Paper)
ISBN: 978-1-60381-253-5 (eBook)

Library of Congress Control Number: 2014951786

Printed in the United States of America
10 9 8 7 6 5 4 3 2 1

For Kari and Decker

Acknowledgments

SPECIAL THANKS TO Phillip Vaiimene of Avarua, Rarotonga, for helping with so many small details. Thanks to Tammy and Michael Winser who gave us a real volcano we'll soon call home. My love and gratitude to Kat, Tylea, Amy, and Regan for making me believe in invisible things. My deep appreciation to Ellin O'Hora for teaching a special game that will last a lifetime. And my thanks to Catherine Treadgold, the most patient and gifted editor on this extraordinarily blue planet.

Also by the Author:

The Bear in a Muddy Tutu

The Turtle-Girl from East Pukapuka

The Spy's Little Zonbi

In the Beginning

—

THE VOLCANO BECKONED with pale smoke that curled into slender fingers at its far reach. The giant brown teat ascended from the blue sea, its milky ribbon spilling across the late-day sky. It was irresistible, despite a fuel needle dancing near the dead zone and a sun barely two fists above the horizon.

"We have time, mate. One pass ain't gonna hurt, but keep her nice and wide. I don't wanna spoil the surprise in case somebody's home." Red's hands itched from nervous energy, jagged knife scars turning crimson as he kneaded a shiny spot into his soiled khakis. He lived for the hunt. Paydays were sweet, but it was the hunt that got the blood pumping. It made the hair over your collar stand up and put the taste of copper on your tongue's fat end.

The man at the helm steered through the heavy rollers, white water kicking off the bow and spitting across the windscreen. Wending in and out of the volcano's shadow, they made their way counterclockwise around the teardrop-shaped island.

Red could sniff out a nest from twenty klicks, and sure enough, he was right on target with this honey hole. Rising and falling on the deep-water side of a protective reef were four canoes.

"We got savages," he said, not relinquishing the field glasses to the reaching hand of the man in the helm seat. "I don't see weapons, just bare-ass fishermen in dugouts."

Red glanced behind him to size up the western sky. "They ain't seen us. Leave the sun on our backs, and let 'em show us where the reef break is. You feelin' like a big bad wolf, Slim?"

Slim chuckled. "You *know* I'm feeling like a big bad wolf."

"I sure would like to find me a Little Red Riding Hood. You think there's a sweet young bird stashed away in them trees?"

Slim drummed the boat's metal steering wheel. "Only one way to know, Boss."

Binoculars back to his face, Red scanned the treetops for signs of cook fires. Four boats meant a village of at least a few dozen adults, which gave fair odds of finding high-value quarry. He hocked through a side window and shook a smoke between his teeth. The market for boys was bone dry, and that was fine and dandy in his book. Boys were a pain in the arse, always with half a mind to jump overboard when they weren't trying to sink their pointy teeth into anything you left close. And he wanted to puke from dealing with ratbag Euro businessmen who sweated like pigs and stank of perfume. He'd like to gut one or two of those slimy fuckwits if not for the rep it would cause.

Girls were a different enterprise, with their easy fear and the way they clung, once land was out of sight. The lost pups were ripe for training, and it was a wonder they got them to port in one piece. More than one little sprog had fed the fish after his boys got carried away, but that shit didn't pay the bills and he put his foot down hard.

Red watched the fishermen at work. In the undulating waves, their narrow skiffs appeared and disappeared, rocking tip to tail in what looked to be a dodgy spot. Too many hungry tiger sharks to be out in heavy waters. Not in dinky, hand-carved paddle boats, anyway. You had to be mighty brave or mighty dumb.

A flock of circling gulls swooped in close when the fishermen dropped to their knees. The four wiry torsos twisted in fast rhythm, as if moving to the same music. "They're hauling lines," Red hollered, then cleared his throat to calm himself. "Let's saddle up, but keep the hardware low. We'll go in friendly 'til I'm sure what we got, but I don't reckon anything more than spears and arrows. I'll take the wheel."

Red flicked his cig and shimmied onto the cracked vinyl. The engine was a low rumble as they came about, the sea below the bow turning to soot in their hulking shadow. Less than an hour until dark, and these backwater shithole folks were known to get crafty with their home-field advantage once the sun fell under.

"Nice and easy, girl." He inched the throttle, feeding the engine and squeezing the gap. Three hundred meters, give or take, and still out of earshot. No need for introductions just yet. The sun kept them invisible as the primitive crafts fell into a single line, paddling south and then hooking a sharp turn through the reef opening. "Bingo. There's the front door, thank you very much."

Red kept tabs on the depth finder as the skiffs angled north to skirt the coast. There was plenty of draft, a steady five meters after they sliced into the protected water. Beyond the sagging whip aerial was a jetliner reflecting sun on the cold highway ferrying Aussies and Yanks. The volcano's upper third remained visible over waving palms. Smoke above the cone blinked orange, as though this might not be such a habitable place before too long. "Hello, Mother," he whispered. "I think you have a present for me."

Losing sight of the fishermen wasn't a worry. They'd beach in a cove or along the shallows, and he and his six men would roll on up with how-do-you-do grins, like they were new neighbors coming by with a plate of jelly slices. And it would be damn fine to stretch his limbs on solid ground. The world tilted off center when you hadn't sent a soul to heaven or hell for too long a stretch.

"Let's keep focus, boys, before the good light gets scarce," he called over his shoulder. The 44-foot Waveney was American made, but outfitted for the Australian Coast Guard. Its V6 Cummins growled like a bear, so there was no way of truly sneaking up on anything with a pulse. "Shoulder your rifles and tilt up your brims. I don't wanna spook the natives and cause any unnecessary bushwhacking."

There was a decent enough channel twenty meters out, although they took a nasty scrape coming up on the men hauling their boats onto the sandy scrub. Each looked up, eyes narrow, skin reflecting the late day glow. The fishermen stood frozen in mid heave as Red leaned the painted steel against the island's stone hip and throttled down. The engine cut out with a wet belch.

"Candy from a baby," he sang under his breath, turning from the instruments and shouldering the Kalashnikov he kept racked in a dry spot over the visor.

One of his men already had wet knees tying them off when Red stepped up to the gunwale and gave his best aw-shucks shrug to the not-so-certain looking locals, two standing in drooping, western-style underpants the color of their skin. Each skiff sported a bloody mound of silver-bellied fish, but the only cutting tool in sight was a rusty blade, nothing more than a pen knife. And while some heavy-handed coercion was always entertaining, the clock was ticking.

"G'day, gents." Red gave a cordial wink, then pulled a handkerchief from a back pocket good and slow, a magician beginning a well-practiced trick. He lifted his bush hat and wiped away beaded sweat. He knew the effect his shock of red hair had on these sorts. What once got his bum handed to him in the schoolyard now made him a god. The thought was a hoot and a half, but these simple fucks would bow down to a turd pile if it steamed just so. "I was gonna ask how they was biting, but just looky there. You sure got into them today."

Red measured their faces as they turned toward each other. The man on the far left—the tallest and broadest at the shoulders—jabbered to the others in some dipshit bird talk. Good so far. None looked ready to sprint off to their mud huts to scatter the tribe into this godforsaken jungle. Red hefted a boot onto the rail and rubbed his jaw whiskers, rifle butt tight against his shoulder blades. It was a quiet spot away from the breakers crashing out over the reef, and the night critters hadn't started their usual chatter. He turned his ear to the slight breeze coming from a black opening in the canopy beyond the fishermen. It was a tunnel hacked out of thick greenery. A lesser hunter might have mistaken the high-pitched sounds for feral pigs or those quick little giant-eyed monkeys. But Red recognized the distant clamor of blissful children, a choir of ten or more angels engaged in some game or sport.

The hunter's mouth turned wet enough to wipe one corner. He took a deep breath of salty air and leaned his weight forward.

"Maybe one of you blokes has a map of these fine and lovely parts?" Red showed the four men a toothy smile that he hoped wasn't too wolf-like. Not quite yet. "To be honest, we got a little lost on our way to Grandma's house."

Chapter 1

———

DASH DID CALCULATIONS in his head. He guessed they had about four minutes to live. Not that he was an aeronautical expert—or any kind of expert, for that matter—but sitting alone in the upright position, he had nothing better to do after the engines went silent. When he'd attempted small talk, the elderly woman in the aisle seat had responded with an unfriendly grunt.

He shielded his eyes and craned for a view out the oval window, searching for flames and sniffing the air for trouble. Perfume and sweat. Someone close was a smoker. Setting fire to model airplanes as a kid seemed less cool now that he was aboard a full-size jetliner about to crash.

He had rubbed the fingertip pads that turned rough from pungent glue those summer days, hands trembling as he tied string to one wing and then held a lighter to the tail. He turned fast circles, flaming goo spraying across the lawn, black smoke curling into the trees.

The cabin speaker was full of static, and then a mouth came close to the microphone. *"Cindy?"*

Dash looked at his row mate. She was too old to be 'Cindy.'

Cynthia, maybe. The woman caught him staring and glared back. He tried a smile.

"Are you there?"

The massive plane had become an unwieldy glider six miles above the Pacific Ocean. Dash kneaded both ears, worked his jaw to pop the right. He'd been dozing when the captain had first clicked on his mic to report in a silky, overnight disc jockey voice that they should expect light headwinds and an early arrival. Local temperature in Sydney would be a balmy thirty degrees Celsius, perfect weather for a chilled mai tai or a little sex on the beach, ha ha. A real hoot if they recover the black box. Maybe not replay that sound bite at the press conference.

"Please come forward."

No velvet edge to the voice. Maybe even a hint of desperation.

"Cindy?"

Dash watched heads turn, but there was no Cindy, or she didn't want any part of this. Nobody got up to pretend to be Cindy.

The relative quiet following hours of mechanical howling created its own dimension of noise. Dash shifted in his seat, tilted his chin, and whispered the lullaby his increasingly bat-shit crazy mother had been singing while she fed cubed tofu and miniature pickles to her porcelain dolls during his last visit. She cooed and sang, only knowing half the words, filling in the blanks with whispered obscenities—proof nothing had changed since he was a boy.

"Papa's gonna buy you a piece of ass," Dash sang.

His row mate pursed her lips, wrinkles everywhere.

He'd been sent to the principal's office in second grade. He was seven, and it had been his mother's word against his.

And then Sarah's icy breath took over. Scented puffs of frozen moisture contained news that she couldn't wait to be married. We'll live happily ever after, a fairy tale everyone will envy. They'll wish they were us. Imagine the gifts, the cash, and all the new … the new stuff! Love will be easy. We'll honeymoon someplace exotic, warm.

Thirty degrees Celsius. Balmy enough for string bikinis. Sarah should be on this doomed fucking plane. Mom and her both.

There were grumbles from his dead father, another visit in spirit only, but Dash wasn't ready to listen to the old man's excuses. Prick. He tuned his father out and sat up, allowed the buzz from five hundred passengers to smother whatever his father wanted to report from the grave.

The voice: "*I can't.*"

Can't find Cindy? Can't live without her? Can't die without her?

Cloud tops attracted his attention, a calming distraction. Puffy white things on the other side of the scratched window formed an entire encyclopedia's worth of farm and zoo creatures in boundless quilted serenity.

Dash tapped the window with a middle knuckle. "A one-armed zombie." He looked at the lady in the aisle seat and winked, hoping to cheer her up, work his way back on her good side while there was still time. No more swearing. But her eyes were too wide open and her mouth formed a lipstick-red circle. Seatbelt lights were flashing bright yellow reminders all around. He looked back out at the cloud. "It's riding a unicycle."

Someone close muffled a sneeze and another asked what was happening. A gorgeous flight attendant jogged up the aisle. Dash watched her long fingers brush each headrest, her nails bright white flashes. Authoritative and compassionate, she provoked a longing in him such as what he'd felt for his fourth grade teacher and the trooper who last handed him a speeding ticket. No nametag to solve the Cindy mystery, so he was left to imagine the smell of her neck, and how her rounded spots trapped beneath the slick material of her blouse might feel. Her crisp blue uniform disappeared through the curtain

separating coach from the rich people. Only a single strand of
blond hair was left behind, wafting toward the carpeted floor.

Passengers half rose from their seats, thumbs jamming
overhead call buttons. Click, click, click. Dash looked up at his
own set of controls. There was a reading light, a tiny stream
of forced air that had tickled his palm, and the button that
summoned the flight attendant. He thought of calling back the
pretty woman, maybe tell her about the hair she'd left behind,
how it seemed utterly magical.

"Are you Cindy?" he would ask. "Can you tell me about her?"

One section of the cabin began crying and another prayed,
two rapidly spreading contagions competing for bodies,
gobbling the weak first. Dash, looking out his window at a
butterfly chasing a three-legged giraffe, settled back and tried
to shut them out.

"I've never flown." It was a small voice that came from the
woman too old to be Cindy. The middle seat held a canvas tote
overflowing with wads of bright yarn. A candy color rainbow
of fluff impaled by a set of knitting needles he assumed had
been missed by the screener who confiscated his four dollar
water bottle.

He nodded down to the seat occupied by her supplies. "I'm
on my honeymoon."

There was a heavy bump underneath. A rabbit or slow
moving turtle. Would a cloud leave blood and guts? It forced
simultaneous hiccups from all around. Dash squeezed his
armrest with one hand, rubbed his face with the other.
Perhaps they'd boarded a plane driven by one of those boozed-
up captains who made the nightly news in gritty airport bar
surveillance videos. It was a high-pressure job, but why not
cocaine or some other drug that enhanced concentration and
helped get these giant rubber tires back on solid ground? He
also knew from his recent run of bad luck that the trouble
could be terrorist related, maniacs in clever old lady disguises,
throwing off shawls to stab the flight crew with knitting

needles, screaming how Allah was great.

Dash pushed away thoughts of al Qaeda, let them wander back to the clouds.

"A giant skyscraper," he said, "and an airplane."

The lady scowled.

The plane they were inside was the size of his town's elementary school, with twice the souls on board. He counted both engines a half dozen times. There were probably two more bolted onto the other wing. That made four. He'd heard plenty of stories in which big jetliners landed under the power of a single engine. And these couldn't all be broken. Surely someone put in charge of such an expensive piece of equipment could get one motor to turn over?

Two minutes to live.

Another jolt tilted the nose down, making the seatbelt dig into his hips, and new humps in the floor forced the seats askew like rows of bad teeth. The disconcerting effect was multiplied when oxygen masks dropped from above to hover like dancing spiders.

Dash looked back to his row mate. "Do you need help?"

The old woman shook her head and put it on wrong. The band fitted properly around the back of her stiff hairdo, but the yellow cup covered her throat like a diseased Adam's apple.

Another bump and pieces of the cabin interior shifted, panels separating at their seams. An overhead compartment unlatched and dumped carry-ons into the aisle, where they sat unclaimed. Dash inspected faces near the mess, watched passengers suspiciously eye the bags and then each other. *Someone should fix this; it isn't right. That one's too big. People are selfish. They're not mine. Are they just going to be left there?*

The cries and prayers were muffled as brand new noises commenced.

The seal around Dash's window formed a hissing gap. They were roaring across the heavens with a view only meant for angels. Daredevil angels, with helmets and parachutes in case their wings failed. The sea below was a soiled blue rug frozen in a snapshot. Monstrous oil tankers were mere fly shit specks, nothing more than granules of instant coffee left on the spoon.

Then the plane, rattling through the sky, began its harrowing descent in earnest.

The fuselage against Dash's right shoulder billowed and crackled, making sounds that reminded him of stage hands waving sheet metal to create thunder for dismal scenes. The wall peeled away from one side of his window frame. It produced a harsh sucking noise that drowned out the screams. He put his fingers to the seam and it was as though his thumb found a powerful vacuum nozzle, its suction intense but not painful. Was it eighth grade when his buddies were goofing around after school, smoking stolen butts and bullshitting about clever ways to whack off? Dash secretly attempted the vacuum cleaner method but had gotten stuck, pubic hair ripping out, eyes watering like crazy as he fumbled for the off switch. It had been his only such attempt.

Dash glanced back at the old lady, whose head rocked side to side in an arc, right cheek then the left touching the seat. The mask was still attached to her throat, the cord a hangman's noose. He imagined her leaning forward and executing a horror movie-style full rotation.

"We'll be okay, ma'am, I promise." He kept his voice calm, thumb stuck in the window seam, his own mask dangling untouched. He wanted her to like him, to need him, maybe even love him. "I'm sure this happens all the time. It's probably a drill."

"Ladies and gentlemen, this is your captain." It was the voice of a man maintaining aplomb while hefting a thousand pound weight, a worthy hero. "Please tighten your seatbelts. Put your knees together and feet flat on the floor. I need you to lean forward and brace for impact. God bless us all."

"Impact?" The woman's voice accused Dash. "You said this was a drill."

He should have kept his mouth shut, left sturdier hands in charge of comforting the weak. The silent engines and falling elevator rush had been dead giveaways that things were going all wrong. They were dropping out of the sky like a broken kite.

"I'm sorry."

He reached a hand across, but it was blindly swatted. The woman's eyes were locked on the ceiling, head still moving, lips signing off on a final prayer. Obeying the captain's orders, she lunged forward and grabbed at her bare ankles beneath the hem of her flowered dress. Dash noticed the worn carpet. It was the same blue as the attendant's uniform, but faded where passengers' feet had rested. There were loose threads and rust spots on screws that locked seats in place. The closer his examination, the more tattered it all appeared and the stronger his sense of doom.

The plane rolled and caused a chorus of different notes. Dash was socked in the jaw by the laptop he'd stowed with the magazines and vomit bag. He didn't need the damn computer. He had no work, and no emails to check. What he had was photos on the hard drive to sulk over—thousands—all of him and his fiancée, who was supposed to be in the middle seat. Strike that. She'd have demanded the window, would still have her seat reclined and tray table in the down position, jabbing at the overhead service button for a fresh gin and tonic right that very goddamn second.

The spiteful thoughts made him feel like crap again. Sarah would have joined the harmony of anguish. She was just as human as the lady grabbing her ankles, despite being a treacherous, black-hearted whore.

The already dim cabin lights flickered, and there was a reek of things on fire. Not wood or paper, or even the smell of a flaming model airplane tethered to cotton string on a humid July afternoon. This odor was sharper—hot wires and melting glass—as though electronic things, maybe even his computer, had begun to smolder.

The vibrations intensified, making the screamers stutter. Some of the praying passengers remained upright, maybe not wanting to point their asses at God just yet. A few seemed to be trying to decide if they should scream or pray by doing both. Dash opened his mouth wide, but his ears blessedly popped before he could try screaming or repeating one of the prayers. It was a wonderful release, like waking from a nightmare with perfect clarity, the certainty of being safe.

The tight motion of his cushiony seat was more calming than terrifying, and he turned his attention back to the sucking window gap. It pulled at his hair, tugged at his breath.

"We're going to die." The voice came from down by the floor. The lady's face was turned to Dash, her mask gone. Tears ran up into her tight gray hairdo. "We've sinned and the Good Lord is calling us home."

If it were true, it wasn't the least bit fair. It is Sarah who deserves to be falling into the ocean from above the clouds, not you and me, lady. The Good Lord should take a peek at the laptop that just whacked me. Flip through the snapshots of everlasting love. We didn't need a million dollars in the bank, only a good hiking trail and a nice view for a picnic. Except, of course, Sarah also needed Tommy Chambers riding on top of her in my bed. In our bed. And we're the ones being called home?

He hated himself again. It wasn't that Sarah had changed from the girl he'd met in college. The problem was that he'd tried changing her. She was a free spirit and he was a miserable anchor whose goal in life was to weigh her down. That's how she'd described it, and he'd believed every word. The irony of her saying it while pinned under Tommy came to him much later, as he stood in the airport check-in line next to his suitcase and backpack.

The plane rolled harder, pushing Dash onto his side, right elbow in the center of the oval framing a rapidly approaching ocean. The sound of rushing air enveloped him as the cabin continued depressurizing. His face tingled, goose bumps spreading everywhere else. The world outside was a giant vacuum cleaner, and maybe his elderly row mate wasn't wrong. Maybe the sinners on board were about to be sucked into oblivion, some headed to the Promised Land, others going with Dash.

Maybe someone would find Cindy.

The vacuum tugged Dash's polo shirt, grabbed it from the one nice pair of dress pants he owned. His seat belt was cinched too tight, threatened to snap ribs. He reached down and unclicked, setting himself free.

"Against the rules," said the lady, and Dash nodded down that he knew.

He'd found Sarah in bed with Tommy, the raddest and baddest guy in all of Northwest Vermont. Man of mystery and grimy fingernails. A man's man who would light a cigarette at the diner counter and dare anyone in the room to speak up. The word 'contractor' spelled with a fucking E on the side of his pickup. He should be on board this plane for that alone.

The fuselage tilted farther and Dash braced against the side of the cabin, knees on his armrest, face plastered to the wall by centrifugal force.

Fucking Tommy Chambers. Dash lost his job a week before the wedding. He'd driven home, unlocked the apartment door, and then closed it quickly so the downstairs neighbors didn't hear the porn flick Sarah was watching with the sound cranked. He hated those movies. The men always knew the exact right thing to do. Touch here and bingo. Put a tongue there and bango. Just once he wished the woman would climb out from under the guy and call him a clumsy loser. That was how it worked in the real world.

Dash now had an uncomfortable boner as he pressed up against the window, which would have confirmed to the lady holding her ankles his capacity for sin if she hadn't been totally absorbed in her own moment of terror. He despised every scene his memory painted for him, but they still had an effect.

"Watch a real man." Sarah's voice was as strained as the captain's, equally committed.

It had been the second worst moment of his life. Finding his father in a pool of blood was still *numero uno*. Both made death by engine failure a cakewalk. "God bless us all," the captain had said. Heartfelt words even to someone like Dash who believed as much in gods as he did Martians. The words were profound, all-encompassing and sincere, made you feel the speaker genuinely cared. They'd definitely play those words at the press conference.

"God bless us all," Dash said.

"Harder," Sarah practically shouted, laughing and bucking her hips, nearly throwing Tommy from the saddle. Yippee-ki-yay. Her laughter was the cruelest sound in the world, crueler than the cry of an airplane wing tearing free from its last bolt.

"I need you." The cabin voice was a desperate sigh, barely audible. Whiskers stroked the mouthpiece in place of more words.

Dash pulled a hand from the fuselage wall, reached to unzip his fly. The suction from the widening gap tugged his penis, did the rest.

"You're going to hell." The old woman in the flowered dress sounded certain, and he was in no position to argue.

The jetliner broke the surface of the water a few seconds later.

Chapter 2

———

Dash sank in the froth, water rushing up his pant legs and causing his shirt to billow. His head was pinned to one shoulder by a heavy chunk of metal that pushed him deeper. He twisted his face to profit from a shrinking air cavity, breathing quick puffs. Down he slid into the darkness, the water colder, filled with objects that deflected off his legs and ass. He filled his lungs with the last of the air, raised his hands and pushed with his remaining strength. He went down feet first, kicked sideways and got free, ears aching, water pressing his sinuses. He toed off his old canvas sneakers and swam toward an orange light.

Two bodies danced. She was already topless, immodest, long hair a shocking corona. He had no hair or face, one remaining arm twisting on a thread.

Our Father in Heaven.

A girl, not quite a teen, wore a pretty dress, an unbuttoned sweater. She had no shoes or legs.

Dash broke the viscous surface, a smoldering cauldron of oil and jet fuel. Burning islands floated in every direction, reflecting their hellish light in the poisoned water. He latched onto the first object not spewing flames, not caring if it was the Devil himself; anything to keep his face out of the toxic mix. Deep breaths pulled in the searing heat, cooking him from the inside. He switched to the quick puffs women in labor did on television, climbed higher onto the demon's spine with blind faith in the thick smoke. The creature was buoyant, the scratchy hide vaguely familiar.

The oven glowed for hours, Dash turning slow rotations, a rotisserie singeing both his sides equally. The fires eventually ate themselves and blinked out, shrinking into gray mounds and dipping beneath the surface. The debris field spread, the water spotted with swirling rainbows. He was submerged to his chest, his legs being brushed by hidden things with no interest in biting just yet. Unmerciful thirst forced a cupped hand into the littered water. He sniffed and then drank the warm, briny liquid. He was adrift in a sea of stale margaritas. Dash shifted more and guzzled a bellyful, then paused when a cramp pinched his stomach in a steel vise. A deep belch nearly knocked him from his host. The retching began and wouldn't stop. He vomited salty water, and every last bit of mini pretzel and gristly meat the lovely flight attendant had served. Tiny fish came to say hello with eager round mouths, greedily cleaning up his mess.

Hallowed be Your name.

Up from the depths rose a human hand, a fleshy stump with manly fingers. It arrived pinky side first then righted itself just beneath the surface, luring away the hungry fish. The hand didn't seem to belong to anyone, had struck out on its own. A dull flash showed off a gold ring.

Dash drew a painful breath. "How's married life?"

The hand did not answer, only stood upright with its three middle pads tickling the oily surface.

"I'm going a little crazy now."

He collapsed, leaned his cheek on a forearm, chin stirring the water. He tried his best to ignore the hand, its constant waving, the monotonous hellos or goodbyes. Thirst came back worse than before, and he couldn't fight the impulse. He tilted forward, took noisy gulps, swallowing hard. He wiped his arm across a burned face and cold tears, braced for the spasm building deep in his gut. The pain subsided when his mind latched onto a better place, in a different time, one with a more peaceful view and better margaritas.

Your kingdom come, Your will be done ....

THE MUSIC HURT his ears even after he finished chugging an icy thick margarita from a beer stein dipped in salt. The Omega Psis were rich pricks who spared no expense at party time. Live bands, top-shelf booze, a level pool table with no rips, and juicehead goons on barf detail ushering woozy partygoers to the front of the bathroom line.

One of the goons stopped Dash in the act of retrieving his coat from a second floor bedroom, stepping in front of the door, latching one giant hand to his shoulder. Sausage-like fingers from the other hand dangled in front of Dash's face.

"Waddya see?"

"A peace sign."

"Not what I'm lookin' for."

"I need my coat." Dash tried to twist away from the hand pinching his skin.

"I think you're an asshole."

"You're not alone."

"You puke in Dicky's room and I'll make you eat it, asshole."

'Eat the room or the puke?' Dash nearly asked before foreseeing the consequences. The goon let him pass with a wave, eyes locked on the next target, a tipsy co-ed with untied shoelaces leaning into a wall.

Beyond the door was a room that had grown two igloo-size mounds of winter outerwear, one on each twin bed. Dash chose to hunt the nearest pile, stomach churning from the goon's power of suggestion. He peeled back layers of expensive down coats and handmade scarves, looking for signs of his Army surplus parka. Nearing the bottom, the material shifted, came alive. He unearthed a miniskirt with a tanned leg. Parting two leather jackets, he found a girl with curly blond hair wearing a t-shirt with the word CRAZY in large letters across the chest. She smelled of cinnamon gum and fruity perfume and made purring sounds in her sleep.

He put his full weight on the bed and she stirred, turning to look up through foggy eyes. Her lips parted as if to speak, but then her lids dropped and her head lolled. She began snoring. Dash couldn't help but notice that her skirt had hitched up to expose the first shaved crotch he'd seen outside of magazines. It grinned at him sideways, and he resisted the temptation to reach down and make it talk the way he did his niece's chubby belly.

"Hello, how are you?" he'd made his niece's belly button say. "My name is Boo Boo."

Dash knew the sleeping girl's name. He'd heard the guys talk about Sarah the Fuck Machine, the school's gold medal tramp champ. Just wind Sarah up and watch her blow. But this Sarah was quiet and lovely, and Dash knew how full of shit guys were because of all the lies he'd told personally.

Did respectable girls shave their privates? He knew for sure they tended pits and legs, but he had no experience with hair down there. The missing panties might be an indication of her habits, but he only had rumors to go by. He sure as heck never witnessed her using her mouth like a Hoover on half the basketball squad, JV included.

Her cheekbones were rounded and soft, lips thin and fragile, meant to whisper, not service athletes. It was an innocent mouth, nothing like a household appliance.

"I think you're beautiful," he told the lovely Sarah, whose face was nestled in black leather and silver zippers. He leaned forward and brushed golden ringlets from her forehead, trying his best to ignore her intriguing crotch with its tantalizing smile.

Again she responded, opening her eyes and then her mouth, first looking at him as though startled, and then turning away to projectile vomit across the coats he'd stacked. Dash glanced at the door, where he'd promised Godzilla there'd be no such crime. Luckily, it didn't touch any of Dicky's stuff, he imagined telling the goon. Not a speck hit the mattress, not a single chunk on his tasteful shag carpet. But Dash knew it wouldn't fly.

His fingers touched her collarbone. "It'll be okay."

Sarah's head tilted back, eyes dancing over his face like a moth afraid to land. She squinted, perhaps searching for a name, or maybe his position on the basketball court. "I'm a mess," she said, eyelids again drooping. Her breathing turned smooth and deep, and Dash lightly stroked her bare arm after flicking a wad of gum from the letter *Y* over her left breast. He pulled a high school varsity jacket from under his butt and used its soft cuff to dab the corners of her mouth.

"I'm sort of a mess, too," he told the sleeping girl, then tossed the jacket onto the floor. Fuck you, Dicky. Fuck every basketball player who ever lived.

Dash then did something that would cause guilty pangs over the coming months and years, shame that would haunt his conscience late at night. He considered confessing, but there was never the right time when Sarah might understand his loneliness, might not turn and leave forever. He had betrayed her on the night they'd first met, and there would be no forgiveness if she discovered he'd maneuvered over her partially naked body, then shifted her hips. In a total breakdown of his moral self, Dash had gently touched her shaven parts with trembling fingertips.

"I love you," Dash said, his voice quaking.

"I love you, too," he made her labia respond. Then he turned her puffy lips into a smile and kissed them goodnight.

DASH PUCKERED HIS cracked lips, tasted salt. He determined he was floating chest deep, legs prickly numb, arms folded over some kind of soggy cushion. His face throbbed, was full of needles when he pressed a cheek into his forearm. He could barely force one eye into a blurry slit. It was sunset, or maybe sunrise. An orange ball was out there, low on the horizon. His stomach was shit, abs strained as if he'd been throwing up all night. Yeah, that was it. Some part of him made sense of the situation, and relief settled in. He was in the Omega pool, experienced enough at drinking himself into oblivion that he hadn't relinquished hold of the cushion. And while dumb enough to wind up in the deep end, he'd remained at least one beer shy of drowning.

It took mad skill.

On Earth, as it is in Heaven.

Dash heard the flapping an instant before the bird found his shoulder. It was a hard landing, and the damn thing's nails dug in while finding its balance. The cushion dipped and a cold wave splashed over him. It was salty, stung his barely open eye. Maybe it was the Kappa chicks' pool, since they owned a parrot. Yo, ho, ho, and a barrel of rum, vodka, and Everclear. His stomach lurched, and up from the darkest depths of his belly came a wet burp that sent his companion airborne with a squawk.

It was a seagull, not a parrot. He could recognize a seagull's complaining voice from a mile away. Maybe it was the Omega pricks' pool after all. The guys were pigs with their trash, driveway dumpsters attracting gulls year round. They'd been threatened with losing their charter for all the garbage fanning out over campus.

He tried pulling higher up onto the cushion, but wasn't able to kick his feet. Both were shoeless and swollen, neither ankle wanting to flex. He willed his right knee to bend, but was distracted by a new flurry of wings and braced for another impact. There were more gulls this time, some landing on his back and shoulders, others on the cushion near his face.

Words erupted in a dry croak. "Get away," he said, shooing with one hand, sensing yellow beaks about to pluck out his eyes and snip his ears. He'd witnessed their work, an Omega gull once prying open a can of pork and beans and nearly fighting to the death with others over every morsel. Dash shrieked when something caught his pinky, began to twist. He jerked his hand, nearly losing purchase on the cushion. He scrambled back up by rocking his shoulders, then buried his face and hands, hunching forward to protect both ears.

"Fucking Omegas," Dash shouted into the soggy cushion. "You guys are fucking slobs."

His tongue had grown fat, made it a struggle to swallow. He hoped the bastards lost their charter and their house burned to the ground with Dicky and his goons still inside. He'd cheer when the dumpsters erupted in flames, raise a beer from his soggy cushion, and toast the embers.

Gulls poked at his neck, tasted his hair. He feared for his earlobes, rocking his head back and forth to present a difficult target. He stopped only for peeks at the enemy, who seemed to mostly bicker at one another, hopping on orange webbed feet instead of coming in for the kill.

Dash was dizzy when the sun dipped into the horizon and sent the world into blackness. The cushion lightened as bird after bird grew bored and quit the game. Each took wing in a noisy flourish.

Give us this day our daily bread.

He shivered into the night, cold and alone, as a full moon rose and showered blue-tinted light. Waves of depression descended, consumed him by midnight. The stars changed places, and he eventually missed the seagulls, convinced they could have somehow coexisted on his cushion's meager acreage. He tried staying awake, knew it was the safe thing to do. Rescue would come. He would hear the car doors, the drunken laughter, the sound of bottles being uncapped. Someone would switch on the stereo. The back door would swing open, one of the guys dragging an overflowing trash bag. Or somebody would be in the mood for a swim, come running across the concrete patio for a monster cannonball.

Something moved in the water, only a shadow at first. Dash squinted into the reflections, allowed his eyes to adjust and make sense of the shape. Bobbing just beneath the surface of the pool was the human hand. It floated upright, as if awaiting a high-five, or perhaps waving goodbye to an old friend or lover.

And forgive us our debts, as we also have forgiven our debtors.
"I know you." Dash spoke in a whisper, energy depleted. He struggled to hold out his own hand, index finger reaching, tantalizing close but not quite touching. He smiled over a bittersweet image of his father's cramped workspace, a modest desk and wooden chair, a single bare bulb suspended from a leather cord. The only decoration was a Michelangelo print of *The Hand of God*. His father had explained the picture of Adam's limp hand, weak and languid, awaiting the infusion of life from God's touch.

An airplane had fallen out of the sky. *His airplane.* He swam through dancing bodies with missing pieces because he wanted to live, to be different than his father.

The submerged hand remained out of reach, and the water rocked him to sleep. He held onto his cushion through a dream in which he kept glancing over his shoulder, searching for Sarah's face as he was herded down the loading bridge to the waiting plane. She hadn't cheated on him in the dream, and they'd had a beautiful wedding. But where was she now? Why was he boarding a plane alone? He tried calling for her, but could not speak. His tongue didn't work, nor did his lips or jaw. He shifted his pack and reached for his face with both hands, but there was mostly empty space where flesh and bone had been torn away. His fingers fumbled across something hard at the back of his ruined mouth and he couldn't resist prying it free. He held his last remaining tooth in his palm, embarrassed by its yellow shade. *You'll still love me because this is a dream*, he tried saying, but only managed animal grunts that turned into a cadence, became the sound of a beating heart. He listened instead of trying to say more. He knew he was alive as long as the rhythmic thumps continued. *You'll still love….*

Thump. A quiet pause. *Thump.*

Everything went black, and he might have felt one eye tumble down his cheek and ricochet off his forearm. Everything went silent when both ears came loose and bounced from his shoulders. Did they make a noise when they struck the water?

I can't hear my heart.

Dash let the tooth fall from his hand. And then he let go of the cushion.

And lead us not into temptation, but deliver us from evil.

Chapter 3

—

THE WALLS WERE close, the air cool and damp. The echo was a familiar voice.

"I love you."

Quiet for a while, and then it came again. A simple, emotionless declaration from an old tape recorder's battered speaker. But the words changed his heart's rhythm, caused a skipped beat as he anticipated their return and imagined the soft hand accompanying the message. They were three words wielding so much power, no matter the energy behind the delivery. He fought growing anxiety, tried calming his noisy insides, and listened to the empty darkness disrupted only by dripping water. He wanted to believe it was an angel's voice, rather than his own parched throat's raspy plea.

He dozed until something landed and scuttled from brow to chin. He jerked to life and wildly swiped the air. He felt his mouth and jaw, touched the outline with hands that were impliable and benumbed save for two fingers he used as beacons. Spots of raw flesh on his cheeks, open wounds with crusty edges. One motion brought spectacular pain, bone against bone, and he swooned, nearly blacking out as the room lit up in pure white. Back in pitch darkness he was left with throbbing aches that spread deep into his ears, into his skull. He sensed his screams long before he heard them winding down. His live fingers crawled to his chest, felt the thumping. He covered his heart as if to protect it.

A small, distant voice said, "I love you."

Dash imagined Sarah's hovering face, her warm breath across his damaged skin. But her perfect blue eyes narrowed, and he sensed her contempt. His own eyes turned wet with tears.

"How could you?"

He fought the urge to wipe his itching eyes, allowed tears to draw uneven lines and fall into his ears. Either he was blind or the night was pitch black, but he was blessedly out of the poison water. Solid ground cradled his broken body, although he hadn't completely escaped. The drips fell hard and flat in unrelenting cadence. Despite his thirst, he never wanted to see water again, not even in a glass. Not in a fountain, not in a wishing well. Each drop was a hammer into a coffin nail. The flinching wore him down.

Sleep and dreams of water. A hand too large to be human touched his wounds, stripped off his clothes, and forced his head under the surface. A naked infant floated close enough to touch, an ivory balloon trailing a purple umbilical cord. Tiny fish were in pursuit, tasting or maybe trying to inflate. The fish came to him, offered their bodies to his tongue. The hand reversed, brought him to the air for a single breath, and then plunged him deeper. Are you clean? Are you saved?

Dash kept count, each dream a new day. A week passed.

His skin was no longer cold or burning hot, although the air grew worse, stank of mould and sewage. Sometimes he woke understanding his circumstances. He'd drunkenly stumbled into a bathroom and fallen in the tub. Bad things had happened. Makeshift first aid performed by one of the goons who didn't want any unnecessary bloodshed. Dash imagined the guy biting his own tongue in concentration, yellow *Tourniquets for Dummies* book propped in one hand, Dash's gushing wound squeezed off in the other. From the way his blood pulsed in his forearms and shins, he had no doubt that his body parts were tightly wrapped. His knees were bent, his neck tilted for his head to fit. There was plenty of room on either side because he'd lost all his fat after finding Sarah under Tommy. The rotten fiancée infidelity diet had worked like a charm.

Ten days gone.

Not flushing the damn toilet was something new, a definite step backward for a drink-to-oblivion phase. He was disappointed to have an instinct let him down. Not cool. It went on the list, along with puking on your own shirt and drinking from a glass being used as an ashtray.

Two weeks.

Taunted by the rhythm of the drops, Dash began questioning his circumstances. Doubts rose with images running across his black vision. He saw the small dial with a pointed nipple in the center, knew that twisting its grooved ring created a jet of air. An old woman was bent over, grasping her ankles in a strangely erotic pose.

"I need you to lean forward and brace for impact."

He recalled his erection.

"Only pieces."

"Pieces come from many people."

"Send them back to the Sea God."

"Volcano wants this white man."

"We wait for her to speak."

Dash answered weakly. "Cindy?"

The pictures morphed into movies, a bird's-eye view of recent events. He stuffed clothes into a backpack—clean underwear and dirty socks, a damp swim suit. He grabbed his passport from next to the coffee pot and spotted the creased note attached to the tickets from his crazy mother. It said to have a wonderful honeymoon and be sure to bring back a grandchild.

"Whose grandchild? Grab one off the street?"

Trudging through the airport, the pack slung from a shoulder and his laptop wedged beneath one arm, he twice stumbled into the person in front of him. A man cursed.

Burlington to Detroit, then Atlanta to LA, a flight path resembling an advanced mathematics sign when looking at a Google map. The last leg to Sydney was more than half the twenty-eight hour trip. The captain's voice had been friendly but professional, reassuring to a novice flyer. It was a doctor's voice explaining there was only a slim chance of cancer, and the next forty years should only deliver a few minor cuts and bruises. The captain let everyone know their cruising altitude, the temperature, and the local arrival time. The only visible land once they got out over the Pacific would be beautiful Fiji, a destination to consider for their next trip. "Beautiful Fiji, the Hub of the South Pacific. It consists of 322 islands, with 522 smaller islets, each more tranquil than the last. They'll be visible on the right side of the aircraft if the weather cooperates." He'd remind everyone to have a look once they were closer.

Fiji never happened. The captain spoke. The airplane fell.

Twenty-one dreams, twenty-one days.

He tried shifting his back to stretch, but a flash of pain took his breath. A knife was buried, or maybe a knitting needle. He touched his face, noticed his palms and wrists were wrapped in strange gauze that smelled like muddy grass. He sniffed and touched one hand to his chin, discovered it *was* mud and grass. He remembered the sucking fuselage wall and reached for his penis, but trying to scrape off the concoction brought electric jolts zipping up into both funny bones, a sickening agony that roiled his stomach. He drew deep breaths of fetid air, then turned and vomited next to his ear. He'd stuck his dick into a hole on a doomed airplane. It wasn't a nightmare; it had really happened. No, check that. He was now living in the definition of a nightmare. I have fresh puke leaking into my ears and my dick is gone, and some funky awfulness is happening to my hands. I'm blind and buried in a cave or some primitive toilet, and never once have I heard of a penis growing back.

He fought for control, tried to steady his hitching body with deep, even breaths because the sound of grinding bones was worse than the dripping water.

"The fucking sun will come out tomorrow," Dash tried singing, needing his mother's comforting voice, but his mouth would not work, would not bring her closer.

Any hope for his vision was lost, not that there was anything to see at the bottom of a leaking grave. Dizziness swept over him, a sensation of falling from the tops of clouds, from six miles above an empty ocean. He vomited again, and then mercifully passed out. He dreamed he was lying next to Sarah in the gloriously cold snow. They were at arm's length, about to make snow angels, his dick shrunken from the Vermont chill but still fully intact.

A month of dreams.

⌀

"IT IS CRUCIAL we retrieve every piece of wreckage."

The voice was female, but masculine and heavily accented. Not British or Irish; it was more like the Aussie action movie hero, or the poor crocodile hunter TV guy whose daughter would never get to know him.

"You crazy. No way to fix airplane. Broke in too many pieces."

It was a man's voice, authoritative, also perhaps Australian, but the sentences came in short bursts, the way Tonto spoke to the Lone Ranger.

"They need to be examined to find answers for the victims' families."

"Your airplane killed our fish, turned lagoon to shit. Fish go belly up, taste like bad clap-clap," said the man.

The accusatory words entered and bounced around the walls of Dash's grave, made him wonder about good clap-clap. His head no longer ached, and his stomach was empty. He was hungry despite the piss and mildew smell.

"The airline company will make restitution. They'll pay for the damage. Their environmental team is the best in the world. My concern is with wreckage, anything that may have washed up on your island."

The man grunted and his language changed to something flowery and sing-song, nearly all vowels. His words set off a stampede of bare feet, followed by a long pause.

There were murmurs—small talk that sounded more like tropical birds and communing insects. It slowed time and nearly put Dash to sleep.

Feet slapped the ground, heavier and much slower. Dash heard strained breathing and the sound of rustling, two plastic buckets dropped onto stone.

"One million dollars, small bills," said the man.

"With all due respect, Chief, I can't imagine what your people would do with currency." Exasperation tinged the woman's words, and Dash felt sorry for her. "We need to salvage airplane sections, plastic or metal. Segments we can piece together."

"You take good look at my island," said the Chief. "You see mini pretzel factory under breadfruit tree? These come from your plane. Bags say these are savory treats everyone loves. Mini pretzels *are* wreckage. One million dollars."

"These are food snacks. And that bucket is filled with sanitary napkins." There was more rustling, and Dash pictured the woman taking inventory. "Passenger headphones, airsick bags, magazines."

"Half million dollars; you keep buckets."

French words were exchanged among the woman's clan.

"*Merde*," said one. Dash knew it meant 'shit.' One of his high school pals had also taught everyone how to say fuck, handjob, and tits.

"I'm very sorry for what's happened to your lagoon. We have sixty kilos of rice and a fair amount of coffee. It will be our gift. We'll bring it from our boat with help from your people."

"You pay one million dollars if we find metal pieces of airplane?"

"We don't have money, Chief. Our job is to investigate the cause of the accident."

"What you pay for people?"

"Did you find human remains?" The woman's voice was skeptical. Too skeptical, as far as Dash was concerned. "Did a body wash up?"

"You have one million dollars?"

"No, I'm sorry. Just rice and coffee."

"Then we only found what's in buckets."

❧

DASH DRIFTED OFF to the intoxicating smell of fresh brewing coffee and melodious chatter in exotic tongues. He dreamed his own feast, though his jaw required help from strange hands that smelled of coconuts and slightly sour milk. Every joint was a rusty hinge as he gobbled spoonfuls of steaming rice heaped with tiny whole shrimp and a fishy sauce. He was a voracious Tin Man with no can of oil, itchy hands, and a missing dick. A metal body polished by busy bees with coarse rags, although each bee was a non-stop complainer in clunky English phrases.

"Cries more than sick baby."

"Smells like old squid."

It's the fault of these grass and mud mittens, he yearned to respond. It's these corroded knees and dented feet. I'm trapped, lodged in this too small tub. The toilet might as well be on the moon. I try to hold it in!

"I'm a mess," Dash whispered to the hands that had quit polishing, had left him in the dark.

A ghost barged into his sanctuary before he could drift back into his dreams, interrupting his loneliness. The apparition was tall and square shouldered. Light from a single eye cast a white glow from head to toe. A rag was draped over one shoulder, stained with something like blood and gore. The creature stank of ammonia, things found under kitchen sinks. Dash drew a breath and watched it peel one hand off in its teeth, then reach down with the remaining stub to part the flesh beneath its bulging stomach. It pulled out what resembled a human penis that created an arc of yellow fluid. Whistling noises emanated from a scabby face, a tune resembling Led Zeppelin's "Stairway to Heaven."

The creature shook its phantom member, made a farting noise, and dissolved into the black wall as though it never existed.

"Stairway." Dash once loved that song, had sung along with Sarah each time it played on the classic rock station out of Burlington. He sniffed hard, cleared his throat of the lingering ammonia. Maybe there was hope for his vision, if only to watch pissing goblins in hell.

He began to hum about a lady and things made of gold.

Chapter 4

—

A HAND PRODDED Dash's face, pinched his nose, and shook
it from side to side.

"Wake up, Cracker, no more cleaning your filth."

"That hurts."

The hand drew away when Dash reached. Long nails with
dirty crescents in a flickering candlelight. The mud and grass
bandages were gone. The pain was gone. He wiggled five pale
fingers. No scars on his wrists.

"You okay now to wash own ass." The voice came from above
and was followed by a sharp hand clap. "Let's go, let's go."

Two women in matching men's underpants and white sports
bras grabbed him under his armpits and lifted. He stood
wobbling, weak and pathetic, leg and back muscles threatening
to give out. He was naked except for the same style underpants
as the women. His were saggy, pastel, maybe light blue.

Dash remembered the female voice: "They need to be
examined to find answers for the victims' families."

He grabbed at his crotch, found numb resistance beneath
thin material, the sensation of touching someone else, a
corpse, perhaps. He wedged his hand into the fly, digging until

he located a shriveled, lifeless member. *It might be asleep*, he reasoned, and squeezed as hard as his muscles allowed. There was nothing, no pain, not a distant tingle. He kneaded, groped his testicles.

"You do nasty stuff on your own time," said the woman on his right, who began moving them forward, leading the way out of a place that had no resemblance to a bathroom. It was a stone chamber, a cave with charcoal walls, barely head high, but wide enough for them to march three across. It dog-legged left and the sun struck him like a fist, his vision exploding in a white flash, heat searing his face and chest.

Dash whined, his knees buckling. The women grunted, struggling with their awkward load. "Come on, Cracker, you too big to carry," said the woman, propping up his left side.

"And too stinky," added the other.

"Even flies scared to land. You gonna walk or crawl, but Manu wants you washed up to eat."

He kept his balance, squinted into the hellish glare. Each arm draped over a squat woman. *Wait a second.* Did this Manu person intend to eat him? What kind of crackers were they talking about? If he could see, and if his legs could manage a few good steps, he might have considered running.

Instead, he allowed himself to be shuffled blindly forward. With no escape from these women, he confronted his fate. "Are you going to eat me?"

"You dumb as you look." The woman hocked and spit to show her disgust. "Nobody eat people for long time."

"Especially white man who smells like rotten fish," said the other. "The girl will come for you when food is ready. You need to wash first. Give some stink back to the sea where you came from."

Dash stopped the forward momentum when his toes hit water. He struggled against the women's grip, tried backpedaling. His vision returned in time to see the enormous expanse of blue water. He might have come from the sea, but he wasn't ready to return. He had images of fire and demons, terrible things lurking below the surface. It took a ruthless shove from both cantankerous women to send him splashing into the water.

He tried turning, twisting his arms and bending at the waist, but they were too strong, or he was too weak. "I don't think I can swim," he cried out in voice so pathetic that even he was embarrassed. Dash was being overpowered by a pair of short female cannibals and was on the verge of tears. Nothing out there was burning, he told himself, and he was too easy pickings for any devil to bother with. He looked down at his spindly legs, his knobs for knees. He worked to get hold of himself, recover a sliver of dignity despite his smell and dirty underpants.

His captors grunted, forced him deeper into the lapping water. It felt like a thousand tongues. He tried not to look.

"You gotta wash, not swim," said the woman on his right. "White man is a big baby when he don't have a gun."

Dash wanted to tell them he'd never owned a gun, never even fired one. He had friends who shot deer and even moose up in Maine. But they weren't good friends, just people he knew, really. You might even call them strangers. Sure, there were rusty antique weapons hanging in his father's shop, but Dash only wanted to fish as a kid. He was a boy who set model airplanes on fire, left the real killing to others.

He was pushed deeper.

"I just wanted to fish."

The heat was stirred by a headwind that carried the noise of seagulls and distant waves crashing over a partially exposed reef. The shells underfoot were all razors and broken glass, shredding the pads of his delicate feet and surely tantalizing the deadliest species with fresh blood. The trio splashed into water that surged and pulled, the bottom becoming slick rocks and sea grass that tangled around his ankles. They stopped when he was waist deep, rolling waves pushing at his damaged crotch, extra material an underwater cloud, a blue jellyfish hugging a too pale man.

The women loosened their grip, allowed him to take two more steps forward on his own.

Dash swayed in the cool water, all the color returning to his world. He dropped open hands to the surface, fingers spread and palms slightly cupped. He turned slowly, creating a light wake behind each hand, careful not to slip on the unstable bottom. His back to the sun, he saw the world come into full focus. Framed by his two escorts—both frowning, middle-aged women with chocolate skin and wild black hair—was a panorama of unimaginable beauty. He stood gaping at a tropical paradise as the woman to his right fumbled a hand into her bra, produced a sliver of soap, and tossed it at him.

"Be sure to scrub that calf meat real good." She licked her lips, then turned and trudged back toward dry land.

"Yeah, and get both them ears clean," said the other, gripping her own ears and waggling. "They good and chewy."

He began to lather his whole body.

⤫

DASH SCANNED THE heavens beyond the clusters of puffy clouds, numb penis in his right hand, soapy underpants at his knees. He tried recalling a snippet of prayer from one of the half-dozen times his grandmother had bundled him off to church without his father's knowledge, but too many years had passed, and he'd been too young. He'd only hoped for something generic, since no rural Vermonter had risen in church to ask God's help for his sort of ailment. He mostly remembered the shiny pews that made your thigh skin squeal when you slid in shorts and the smell of hair tonic. Even the songs he'd stood up to sing next to his Nanna were long gone.

There was nothing in the sky but clouds and the airplane

cabin's fading image. An old lady hunched over, hands below the hem of her flowered dress, appalled by what he was doing. He couldn't stop himself any more than she could have stopped praying. They'd faced death via two different paths. He should be grateful his parts were still attached, and that he'd washed up in a paradise inhabited by cranky natives instead of on the shores of hell.

Where was the lady? Probably with Cindy at the bottom of the ocean.

A girl was sitting in a patch of black sand drawing with a twig when Dash hauled himself out of the water, exhausted from fighting the slight current. Had she been there during his examination? No cuts or scars, and it remained the same pink color. But the entire package was devoid of feeling, tip to testicles. He'd used his middle finger to flick the end, but felt nothing. He'd shaken and tugged, then stopped to catch his breath and fend off panic. He slapped his member against the water, threatened and then pleaded for its forgiveness.

The girl's large brown eyes found him, and he was embarrassed about his drooping underwear and what she must have witnessed.

"Food's not ready." She tossed the stick and wiped away her artwork. "I came early. Men are drinking clap-clap and are all piss and wind."

"My name is Dash. The women said you'd come."

"I'm Tiki. You looking for your airplane?"

"I don't know what I'm looking for, but it's beautiful here. This is an island?"

The girl nodded.

"I'm sorry the airplane killed your fish. I was only a passenger."

"Not your fault. Manu says the Volcano was angry. She threw a stone and made your airplane fall. There's another." She pointed past him, and he turned to look up at shiny hints of distant metal, long contrails beginning to twist apart at their far ends.

He made old man sounds when he dropped onto a mound of hardened lava, knees popping. "Did anyone else survive?"

She shook her head. "You're the only one. Fish ate what the Sea God didn't want."

"The volcano erupted?"

"Just one stone." She used her thumb to indicate the barren mountain rising from the center of the island, a soaring brown monolith producing a ribbon of white smoke.

"I've only seen volcanoes on television."

She leaned toward him to whisper, "She has a bad temper."

"It's incredible," he whispered back. "I guess the smoke means it really is active. That it's alive."

She tilted her head at him. "How else would she throw stones?"

"Right," he said, reasonably sure the engines had been starved of fuel, or died from a catastrophic failure of a bad wiring job. Or terrorists. "I guess that makes sense."

"People who hunted for your airplane pieces said we should move far away. They said the Volcano will kill our village soon. Manu told them people can't hide from a god. God want to eat you, then you will get eaten no matter what island you go to. Manu said those people had nice clothes and fancy boat, but were dumb as shitter bugs." She wrinkled her nose. "Ever see what a shitter bug does?"

He shook his head. "Has it been smoking like that for a long time?"

Tiki shrugged, got to her feet. A pretty child—maybe ten years old—with wide eyes and smooth skin, she had a mass of thick hair halfway down her back, brushed to a deep shine. She wore the same style underpants as everyone else.

She leaned in close again and lowered her voice. "She smokes when she's angry, which is most of the time. Her temper is worse than boy warriors who drink too much clap-

clap. Warriors get angry because they have nobody to fight.
Maybe it's the same thing for the Volcano God."

"The volcano wants to fight?"

"She is surrounded by water, has no enemies. Eating people
is the only thing left to make her happy."

The narrow trail of smoke was an unbroken line connecting
the mountain to the horizon. Would it bring rescue? How far
did it hold together for people to see? If it really came from the
mouth of a god, maybe it traveled all the way to where they'd
lifted off, the perfect white smoke mixing with the yellow smog
over Los Angeles. The thought made him feel less isolated, if
only for a few seconds.

"Should be time for food," said the girl. "You look hungry as
a volcano."

She was looking up at him, smiling with a flawless set of
round teeth that he caught himself inspecting for bits of
human flesh.

✝

THE PATH BROUGHT them up a slope toward a thick jungle,
where soaring palms with clusters of heavy looking fruit
stood sentry. Dash had researched exotic honeymoon spots,
read trivia with regard to the number people killed by falling
coconuts. One writer compared the fruit to dangling bowling
balls, taking many more lives than great white sharks.

Tiki plunged them into humid darkness. Vines hung from
a low canopy that had been chopped into a tunnel, brown
cuttings lining the way. He struggled to keep up, legs and lungs
pushed to their new pathetic limits for a man who'd lived his
entire life in a mountainous state. Rivers of sweat poured from
his body, clumps of tiny bugs riding the rapids. He eyed the
girl's bouncing hair as she skipped and did pirouettes, naked
back dry and insect free, apparently too young for the bra tops
worn by the cranky women.

The path leveled and they emerged into a sunny clearing. He bent at the middle, grabbed at his sweaty knees, suddenly sure his heartbeat would never slow. Through his straggly hair, he could see they were at the perimeter of a village composed of dozens of thatched huts. Busy brown people were doing chores in similar Western-style underwear. A boy probably seven or eight ran to Dash, who half straightened for a greeting. The boy grinned and kicked him in the right shin, then turned and sprinted toward a group of children standing around a lopsided ball.

"What the hell?"

Dash hopped on one leg, but it gave out and he fell hard. The ground was a layer of crushed shells that stuck to his skin. He clutched his shin with both hands and waited for the pain to ease.

Tiki squatted and picked away shards one at a time. She patted the top of his head. "John John hates white people and can kick pretty good for a boy. He's our goalkeeper."

Dash looked beyond the girl at women tending black pots suspended over wood fires. Others swept dirt from interiors or sat weaving fibrous material into coiled piles. Nearly all the women appeared pregnant. He gave his shin one last squeeze and Tiki stepped back.

"You really don't eat people, right?"

He had seen all the movies where an explorer is met by a greeting party, strings of flower leis draped over his head by dutiful, bare-breasted women with lowered eyes. Intricate carvings and valuable beads were gift wrapped in wide green banana leaves, left at his boots. Drums would thump in the background—some official tune for an honored guest—a line of hula girls with swaying arms off to one side. Men in traditional face paints would hold bamboo weapons to port on the other.

None of this happened. Nobody except the one mean little boy had taken any notice of Dash, who struggled to his feet, brushing away shell fragments.

Tiki led them across the village compound to a gathering of men sitting on the ground outside the largest hut. The group was in a shady spot, circled beneath a narrow palm growing at a steep angle. The girl cleared her throat for their attention then ran off to where children were playing. Dash noticed their eyes were all glassy, each man suffering a slight wobble as a cup was refilled from a wood jug and passed around. Outside the circle were more jugs. Two were apparently full and ready, while four lay spent on their sides.

"Sit, Cracker, before another child knocks you over." It was a voice Dash remembered, the Australian accent cut into short bursts. The chief was directly across the circle, the oldest looking of the bunch. Elevated by a stack of large leaves under his rear end, he was the only one not sitting directly on the crushed shells.

"Thank you very much." He brushed his hands, then stepped forward and dropped to his butt when the circle parted to make room. "My name is Dash."

"I am Chief Manu."

Dash offered his best polite smile. "I'm honored to meet you."

"There is no honor left, only age," said Manu, who leaned toward a muscular young man next to him—one of the warriors, Dash guessed—and spoke in the native language. The warrior nodded once, hopped to his feet, and left the circle. "Other business," said the chief, waving a hand. "Time for rest will come when our bodies are cast into the sea."

"I'm grateful that your people took care of me."

"You killed our fish," said the old chief.

Dash looked around the circle. Some were nodding enthusiastically, while others seemed nearly comatose, leaning hard, hands planted for stability. The man with the cup took a sip and swallowed. He then spit into the remaining liquid before passing it along to the man on his right. The ritual was repeated.

Outside the circle, Dash saw the warrior emerge from one of the huts tugging a skinny teenage boy. Difficult to see in the harsh glare was the cord binding the teen's wrists.

"Your airplane poisoned our lagoon," said the chief. "Even men who came dressed in white bags and used big towels did no good. They brought barrels of medicine for the water and dirt, but made nothing better. Your people did not bring our fish back to life."

"I was a passenger," Dash said, an innocent victim up until that point. "I was on my honeymoon. Row 22, seat F."

"Your honeymoon killed our fish."

Dash opened his mouth, but couldn't speak. The chief's face was so wrinkled it was impossible to read. Maybe they were going to eat him out of spite.

The man to Dash's left spit into the cup and handed it to him. It smelled like lamp oil with a hint of rotten fruit. "Makes you strong," said the man, words slurred but chin jutting proudly. He stuck out a bent arm, flexed a rubbery bicep. "Keeps them little sprogs from kicking your arse."

Dash took the cup. As he did, he watched the teenager manhandled across the compound, the big man jerking hard on the cord, impatient with the boy's resistance. The man slapped the back of the teen's head twice, sending him to his knees once. The warrior stopped at a pile of large stones and wood stumps just shy of the soccer players. The children ignored the pair, but shifted their game to the far end of the field.

It was a mouthful of sugary high test gasoline that closed Dash's throat, made his stomach muscles contract. He shook his head furiously while trying not to spill, knowing the punishment for such an offense might very well be death.

The circle of men snorted and laughed, clapped their hands when Dash finally managed to swallow and keep it down. He remembered to spit into the cup before passing it along. He caught his breath as the laughter died. His throat was coated in something similar to candle wax. "Your island is beautiful," he said, nearly barking the words while trying to relax his gag reflex.

"Used to be called Moku Siga, which means No Hurry. Now it is called Valelailai," the chief said, holding the cup while another man poured it full. He took a sip, swallowed, and spit. "Men of white cracker god called it that and the name stuck. No big deal. One name is good as any."

"It's a pretty name." Dash's legs were cramped from sitting pretzel style, what his ancient kindergarten teacher had called 'criss-cross applesauce.' "What does it mean?"

The chief took a much longer drink, then spit another phlegmy gob. "Means toilet. That's what white people called our home. We need to talk about the fish you killed."

Dash watched the warrior force the teen back to his knees, then reach out to untie the cord. The big man stayed close, made growling sounds into the boy's face and began jabbing his finger at the top of one stump. The boy looked down, unmoving for a few seconds, and then obeyed. He lifted his right hand and placed it flat on the stump's surface.

The warrior reached for a stone twice the size of the soccer ball.

"I'm sorry about the fish," said Dash.

The men on either side of Manu leaned forward and spoke in their native tongue—angry, rapid-fire words, their hands flailing and nearly hitting the chief. They were the largest and youngest of the group, broad shoulders, and matching black underpants, the same as the man terrorizing the boy on the field. Dash's stomach rolled over when they turned and pointed at him. Their eyes were wide and accusing, lips pursed in the same manner as the old lady in the aisle seat.

"They think we should sacrifice white man to the Volcano," Manu told Dash. "Only way to make fish come back."

It suddenly dawned on Dash how often those movies where the villagers greeted explorers with open arms had turned tragic. Brave adventurers burned at the stake or chopped into bait for crimes far pettier than decimating the fish population.

Out by the soccer field, the warrior lifted the stone above his head, sweat cascading from brawny shoulders and raining down on his cowering charge. The boy made no sound when the stone fell.

An elbow stabbed Dash's ribs. The man on his left held out the cup as the teenage boy slid to the dirt. Dash could feel his heart pounding, could see the boy's blood pouring from a flattened hand that seemed to be missing fingers.

Unimaginable beauty, he'd thought. A tropical paradise.

The chief spoke slowly in his sing-song language, and even the men who could barely sit upright nodded their heads. Dash was certain he was telling them how they'd lash the cracker to a bamboo cross, march him up the volcano's brown slope, snap Roman-style whips across his body for encouragement, and finally boot his pale ass down into the molten lava. The old chief paused and the faces turned to Dash.

"My legs are getting too old for climbing her back." Manu used his leathery chin to indicate the volcano. "Dreams will show me what is best. We won't feed you to the Volcano yet."

Chapter 5

———

SMOKE AMASSED IN a hazy dome over the village, trapping and mixing peculiar food smells with the sickly sweetness of decomposing flowers. The sun was somewhere low over the treetops when a woman came to kneel behind the chief and speak into his gnarled ear. Manu nodded and she reached under his armpits to hoist him to his feet. The other men also rose, although two stumbled forward, pitching onto their foreheads and flopping to their backs. There was laughter, and nobody came to their aid. Both resembled upside down turtles, were left behind drunk and helpless, pushing dirt into a dusty cloud.

The drinking circle formed an uneven line that weaved across the mashed up shells. They reconvened on a long strip of woven mats near the fires, where a dozen women were busy with food. Manu's bony fingers jabbed Dash's shoulder, pointed for him to sit among the scrum of children at the far end. But then the old man put his weathered face close, noxious breath whistling in and out, chest so frail and malnourished that he reminded Dash of the neglected animals in fundraising commercials.

"Better you eat away from the warriors," Manu said. "I don't want you killed before the Volcano speaks to me."

Dash began forming a protest, or some kind of apology that would make a difference, but his tongue was too clumsy from the alcohol, and the woman who'd lifted the chief was now settling the old man between two warriors. Better to take his chances with the boy who kicked him than draw further ire from hand-smashing lunatics who considered him a fish killer.

Dash headed toward the shrieks and youthful bickering, as they took their places facing what appeared to be a stage and a gigantic palm frond curtain suspended from a bamboo frame. They sat with their backs to the jungle's low hum, men speaking in slurred but hushed voices, sipping from coconut shell cups. The children around Dash fiddled and played hand slapping games under the stern gaze of one old woman who kept the noise down with slaps of her own.

The dirt stage was about a third the length of the mat, black lava rocks delineating the rectangular area in front of the curtain. Smoldering metal pots were at both front corners, either for effect or maybe to ward off mosquitoes.

The women in charge of the food filed back and forth from the hut nearest the cooking fires. All had round bellies, in some phase of pregnancy, hefting enormous turtle shells piled with steaming fare. The shells were deposited up and down the mat and set off a flurry of bare hands that filled wooden plates in a mad rush. The boy who'd assaulted Dash wrestled a whole fish from another, clumps of rice and other bits of food flying. There were platters of what appeared to be barbecued bats and long-legged frogs, and plates stacked high with charred rodent-shaped creatures. It was hard to be sure what things were because the pieces were burned to a crisp, but the food smells were good and the clap-clap had left him prepared to devour anything.

Squeals and pig snorts came from a bamboo corral on the far side of what were probably outhouses, where an alcove had been hacked into the thick jungle.

Tiki squeezed next him and sat. "Boys and pigs are the same," she said, and scooped colorful fruit onto his plate. Banana slices were the only items he recognized for sure. She added a handful of thick fish stew from another bowl, meaty gray chunks that bristled with hair-like bones.

"Tastes better than it looks," she said.

"It all looks good." Dash arranged his food, keeping the fruit separate from the stew as the jostling continued on his other side. He took a bite of fish, and fine bones immediately caught in his throat. He gagged and forced a hard cough, tears streaming, much to the amusement of the boys. He tried massaging his throat with one hand and fumbled for a cup with the other.

"Here." Tiki scooped fingers into a bowl heaped with something like mashed potatoes, then grabbed a handful of his hair to steady him. "Makes the bones go down easy."

He allowed her to scrape the bitter paste on the back of his lower teeth, then managed to hold his gorge and swallow. The bones seemed to dissolve, the paste leaving an odd tingling sensation behind his Adam's apple.

She patted his head and began stacking food on her own plate. "Maybe just eat the fruit."

The sky was nearly dark when the clap-clap jugs were fetched. Manu took the first drink and passed the cup. He gave a command that sent three young men to their places behind wood drums and a fifty gallon metal container lying on its side. A boy hopped to his feet, darting to each of the smoldering stage pots to deposit palm-sized leafy bundles that sizzled and caught fire. They caused a loud hiss and eruptions of smoky white plumes. The drummers went to work.

Dash leaned toward Tiki. "What is this?"

"A story," she said, shifting onto her knees. "The pageant of beauty."

"Nice." His head was heavy from the booze and food. "It's like dinner theater."

She frowned and put a finger to her lips.

"Those are the white soldiers from a faraway land. They come to our island once a year, unless the Storm God steers them away." She pointed to a line of six villagers coated in what looked like gray ash from head to toe. They held paddles and stroked imaginary water, taking short, shuffling steps along the stage perimeter. They stopped with their backs to the audience, a bamboo rifle hanging from thin vines over each man's right shoulder. The smoke from the pots lifted into the overhead haze.

"Those are guns," said Tiki. "White men use guns and crosses for weapons." She held her index fingers in the sign of a cross in front of her nose, and turned to show him.

"I don't," he said, and she put one of her fingers back to her lips.

"Those are the first contestants." She nodded toward five of the fattest village men who had stepped through the curtain. Wild grass wigs were perched cockeyed on each head, lips painted bright red, diva-like. Their sports bras were comically stuffed, and grass skirts that came to their feet dragged along the dirt stage, pudgy knees exposed. Those still eating began to heckle in their sing-song language. A few blew raspberries and booed.

The line of white men lifted the rifles from their shoulders to brandish at the men in drag, the drummers doubling their efforts. The soldier farthest from Dash disappeared behind the curtain then returned with a cowering herd of little boys he ordered to sit between the ridiculous contestants and armed men. The drums cut off and the middle soldier turned to face Manu, who had just taken a drink and was spitting into the cup. The chief raised an arm and wiggled his fingers for them to continue.

"This is the punishment for offering girls not pretty enough," said Tiki. "Boys are killed."

The soldiers opened fire on the boys, who jerked from the

gunshots, flopping on the ground and groaning from pretend mortal wounds. Some died five or six times, coming to a final rest in chalky piles. The drummers resumed their beat when the last victim was still.

"That's not how boys really die when they are shot," she added, and Dash wondered how she knew.

Hysterical women scampered on stage with flailing arms and hands. They cried to the heavens before kneeling to scoop up a murdered child to show the audience the depth of their loss. Giggling faces were smothered in kisses before the women retreated behind the curtain.

"Those are the mamas."

The men in drag slunk backward into the curtain and also disappeared. The drums slowed to a steady pace.

"Now come the pretty girls." She pointed to the parting curtain as five girls, all younger looking than Tiki, took the places of the fat men in wigs. They touched their own faces, preened their hair, and struck poses for the soldiers, who shouldered their weapons. The men in the audience cheered the girls, whistled between fingers. Boys jumped up and down, clapping and stumbling across the remaining dirty plates.

"Now they take the winners away," Tiki said, as the girls stepped forward into the imaginary boat. The soldiers paddled to the drum beat, made a slow lap in the opposite direction from which they'd come, and then disappeared behind the curtain with their new cargo.

"Where do they go?" Dash felt a sudden need to know, but Tiki only shrugged and pushed her plate to the center of the mat. "What happens to them?"

"It's the pageant of beauty," she said, as women began clearing the mess and the male actors returned for more clap-clap. "Girls who are ten years old are taken from our island by the soldiers. But only if they are pretty enough to be chosen."

He looked at the girl, examining her more closely. Her skin was flawless—no scars or marks. Her eyes were as bright as any, but her lashes were long and curled. Something about her was different from the other children, the other girls. Her hair was full and gleaming even under the cruddy haze, as if it had been combed longer, readied for some place other than an island jungle. He wasn't much of a beauty pageant judge, but she was surely the prettiest girl he'd seen.

He knew the answer before asking. "How old are you?"

"I'm ten." She smiled, again showing her perfect teeth. "I'm the next to go."

Chapter 6

——

TIKI LED THEM back toward the ocean by the light of a honey-colored candle. Dash was banished to his cave until the old chief sorted out his dreams. He hoped it wouldn't take long, and he also hoped it would take forever.

"Manu says you're safer away from the village," she said, body tilted from a bucket of fresh water she shifted from hand to hand every few yards. "The young warriors don't listen when they drink. They hate your skin."

Dash was trying to balance his load while slapping at cobwebs and floating booby-traps of mosquito clouds.

He understood the fear of outsiders, had grown up with bigotry aplenty. Change was something to hate in his corner of New England. Entrepreneurs considering shops catering to tourists faced insurmountable town meeting battles, stone-faced selectmen convinced of the type of people a fancy bookshop would draw. Candles and maple syrup were barely acceptable, but crafts and pottery would bring the hippies and pedophiles, heathens from the Internets who were thieves of souls and worse. The town hall regularly erupted into shouting matches.

"Photography? Them rag-head bahstads will be makin' phony IDs. They'll have cousins of cousins showin' up at all our gawdamn front doors with cah-sized bombs 'fore ya know it. Why bring 'em here? Plenty utha places in the world for them ta be."

The middle-aged woman who wanted to renovate her garage and take baby pictures was a Boston transplant from some thirty years earlier. She was still an outsider to most.

Dash's father—who sat at the fringe of these meetings, bringing his son along for civic lessons—never spoke up. Dash was glad to be near an exit, one foot in the aisle, ready to run, not trusting his father's silence. His father was a man who would emerge from a closet with an obscure nineteenth-century hand tool, challenging his son's friends to identify the item. And the object would invariably have some bizarre purpose, engineered to remove chicken beaks—"slices like warm cheese"—or it might be monstrous tongs for castrating hogs, "comes off clean as a whistle." His father would hold up a set of imaginary pig testicles then work the medieval-looking contraption with lusty exuberance. The stories circulated, but the antique shop wasn't meant for locals anyway. No dairy farmer or auto mechanic ever stepped inside his father's shop. These people had their own antiques, which were mostly still being used. Dash's father's crime was to put a ridiculous price tag on junk. Twenty dollar canning jars? Being an outcast suited his father just fine because the customers rolled into town in freshly waxed foreign 'cahs.'

"They want to kill me," Dash said to the back of Tiki's head, thinking about the guffaws his father had inspired over an antique dung scraper, followed the next day by the not so hilarious ribbing Dash had received at school.

"They worry because the Volcano is shaking the ground. The village will die if she spills her blood. Feeding you to her will make her calm, stop the shivers."

"Lava," he said, trying to step as lightly as possible on the dead foliage carpeting the tunnel. "Her blood is lava, right?" Some of the chopped vines stood up in spikes. He hefted supplies bundled in a woven mat one of the warriors had shoved into his arms. It was stuffed with wood and rock items, along with candles and a magnesium fire starter in its original package.

"The missioners called it 'lava,' but it comes from her heart, is her blood."

"Her blood, then. Tell me about the ceremony. Who were the men with guns?"

"White men like you."

"Where do they take the girls?" Anxiety rose at the idea of losing his sole ally, the only person not interested in throwing him in the volcano or smashing him with heavy stones. He hoped he'd misunderstood the ceremony, that it was a reenactment of something from a hundred years ago—Washington crossing the Delaware in lousy weather, for instance—and she was just another kid wanting to be on board to wave the stars and stripes.

She ignored the question, kept walking, water sloshing. "It will be safe down here. The warriors are only brave when they are drunk, and all of them are afraid of what lives outside the light."

He searched the living walls by the dancing light of the tapered candle, noticed all the dark hiding spots and noise-filled divots. Their progress was slower despite the downhill pitch. Bats had twice swooped down and nearly touched the flame. Didn't some bats drink blood? He wondered what the tunnel would be like without the candle or bright daylight at each far end, the walls closing in to swallow them whole. The droning was energy filled, an electric pulse from countless insects. The intensity was near maddening, even though it wasn't particularly loud. It was a power plant with a breached core making his fingertips ache, his toes itch.

He would sleep with a nightlight and can of the deadliest bug spray for the rest of his life once rescuers took him away.

"Is the noise always like this?"

She spoke over her shoulder. "The jungle knows when the gods are upset. It talks all night and doesn't sleep good in the day."

She lifted the candle higher, the flame parting another floating black swarm. The formation regrouped behind them and faded into the darkness.

"The jungle was curious when you came. It would have eaten anyone else left on its edges. The jungle even reaches into the sea for scraps. But it let you live. That is why Manu knows you have a special use."

"All this eating," he said. "The ocean, the volcano. And people are scraps?"

"We all ate tonight." She stopped and turned, the candle under her chin casting terrible shadows. "The eating never stops, whether you are a shitter bug or village chief. It never stops until you are made of nothing, until the fish pick you clean and the Sea God swallows the bones."

The moon at the end of the tunnel was high and nearly full. They arranged the supplies at his cave's yawning mouth, a lava tube exit hole somehow attached to the active volcano. Dash inspected the rolled sleeping mat, which would provide immeasurable comfort. He'd also been issued a three-foot-long bamboo spear, and flat round stones with razor sharp sides, perhaps to gut fish he'd be required to hunt on his own. Tiki quickly gathered brown leaves and pieces of dead vine.

"Watch me."

She jammed the candle into a crevasse, then used her teeth to tear open the fire starter package. She separated the striker from the silver block labeled magnesium. "You shave some from the block then use the other side to make spark. It looks like magic, but isn't."

A flick of her wrist and white hot sparks jumped from the bar onto the kindling, a curl of smoke rising from a yellow baby flame. She reached for a new candle, ran the long stick under her nose with her eyes closed, then put wick to flame.

"Bees make candles." She handed it to him. "I'll show you in the daytime. And I'll show how to rub your teeth with charcoal to keep them clean. Missioners brought the fire starters to make us civilized. Light, Jesus Christ, and shiny clackers make you righteous. They brought soap and these clothes because the Son of God doesn't want to look at lady bosoms and filthy bums." She snapped the waistband of her underpants. "There aren't new ones because they've been gone so long. You have Ooba's. He fell out of a tree and was sent into the waves. We'll all be naked again soon. I guess it was meant to be."

Dash touched the waistband of the dead man's underwear. "The missioners taught Christianity?"

She nodded. "And that clap-clap and pagan gods send you to a fiery hell at the bottom of the sea."

He tried breaking a length of bamboo over his knee, but failed and had to add it to the fire whole. She collected rocks and shaped a small fire pit. They sat upwind of the smoke, on a bench of smooth lava that grew tiny ferns where dirt had collected in cracks.

"Your people didn't stop believing in the Volcano God."

She shrugged. "The missioners think their god stays alive inside a book. They open the book to give him breath, and to release his love in song and prayer."

"It's not the missioners coming to take you away."

"No, those are the white soldiers. They have guns. Not all the missioners are white, but all the soldiers are. That's why the warriors want to feed you to the Volcano. White skin is a special evil that brings sorrow to our people."

Dash hunched over his knobby knees. Every explorer he'd learned about delivered disease and death. They discovered what had already been discovered, planted flags in soil mixed with bones of other people's ancient ancestors.

"You talk different than other white men. Same language, but different sounds. Maybe that's also why Manu is waiting to hear from the Volcano. She brought you here, and other gods did not claim you. Manu believes there is always a reason for things to happen."

"I'm from America. I guess the missioners taught English?"

"They were from a church in Australia, but their houses were in different places. Some lived next to elephants and had the same color skin as me. Australia is an island this big." She held her arms in a circle. "There was a book that showed maps of the whole world, but it burned in a fire when I was little. Our teacher drew maps from memory. America is far away. Many months by boat, she says."

"How often do people other than soldiers come?"

She paused as if to think. "Only when a plane crashes."

Dash pictured some sort of Bermuda Triangle, airplanes of all sizes in death spirals, caught by a magnetic field and splashing down like meteors.

"How often do planes crash?"

"Just one so far, but Manu says the Volcano is angry with us. She will throw more stones before she bleeds. Maybe more planes will fall."

"Manu says she's angry because the ground shakes?"

"She punishes him by making his bones hurt, and by making it hard for him to pee."

"Does he say why she's upset?"

Tiki picked a dry twig from the lava, ran it around her toes as if making a chalk outline. "Only that our people are doing something wrong. He is punished because he's our chief, but we feel it too. Not in our pee, but other ways."

"Like how?"

"The fever comes to kill babies and old people. And the hearts of everyone else are made heavy when the dead are put into the sea."

Dash began to suspect who the white soldiers were. Not mythical bad guys from ancient times, but living human beings coming to pick from a new crop.

"The soldiers only take away pretty girls? Never anyone else?"

"Only girls who are ten. The prettiest. They come during the hot season. It's a great honor, but I'll miss Talei and Bulou. We were all best mates."

"And your mother?"

"She was put into the sea when I was little."

"I'm sorry."

"Me, too," she said, feeding the fire with strips of vine.

"Where are the girls taken?"

She took a deep breath, then used her hands again. "To a place with houses taller than a volcano. So tall they touch the clouds. Even the strongest birds can't reach the front door."

Her mood changed, and her eyes lit as she looked directly at him.

"The girls are given a house filled with beautiful clothes, instead of these scungy old daks. They have mirrors more clear than still water, and rows of bottles that squirt perfume more pretty than flowers. The floors are so soft it's like walking on air. The chosen girls can eat whatever they want from a big box that makes cold air and keeps away bugs."

"Refrigerators," he said.

She squinted, leaned toward him. "Did you have one in your house?"

"In my apartment, yes."

"Did you have a kitten? A magazine that didn't burn up has a picture of a kitten eating food from a yellow bowl. It's gray and fluffy and has blue eyes."

He smiled. "No, kittens make me sneeze."

"How?"

"Well, it's called allergies. Something about their skin. It gets in the air and makes some people sneeze."

"I'm going to have a kitten in my house even if I sneeze all day. I'll hold it in my arms while we watch the birds fly below us."

"It sounds wonderful," he said. "A girl should have a kitten. Do the soldiers speak the same English?"

"Yes, like the missioners taught us. But the missioners stopped coming when I was real little. They gave up on us and went other places. Manu says they called us godless heathens, but that shows how dumb they are. We have lots of gods. Lots more than missioners. How many gods do you have?"

Dash was suddenly embarrassed about being a godless heathen. "Pretty much the same as the missioners," he said.

Tiki held out both hands to count on her fingers. "We have a Sea God and a God of the Sun. A Bird, Time, and Dirt God. The Volcano God, Storm God, and Wave God. The Wave God is different from the Sea God. That's eight, and there's one more," she said, frowning, trying to remember.

"Our one god is supposed to watch over everything."

She shook her head. "The world is too big." She put a thumb and index finger together and held them to one eye. "This island is only this big on my teacher's map."

"Having lots of gods makes sense."

She nodded, then spoke in a low voice. "But it makes people worry. So many gods to pull you underwater or make you fall out of a tree. Gods bring thunder to keep you awake at night, and wind to blow away your house."

"What god protects little girls from soldiers?"

Tiki's smooth lips formed a pout, her eyes squeezed into a glare. "How much do *you* want to leave this place? Do you want to grow old in a stinking jungle?"

"But this is your home," he said. "These are your people, your family."

"Mama is gone."

"I can only imagine how much that hurts." When he reached to touch her shoulder, she slapped his hand away with the same blind motion as the old woman in the aisle seat.

Tiki lurched from the stone bench and kicked sand over the fire, suddenly furious. "I'll have two kittens if I'm pretty enough," she said, crossing her arms and turning her back to him.

He groaned as he struggled to his feet. He was tired and everything ached. "I'm sorry. Please don't be angry."

The two lit candles had dripped wax into wide pools, one now only a stub. He hadn't noticed their small flames, had wasted precious light he needed to survive.

"I have to make a place to sleep. Will you help?"

"I'll come back in the morning." She headed toward the path, then stopped and turned. "The Fire God is the one I forgot. He mostly lives inside the Volcano to eat whatever she swallows."

Dash touched his throat. Going back into the fire was a thousand times worse than going back into the water.

"I told you gods were scary," she said, then turned and disappeared into the black tunnel.

Chapter 7

———

SLEEK BIRDS WITH white and black painted bodies patrolled the sky, the calm sea mirroring their aerodynamic designs and sweeping orbits. A slight wind left the water mostly still— flat swells that lifted and lowered with unstirred crests. Dash watched each bird take a turn abandoning formation, shedding elevation until belly feathers kissed its reflection. Dagger-like beaks cut the surface in narrow, car-length incisions, stuttering once with a sideways flick of the head. Graceful wings stroked the salty air, and the bird would ascend with a small fish impaled, its flapping body working like a useless propeller. The birds seemed to never miss.

To his right was the coral reef looming just beneath the waves. It was a protective wall running north into the distance on a parallel track to the island. The reef interrupted waves born hundreds or thousands of miles away. He wondered how far short the plane had come from reaching Fiji. The online maps showed blue almost everywhere in this enormous section of the route. There were more smudges on his laptop screen than specks of land. He was now the proverbial needle in a haystack made of infinite pieces of dried grass because they'd stopped looking. He looked down at the sheltered calm spot where the women had taken him for his first bath. He'd been awestruck by the mountain breathing smoke as though it were a living thing, the exotic leaning trees and untended beaches he'd seen only in pictures.

He stood at the end of the lava shelf, the edge of a black table he supposed was some of the planet's newest land. It was a twenty to thirty yard tongue, depending on the tide. It provided a view of a more hostile world, deep water where anything could lurk, but was also the direction he imagined the ship would come for his rescue. He watched the surging water tumble cream-colored shells, fish chasing bubbles, and tiny skittering creatures with countless legs. Bits of plastic garbage washed up here from ships or other islands, maybe even Australia or somewhere in Asia. He stood a few paces beyond what was currently an anemic blowhole, emitting knee-high puffs twice a minute. The rounded shelf was like the lower third of a surfboard. It cantilevered over a bottom that sloped into the dark. He could only guess how far the sea traveled underneath the island, and never in a million years would he dive in for the answer.

"Where am I?" he asked the tiny creatures taking refuge between his toes, jealous they'd made it to safe harbor. It seemed unfair. The giant over his shoulder who took care of this island wanted to eat him alive rather than offer asylum. Dash was tempted to step back, but didn't. He let them be for now.

The two places he'd experienced the ocean were in New Hampshire and New Jersey. One the temperature of an ice-filled Styrofoam beer cooler, and the other so crowded that hungry sharks would have to eat their way through tons of pasty tourists before posing any danger. The old *Jaws* movie had a lasting effect on New Englanders, especially those in the mountains who only occasionally wandered down to sea level. Dash knew all the things that could slither into a lake.

But oceans held monsters beyond imagination, according to movies and his father's collection of *National Geographic* magazines.

A flash of white against the black lava caught his eye. He padded across the sharp edges, thinking it might be a discarded toy, and pulled one side of a jawbone the waves had wedged into a crack. He turned the bone over in his hands, felt its smoothness and light weight. It held a single tooth at the shorter curved end where the jaw was broken. The tooth wiggled and came free. He cupped it in one hand, and reached to feel his own lower front teeth. They were a close match. He carefully retreated with his find, keeping an eye on the craggy black landscape for other skeleton parts.

Up a short slope was a circular tide pool six feet across, its water replenished only at the peak of high tide, when the strongest waves rolled over the backs of others along a narrow stone channel. On the far side was a perfect stone bench, probably formed when the molten lava met the cool sea during a battle of fire and water. It was a mostly shady spot because of a single squat palm tree growing up behind the bench through a gash in the lava. It leaned with the constant breeze, wide fronds swaying. He sat facing the tide pool, which mirrored the ocean beyond, providing a dual view of the spot where the fishermen paddled their skiffs around the southern edge of the reef. It was the first and last leg of their daily expeditions, return trips sometimes weighed down by bows stacked with big, tuna-looking fish from the deep water.

Behind Dash and the palm were puka trees he recognized from vacation brochures. They were small and bent over, probably stunted from the constant sea breeze that made them all lean toward the leeward side of the island. Another skiff skimmed across the tide pool and the real ocean beyond, as he fingered the sleek bone. Dash looked up and waved, then lowered the jaw onto his lap and jammed the tooth back in place. A fisherman shouted, but the words were drowned out by the wind and hissing blowhole. Dash nodded, held up his right thumb to wish them luck and watched as they turned the corner around the reef to head back north. The long, skinny boats looked no match for such a huge amount of water, not to mention the hungry whales and giant squid. Manu's young warriors might be tough guys, but the fishermen were the truly brave ones.

Dash raised the bone when they were gone, measured it against his sunburned face. It was an adult for sure. The tooth tumbled out again, bounced across the thin layer of black sand. It was yellow, maybe from age or stained from coffee and cigarettes. Could it have belonged to the lady in the flowered dress with the bag of knitting? Perhaps whatever swarmed outside the reef had picked her body clean, recycling the old gal in a way she could never have imagined. He hoped she hadn't suffered, even though she'd been certain he was doomed to hell for violating the irresistible crack in the wall. She'd at least had something to hope for, had somewhere to go. Maybe she was there, or maybe she'd been nothing but one day's nourishment for scavengers.

His penis hurt from thinking about the noisy hole, but touching the front of his briefs proved the pain was a ghost. He was as numb as ever. He stroked the smooth surface of the bone instead, tilting it to examine tiny holes in the harsh sunlight.

The girl had told him the eating never stopped until you were made of nothing. If so, then the woman could be at peace, whether or not heaven was real. But he realized there was still one piece of her left, or two, counting the tooth. He should throw them back into the waves, let the Sea God finish the job.

Perhaps the jaw's appearance was her attempt to communicate from the next life, to remind him of the inevitability of death just as Hamlet had been reminded by his dear friend Yorick's colorless skull. But the all-powerful sea had intercepted the messenger and smashed up her news, or her one last chance to tell Dash he was a dirty, filthy man. Maybe it was the Wave God's work, or maybe the Bird God had filled its belly on her last morsel. Perhaps the Sun God had broiled away every last bit.

Being a godless heathen was easier.

He rubbed the bone as if summoning a genie, held it against his thigh to contrast the color. He tapped it against his numb parts, still feeling nothing. He arched his back and lowered the waistband with his left hand to expose his pathetic member. He thumped the bone directly on the pale knob. "God, smite the sinner with a paralyzed pecker!" he imagined the lady's message was meant to say. He drummed the bone hard enough to bring tears, but his penis was unconscious or dead. The bone became a blur as he beat himself, and then chuckled with an awful thought. He might be in bad straights, but what sin had the woman committed to be reduced to a mere drumstick?

There was another flash of motion in the tide pool, different from the spraying blowhole. He stopped whacking his crotch and looked up in time to see a man lift himself out of the water onto the edge of the shelf. He was immense, with bodybuilder chest and arms, wide shoulders glistening bronze under the high sun. There were no boats in sight. No crashed airplanes.

Dash tried to look away from the man's nakedness when he stood tall and stretched, striking heroic Greek god poses. But the strange object perched atop his shoulders was impossible not to watch. If the man's mouth did not move and his eyes did not turn and blink—and if the small bit of bone or cartilage did not light and flicker over his forehead—Dash would have been certain it was a Halloween mask.

The herculean man with the grotesque fish head stalked up the jagged lava and swept around the tide pool. He sat heavily next to Dash, who could only stare. The man's lower jaw was set in a drastic under-bite; narrow teeth were pointed barbs, made more ominous by wide gaps displaying reddish gums.

His jowls hung from his jutting bottom lip down to a human Adam's apple.

The creature looked at Dash with blue eyes that appeared startled from skin pulled taut and missing eyebrows. What looked to be the front spine of a dorsal fin bobbed freely on a hinge in front of his awful mouth. The tip of the spine was bulbous and glowed. Dash was hypnotized by the creature's dancing light.

"That's kind of weird," said the giant in a clear voice, fish head tilted down to where Dash held the bone frozen in mid-drum over his exposed member.

"Sorry." Dash shook his head, let the elastic waistband snap closed.

"My name is Weeleekonawahulahoopa." He extended a hand. "You can call me Willy."

Dash dropped the bone, allowed the man's fingers to envelope his hand. It was like slipping into an oversized baseball glove left out in a warm rain. "I'm Dash," he said, then to explain being caught drumming his privates he added, "I was in a plane crash and can't feel anything."

"Tough luck. She's a real piece of work."

"Who?"

"The Volcano God." Willy jerked a thumb over his shoulder toward the smoking peak. "I'd lay good odds she's the cause of your current troubles. Doesn't seem fair, I'll bet."

"So she's real?"

"You can't see her?"

Dash couldn't help but follow the bobbing action of the mesmerizing light. It made it hard to maintain a train of thought. "I've never seen a god before. Is that what you are? Some kind of god of the fish?"

"I'm not a god," said Willy, and Dash noticed the light go dim. "I used to be, but I'm done with all that."

"You can stop being a god?"

"Gods are man-made things, my friend. That means they

have all sorts of built-in flaws. And gods are usually born out of fear, with a little hope tossed in. Imagine changing light bulbs for a living, but you're scared of heights. What kinda job you gonna do up on that ladder all day?" Willy paused, looked out over the tide pool at the ocean. "Yep, that's a god for you. A big old mix of fear and hope. And throw in some desperation, too. Afraid of what's out there in all that green and blue water? Then just pray to it. Make offerings and even sacrifices to it. An entire ocean takes a lot of prayers to make a god, but it happened. Same with that bitch?"

"The Volcano God?"

"Right." Willy waved a giant hand in front of his face to shoo tiny moths from his light.

"Why did you quit? Was it all that bad?"

Willy rubbed the sides of his strange forehead, about where temples would be. "My people loved and trusted me. Kids afraid of the dark, and old folks with their days winding down. They believed I'd take care of their island. Bigger place than this, maybe by double or triple. No volcano, though, which was just fine. They offered their belongings, heirloom treasures, to guarantee I'd always protect them, keep them safe from storms and disease. To keep the fish biting. They gave me carvings that were handed down, jewelry that had married great grandparents, all things valuable enough to keep when they migrated across the seas. Fourteen new babies were named Weeleekonawahulahoopa in one season alone. Imagine that?"

Dash nodded that he could.

"They didn't have to give me their things. I wasn't the kind of god to hold out on a sick kid." Willy paused, shaking his head, the light waving back and forth. "But I let them because it was part of the ceremony they loved. Humans are big on ceremonies. Like having gods, they bring comfort, makes them feel closer to whatever they're praying to. And so I kept the worst sickness away, let the rains fall in moderation. The wife beaters fell out of their boats and drowned, and poison snakes were ready to bite any man with an eye on hurting a child."

"Sounds like you were a sheriff, too."

Willy shrugged, and Dash thought he saw a smile.

"I listened to their needs because I loved them, and they loved me back. Even the bad-minded ones were treated with a fair hand if I saw their hearts could change. No one ever questioned whether I was real because I was everywhere. Right up until I let them all die."

Willy's swaying light dimmed again, but his face didn't change.

"I'm sorry," Dash mumbled, not sure what else to say.

Willy got to his feet, enormous muscles flexing and twitching, sweat rivulets trickling through the creases of hard flesh. His thigh was as big as an old coconut palm trunk, skin the reddish color of the last rays of the evening sun. Dash fought an urge to touch the giant thigh, to reach out and knock on it.

"You oughtta know that I can hear your thoughts," Willy said. "They come through pretty loud and clear."

"Yeah, that's okay. I'm used to it. My fiancée could, too. It's why she ended up hating me."

"So much hate out there. Hate and more hate." Willy stepped around the tide pool and walked to the very end of the island without looking back. Dash thought his shoulders were too slumped even for a former god who'd let all his people die. The giant man paused at the edge of the surf, then dove head first, disappearing into the incoming tide.

Chapter 8

—

A SHIP'S DAILY appearance coincided with Dash's sickness. Different than flu or any illness he'd known, it came from depression and hopelessness, combined with the things that had bitten him, the accumulation of toxins. The ship arrived under power of oppressive heat, tanks fueled with his oily fish dinners and mosquito fever nights. His countless hours alone knitted the American flag over the Coast Guard cutter's stern, welded the steel in its hull. Desperation put sailors in crisp uniforms, turned them into busy worker bees preparing a rescue launch from its sturdy railing.

Every detail was correct, from the spinning radar dishes to the single life vest left carelessly on the open deck, all bearing a striking resemblance to the box cover photo on a model received one Christmas from a grandparent.

He could have strolled out across the ocean's surface, feet barely tasting salt, and stroked the orange fabric of the tidy vessel being readied to come ashore. He could have climbed aboard, wondered about equipment and dials, guessed the meaning of things written in cryptic abbreviations. He could have sat next to a warm-blooded man, smelled his sweat and the coffee on his breath. The sailor would be too busy with a checklist for questions.

The mirage couldn't account for the thousands of miles separating the black sand beneath his toes and the waters any such ship would patrol, but it didn't matter.

Passing days blurred the phantom vessel, and the longer he stared, the farther away it seemed. The crew was gone. The red and white paint faded, soon to become the same gray nothing. There was no man or woman to finish lowering the smaller boat dangling on metal arms. It became a ghost ship, and eventually there was no ship at all, only bobbing sea birds where a hundred tons of metal had sunk to the murky bottom of an exhausted imagination.

He was increasingly anxious awaiting Willy's daily visits, sure that something had changed, that his imaginary friend wouldn't return. But then the melancholy former god would swim up out of the waves as Dash sat moping on his stone bench. Sometimes they didn't talk; they were just two gloomy figures casting still shadows.

Each time he heard the village drums, Dash expected an armed procession to come take him away. His cage had no bars, but he was a prisoner all the same. He grew gills in his dreams, and wings in his fantasies, but found how easily hope dried up and quietly died under the heavy sun. The drums mostly sounded in the hour before sunset, but the only one to appear out of the jungle was the girl, usually lugging a bucket of potable water and cooked fish wrapped in banana leaves.

The lava tube cave's main compartment was pear-shaped. Ceiling cave-ins had created a dead end back where the fruit would be fattest. If he were stronger, perhaps he could clear an opening that would lead all the way into the volcano's belly, at least until the heat and gases turned him back. The porous black walls absorbed outside reflections and the light from rationed candles. He lit one candle at a time, always extinguishing the flame when leaving for any stretch. His hands shook when he woke in the pitch blackness to fumble with the striker and magnesium block, drops of sweat complicating his efforts.

He'd spent weeks recovering from the plane crash, and could only imagine the free reign all the creeping things enjoyed while he was unconscious. They'd surely used him as a highway, and probably burrowed into his skin to deposit soon-to-hatch eggs. Light kept things he could see at bay, banished the worst to the shadows, just as he had been sent here to wait. One dream had him wrapped in a cocoon by tiny humanoid creatures that spoke the same language as the islanders. He woke trying to imitate their voices, convinced they'd free him if he could match the right sounds.

Existing on a tropical island was a far cry from reality TV or honeymoon brochures. Foraging meant picking through bug-infested fruit that had become nests of baby spiders guarded by alien-eyed mothers. Fallen coconuts were claimed by cockroach-like insects he'd seen served as toasted side dishes. He was allowed into the village once daily to move his bowels in the stinking outhouses, but he felt watched like an enemy. He did his business quickly and got out.

On his twentieth day of exile, Tiki came with a message from Manu. Dash had been using his stone tool to carve a face into a coconut's outer flesh, crouching over the ground at the very edge of the tide. He'd nicked his fingers in a half dozen spots with the sharp edge, used the salt water to rinse slippery blood.

Tiki cast a thin shadow over his work. "You're bleeding."

He kept carving. "Practice makes perfect."

"Manu will send for you in four nights, when the moon has a big face. All the preparations will be done."

Dash's stomach turned over, and he dropped his tool. The unrecognizable bust of his former fiancée rolled out of his limp hand. "Preparations? Oh, god!"

Tiki spoke slowly, as if trying her best to get it right. "Manu said the Volcano God came to his dreams in the shape of a woman. She spoke of the man who fell from the sky and killed the fish. There is to be a feast in his honor because he will save our people from the soldiers."

"I knew it," he said, head suddenly aching. "A feast of roasted cockroaches, and then they'll toss me in the volcano for dessert."

He rocked onto his butt, soaking his underpants in warm tidal water. After three weeks of fending off spiders and swarming mosquitoes while awaiting his execution, a quick and painless death wasn't the worst of his fears. This wasn't going to be a blindfold and firing squad. No lethal injection while listening to classical music in a room painted aqua. This would be snatched right out of his worst recurring nightmare. The warriors were getting their way, the chance to jab sharpened spears in his back to prod him onto a ledge over a bubbling cauldron. He felt his legs catch fire in the dream, heard his crackling hair, eyes boiling as they went blind. He was certain he'd shared Manu's dream. The Volcano God had gotten inside his head, too.

"Manu says you will learn everything at the feast under the big face moon."

"That's not fair. Why not now?" He had to know. Absolutely needed to know.

"The elders are sick from too much clap-clap," she said. "They spent the morning hiding from the Sun God."

"But you know. You know what they're going to do to me. They planned it all while getting boozed up. Manu is sending the bastard who smashed the boy's hand. What did he do? What could any kid do to deserve that?"

She looked away, hands fiddling behind her back, and he was convinced of the worst. He looked up at the volcano, then out to where there was no rescue ship. How far could he swim? A mile? Probably a hundred yards in the lousy shape he was in. He looked out at the spot among the rolling waves where he'd slip under and drown.

"Please tell me, Tiki. You must have heard them talk. We're friends, aren't we?"

"I can't."

He reached up and touched her shoulder, the brown skin hot from the sun. Her face was hidden, but he thought she'd begun to cry until she swept her hair behind one ear to look down at him. He saw she was trying not to giggle.

"What is it? What's so funny?"

WINDY SPOTS WERE marvelous mosquito-free places. Dash had learned to avoid the water's midday reflection, and that turning over dead logs when gathering firewood meant risking agonizing bites from hundred-legged creatures. He suffered anxious moments following these bites, waiting for signs of poison, wondering if venom was racing through his blood toward his heart. He only hoped the end would come quickly, that whatever god involved wouldn't merely paralyze the rest of him.

Being a castaway meant no aspirin for headaches, no handy plastic bandages for cuts. Being shoeless on a volcanic island changed your pace and stride: each step was cushioned with an extra bend in the knee, a slow motion shuffle across hot coals.

He slumped on his hard bench, chin resting on folded arms. He watched the skiffs return from the deep holes where big ones hid. One fisherman lifted a hand and Dash was about to wave when the man lifted his chin and dragged an index finger across his throat.

A fish rose from the sea beyond the surging tide at the end of the shelf, the human torso and legs underneath coated in white foam. Willy came to sit next to him behind the tide pool, body dripping salt water into a puddle between massive feet. His big toes reminded Dash of the dill pickles his mother used to bring from the deli.

"You could build a raft," said Willy.

"Sure, but where would I drift?"

Willy shrugged, held up his palms. "The currents are weak this season, so it would depend on the Storm God."

"You think it could blow me into the shipping lanes? Or a bigger island with people living in this century?"

Willy seemed to give this question serious thought, took time before answering. "I think she'd let you drift until you were blistered and nearly dead from thirst. Then she would mercifully drown you, or send a bolt of lightning. She's the Storm God, not the Norwegian Cruise Line God."

"Yeah, thanks for the picture."

Willy thumped water from one cauliflower shaped ear. "It would get so unbearable you'd be grateful to her. Some gods are funny like that."

"How do you know about the Norwegian Cruise Line?"

"You looked them up on your computer, remember? Then you clicked on pictures of women with large breasts wearing small bikinis. You moved on to a website showing videos of young ladies being forced to have intercourse with prison guards."

"Okay, I get it."

"That's the century you're looking for, right?"

"It's complicated."

"It seems criminal," said Willy. "The women are already in jail."

"You're trying to make a joke?"

"To tell the truth, I could live without knowing any of it."

Dash watched the life at the edge of the tide pool. Some kind of shell creature, a muscle no larger than the end of his pinky, had opened its hinged body, stuck out a pink tongue to probe the surrounding rock. The creature had been deposited by the last high tide, spent the afternoon in a much smaller world than its usual habitat of the open ocean. Dash wondered if it felt claustrophobic, or if it knew the tide would return. Maybe it relished the calm of the small space, would be content to stay.

"My penis still doesn't work," said Dash.

"So what's the big deal?"

"The girl says Manu wants me to make a white baby. Thinks it will satisfy the soldiers who come steal the girls, and that it'll be enough to keep them away. He makes it sound like an offering to a god, another kind of human sacrifice."

"The volcano gave him the idea," said Willy. "Told him in a dream."

"How do you know?"

Willy rolled his strange fish eyes. "It's not that I want to read minds. Thoughts find me."

"So you still have god powers. You can keep the soldiers away."

Willy held up a dismissive hand. "I'm not any kind of god anymore. And calling those men soldiers is wrong."

"Kidnappers?"

"I'd go with slave traders. And dealing with ten-year-old girls makes them a special kind of evil."

"It's like they're filling orders. But maybe it isn't for sex. Maybe they're some kind of outlaw adoption ring."

"You were a reporter before you got fired and had your heart broken by the town tramp, right?"

"Christ, that's some trick," said Dash. "You even use the words in my head. You'd make a killing working the carnival circuit back home."

Willy ignored him. "What did they teach you in journalism school when it came to the bad guys?"

Dash paused, remembering the theme of the class that made him fall in love with the idea of working for a newspaper. The professor described the career as 'a combination of police detective and mystery writer.' "We were told to follow the money."

"Yes, and they're selling the girls to the highest bidders," said Willy. "The girls are going to wealthy businessmen and pimps, not loving families. No doubt about it."

"You were a god, for crying out loud. They're just humans with guns. Mortals."

Willy turned to him with an oversized index finger pointed to his own chest. "Exactly what do you think I could do?"

"Sink their boat," Dash nearly shouted. "I don't know. Send them over the rainbow in a water spout. Do some god thing. Release the kraken on their sorry asses!"

Willy shook his head. "Not possible."

"You told me you changed the weather, made it rain. You cured diseases."

"I don't exist here," he said quietly. "Not for these people. They don't have a Fish God, never heard of Weeleekonawahulahoopa."

"This is crazy. How does a Volcano God knock an airplane out of sky, but you can't stop a few armed assholes from kidnapping children? You have to. It's what gods are for."

Dash's words hung in the air for more than a minute. Willy stared down at the puddle he'd made.

"I'm nothing but a ghost. You want protection, go see her." Willy bobbed his chin toward the volcano. "She's the almighty one on this turf, but there's a catch. A volcano is like an octopus, tentacles weaving up through the ground and poking holes to feel around. The rest of its body lives far away, with a little brain that's made up of next to nothing. Sometimes she does good things, and sometimes she destroys entire villages for no reason. The Sea God acts that way, too. All the big gods are real sketchy, can be *buku* dangerous. The Bird God is a whole different case. Not many people die from bird shit in their hair."

"How do you ask a volcano for help?"

Willy shrugged. "Human sacrifice gets her attention."

"That's a lousy option."

"You're better off praying to your Penis God to get the old wanker up and working. Or get a Computer God to deliver a new laptop. Those big boobies seemed to work like a charm."

Dash shook his head. "They won't stop taking the girls even

if Manu gives them a white baby. And that's besides the fact that the baby could turn out just as brown as the rest, even if some miracle occurred."

"You're missing the point." Willy unfurled a limp eel that had been curled in one hand. He twirled it between two fingers, then held it over his head and lowered the tail into his mouth. He slurped it down like a spaghetti noodle, wiped his dangerous-looking mouth with the back of a hand and burped. "Manu is convinced they'll be left alone in exchange for a white baby. There's enormous power in belief."

"I still don't understand why I see you," Dash said. "You look real."

"I don't know. You must be a special case. Or maybe I'm only a hallucination. Did you check your daily horoscope?"

"No."

"Good, that shit's all made up." Willy smiled. "Some of the kids see me, too. I scared the bejesus out of two boys hunting sand crabs along the tide line. I can eat a whole bushel of those things."

Dash frowned.

"Crabs, not boys, dumbass." Willy rubbed his stomach, his light surging brighter. "I was relaxing in the shallow water and I might have said boo, or something. Had no idea they'd run screaming. I felt like a heel. Things like that will give a god a bad rep. I've seen it happen."

"So you have no idea why I can see you? I'm probably crazy. It runs in my family."

"You wanna go home, right?"

"Of course."

"Back to where your girl cheated, and you just got shit-canned from a lousy job? Way too depressing. I'd say crazy is a safe bet. Look, I'm really not trying to read your thoughts."

"I appreciate that."

"Humans are filled with mostly monotonous stuff. I'm hungry. I'm tired. I'm horny. I worship you. I hate you." Willy paused to rub his face. "I loved my people, but I never got any sleep."

"I guess I understand," said Dash. "If a village is big enough, there's always someone hurting."

"Sometimes you can't even think."

"What happened to your people?"

Willy's head tilted to the side, eyes turning skyward. "I was idolized in so many ways. It was the best of times before my people were killed. I came to them during a drought, and brought gentle rains. I ushered schools of plump fish into their wide lagoon. And they knelt down before this humble god."

Willy stopped talking and dropped his head into his hands, shoulders lurching. Dash watched him begin to fade as he sat less than two feet away on the same lava bench. The disappearing act lasted several minutes, until only a hint of light hovered where his forehead had been. Then it blinked out and left Dash sitting alone next to a small puddle.

He turned to watch the white breakers roll over the lava rocks. "God," he finally muttered, "I am crazy."

Chapter 9

DASH WOKE FROM a dreamless sleep, climbed stiff from his bedding—like a wild animal, he thought—and headed toward the light. A raw wind swept over the waves to the east, as though rushing to fill a void left by the rising sun. He dipped his toes, let the sideways running tide clean the filth, and began gathering flat stones with good round edges.

The first throw skipped across the breakers five times, nothing compared to what he could do on the tranquil ponds at home, where a dozen or even fifteen touches were possible. The uneven surface launched his best throws skyward, or pitched them down into the rolling troughs with disappointing plops.

He shook out his throwing arm and was stretching his shoulder muscles when a wave tumbled a bulky object he at first mistook for Willy. It rolled up the sloping shore and then threatened to head back out to sea on the retreating surf. He hobbled across the sharp footing to time the next big wave, the blow hole full of energy, showering him from behind. He'd angled his body with one foot forward when the wall of churning whitewater rushed past him, thigh high. He trudged toward the mostly submerged object that was hung up on the very last point of land.

The current pulled back at the moment his fingers wedged under its plastic rim. He planted his heels, locked his knees, and held on with all his might as the ocean changed direction, nearly sucking it from his grasp. His skinny arms were fully extended, butt low, with a river of water blasting against his back and shoulders. He was at the very tipping point of a tug-o-war: either his ankles and wrists would give out, or his body would be claimed by the ocean still clinging to its prize.

A new wave rolled up over the retracting froth and sent him hard to his ass, knocking the object free from the very end of his ragged fingernails. For one brief second he had a perfect view of the row of three connected airplane seats, cushions intact and belts reaching like tendrils. He was overwhelmed by the possibility of losing this artifact of civilization. Panic drove him to his feet and made him lunge chest first, arms wide open, tackling and pinning the seats as the new wave swept back out.

"Please," he whimpered, and then sucked in a deep breath just in time as the next wave rolled and tumbled him over the jagged lava. Another wave slammed down directly over him, driving the seats into his body as if telling him to go ahead and take the damn things. He was upside down when bright stars exploded across his vision. The impact made him forget to hold his breath and he was suddenly choking, spinning in a ruthless washing machine filled with foam and sharp edges. He was rolling, elbows and knees bumping along, until another wave changed his position. He was face down, a slow vinyl record with a needle planted in the middle of his forehead, a great weight on his back keeping him from rising to his knees for air. He reached behind and felt the waterlogged seats that had him pinned, then found his waistband and tugged at the painful wedgie.

He'd been tricked by some rogue god, lured by an enchanting object to the same fate as the small fish attracted to Willy's dangling light. His chest muscles clenched in a spasm, water in his lungs and air all but gone. Would the Sea God go to the effort of baiting the most dangerous spot on the island with something so irresistible as a soft place to sit? He supposed murder might be comparable to sacrifice for gods, a different brand of satisfaction to upset the monotony.

Perhaps it was the god who lurked among white clapboard churches back home, intent on finishing off the sinner, having decided that a paralyzed penis was insufficient punishment for his collective transgressions. Or retribution for violating unwitting female privates in frat house beds. There had been lust and gluttony that night, the remaining five deadly sins to be visited later in the semester. Although he was embarrassed by his mother, had sworn to never forgive his father, it might be worse that he never once believed god existed.

"We've sinned and the Good Lord is calling us home."

Or maybe it was a different god.

Water pressed into his nose and ears, pried at his lips, as if it knew all the ways in.

He craned his neck away from the rocks slicing his face. Through foaming water he could see the blue sky with one eye, maybe even a silver glint of metal airplane miles above. *Watch out for the Volcano God*, he wanted to tell the innocent souls on board. *If I can see you, then so can she.*

Dash opened his mouth, let the salt water rush inside. His tongue floated against the back of his teeth as limp and useless as his arms and legs.

Chapter 10

—

THERE WAS NO romance in the kiss. The embrace was all sandpaper and fish smells, rough touching and the racket from puking and dry heaves. There was a muffled voice through water-clogged ears—something about being all right and trying to relax and breathe. He felt sorry for the poor sap needing those words, had been there plenty of times through college, where the anthem was a mix of Stone Temple Pilots, bubbling water bongs, and retching that echoed from tiled walls and floors.

Dash fell in love the night he dabbed vomit from Sarah's lips in a frat house bed. Ironic how the first and last time they'd spoken was while she was sprawled on her back in a bed. Once covered in winter coats, and once covered in Tommy Chambers.

"I love you, too."

The voice was Willy's, and Dash opened his eyes under a shadow cast by the man's peculiar head. It was comforting despite its fearsomeness. And Dash couldn't risk being choosy about friendships, whether home in Vermont or marooned on an island. Friendships eluded him, and any he found turned out lousy. Sarah had been his best friend, along with being his lover.

Dash squinted and coughed, tried speaking and suffered a retching fit that burned deep in his ribcage. "You love me?" he finally managed.

"I was seeing your words. You gotta stop obsessing over that broad. And her Humpty Dumpty guy sounds like a total jerkwad. To tell the truth, I'd have parted his hair with a hammer."

"Humpty Dumpty?"

"You know what I mean," Willy said, pulling away and leaving the sun's heat to press down hard.

Dash looked at the row of airplane seats that had caused him to drown. They were wonderful, man-made things, all plastic and metal. And fire retardant nylon, too, he guessed.

"I was dead."

"You could say that. No gills." Willy poked the side of Dash's neck.

"Ouch!"

"Tender, huh?"

"Your nails, Willy."

"Most people can bite them." He held one hand out and wiggled beefy fingers.

Dash rubbed the part of his head that had been driven into the rocks. There'd been a flash of anger at God for letting this happen, blaming a deity he didn't believe in for letting more shit rain down. There hadn't even been a white light to walk toward when he died, only the goddamn blazing sun overhead that was ready to bloat his rotting carcass by supper time. And then he was being kissed by a fish and thinking about Sarah. Missing Sarah.

"I wasn't kissing you, dumbass. It was mouth-to-mouth resuscitation. You learned how to do it in high school, remember? You learned it, so I knew what to do."

"I'm sorry." Dash worked to smooth his breathing.

"Don't call it kissing unless you wanna go headfirst back into the water."

"You said you were going to stop reading my thoughts."

Willy knelt back, allowed the sun to fall across the rest of Dash's shivering body.

"Yeah, well, then don't accuse me of kissing you."

Dash pushed himself to his elbows and watched his scrawny chest rise and fall, hair so bleached it was nearly invisible. He was thirsty but feeling better. His breathing sounded less like air being forced backward through a wind instrument. A small crab walked sideways past his feet, one claw held out for self-defense, pincers tapping a warning. Or maybe it was scouting for food, and Dash was a disappointment.

"There wasn't any white light. I think it all just goes black when you die. No Pearly Gates, for sure."

"That's about the gist of it." Willy paused for a minute, watched a gull come in close overhead, tilt its head to scan for food. It eyed the crab on its second pass, circling back and hovering against the wind, but didn't come in for the kill. "Keep it to yourself, though, if a miracle ever happens and you get off this cruddy rock."

"So that's it? You're telling me you know there really isn't a heaven? Not even a chance?"

"Relax," said Willy. "You can still believe if you want."

"That's just great." Dash shifted his weight, propped up on one elbow. "I didn't believe, but at least I still had the option. Like flying saucers."

"They aren't real, either."

"Stop!"

"And Santa Claus," said Willy.

"I get it."

"Bigfoot."

Willy began picking through the scattering of shells surrounding them. "Humans get jazzed up over the whole eternity thing. But what kind of life would there be for a god who had to keep an eye on billions of dead people? Imagine the noise from a million symphonies of human complaints. You'd have the only suicidal god in the universe."

Dash squinted. "So why pretend?"

"The world would be out of control without a promise of an afterlife. Remember when your grandma died?"

Dash had to think. "I was in fourth grade, Miss Tate's class. My father took me out of school and drove us real fast to the hospital. I didn't understand what was happening, but I was afraid to ask while he was turning the wheel back and forth like that. I thought we were going to crash."

"Your folks told you it was all okay, that Granny was headed someplace better. She was off to finally see her husband who died before you were born," Willy said. "Imagine not having those little nuggets to spread when trying to make death sound like a million dollars to a crying kid?"

"Maybe I wasn't dead long enough," said Dash. "And maybe you're wrong, too. I always hoped I'd get a chance to see George again."

Willy shifted, putting Dash back in his shadow. "Your dog when you were a kid?"

"Stop reading my mind."

"No, I swear I wasn't." Willy shook his head. "Everyone wants to see their dog again."

Chapter 11

—

Dash struggled with his lungs, hacking up froth and having to stop every few steps as he dragged the seats up the rocks. He wedged the row in front of the lava bench to face the ocean. He'd have a prime view in a comfortable seat, use the rim of the tide pool as a foot rest, and be able to cool his feet. The lower halves of the seats were out of the shade of the fat palm, the soft material baking in the sun. All parts were intact, including the bottom cushions that doubled as flotation devices and the trays behind, although the magazines and barf bags were long gone from their pouches.

He squatted before the seats, eyes following the curving lines of fabric pulled in place by hands in a distant factory. He imagined the sturdy shoe over a switch that began the machine-gun sounds of heavy thread lacing it tight. The stitches were geometric patterns, repeated and perfect, not like any jungle shapes, not like anything in the waves or the clouds. He brushed bits of sand, pulled away dead strands of seaweed, careful not to leave marks from his bloody fingers.

The cushion was still damp when he lowered into the blissful comfort of what he guessed was an aisle seat.

The sun was down, and he was dozing when Tiki flopped into the seat next to him, a candle made from a small coconut held to her stomach, the flame barely alive. She bent her knees and drew her feet back, then ran her hands over the material. "Manu wants you to come."

Dash rolled his head away from her, the top third of a giant moon just now peeking over the horizon line. "I used to love the moon."

"He said not to make him send warriors. But that's not going to happen; all the men are too full of clap-clap to find the path. They would stumble into the jungle and be food for the night things."

"They're celebrating, huh?"

"The drinking circle formed this morning. Even the boys too young were invited. The cup passed until everybody fell asleep with the sun in the top of the sky. Then they woke up and began passing it again. Some made pee on themselves."

"Sounds like quite a party."

"I like your chairs. They're like the ones in the missioners' boats, but even bigger."

"I found them this morning."

She leaned forward over the tide pool, gazed at her bluish reflection, her head in a half-moon phase. She touched her cheek with the back of a hand. He couldn't tell for sure, but thought he saw teardrops send ripples over the dark water. "When you make a white baby, no more girls will leave the island. It will keep me here forever, until I am old and then die, until I am put into the waves."

Dash wanted to tell her it was a great thing, not just because the girls were taken from their families, but because of the horrific things she didn't know about. But he wasn't saving anyone. He'd stuck his penis in a broken fuselage and lost any chance at being a hero. He was doomed, and so was she. And the villagers were either naïve to what the soldiers did with the girls, or refused to believe. He was just as guilty for not telling her there'd be no kittens.

She turned to look at the sky, then back at him. "The moon is climbing. Manu will be angry."

"All right, lead the way." He groaned, getting up, muscles sore from the battering. A hundred tiny scabs had begun to form on his legs and hips. There was a golf ball-size knot on the back of his head.

He followed her into the living tunnel, the walls vibrating from the intense insect noise. The vegetation pulsated when you stopped and held still for a second. Stepping carefully over the sharp grass, he imagined tossing a raw chicken leg into this part of the jungle to watch the creatures come pick it clean like in a time-lapse movie. Vines would slither out of the rich earth to envelop the bones, pull them under. It was a relief to see someone had recently been through with a machete, had chopped back a layer of reaching hands. If he ever got away from this place and somehow bought a home, he'd pave every inch of lawn, uproot every stick of shrubbery.

They emerged from the outskirts into the smoky village, and Tiki led them across the compound by the light of a large cook fire and glow of the moon. She dropped her candle, turned, and ran to where kids had formed a circle to play keep-away with the ball.

"Sit down, Cracker," Manu said, and two men inched apart to make room. Dash could see in the dim light how tired the old man was, the creases in his narrow face deeper than ever.

The first sign of trouble beyond the stink of urine was a break in the usual ceremony. The clap-clap cup was filled and passed directly to Dash. He stared down at it, unsure.

"Don't just look at it," said Manu, and the dozen other men mumbled drunken encouragement. "Smooth like silk. Comes from the best fruits, and my people's special ingredient."

Dash nearly asked, then decided he didn't want to know. He sniffed the awful mixture, readied himself for the taste of gasoline. When he tipped the cup to his lips, the man next to him grabbed his wrist and the back of his head, making the noxious liquid pour into his mouth. He choked down the entire cup, his vision going momentarily white as if he'd been punched in the nose. The circle of men hooted and laughed while as he coughed hard, trying to catch his breath, his lungs already raw. When the burning subsided, he realized the alcohol was already taking effect. The faces of the men seated across from him drifted out of focus. His cuts and bruises no longer ached.

Remembering the tradition, he leaned forward and spit, even though the cup had been passed on. It brought more laughter and he clapped along with them, then had to concentrate on not falling over. The man who'd grabbed his wrist walloped his sunburned back and made a comment in his own language. It sounded a lot like *mazel tov*, which got Dash laughing and coughing more.

"You are here for a reason."

Dash looked across at the chief, blinked hard to get the double-exposed image of the old man back into a single frame. His forehead felt wet and his mouth bone dry. He had a sudden epiphany regarding the importance of cold beer as a chaser. He thought of the crude old saying about giving your left nut for a cold brew, then laughed again at what a shitty deal it would be for anybody getting one of his testicles. Both nuts were as worthless as the rest of his gear down there.

Then his giddiness drained away. He was like a drunk on a barstool when the lights come up at last call, a broken man whose only value was his death, spending his final days surrounded by people who looked upon him as a barely tolerable enemy. They'd been murdered by whites, and the missioners had condemned their beliefs. He was a eunuch with a death sentence. No son to toss the ball, or daughter to take on trips to the zoo. Overcome with melancholia, he tried turning to where the children were playing their game that was a lot like soccer. He fell over, and it took both his neighbors to set him upright.

He thanked the men, patted one bony shoulder.

"The Volcano God has spoken." Manu's voice was steady, and suddenly sober. Dash stared across the circle. "She says you will make a baby to satisfy the men who steal our children. She says the baby will be worth much treasure and will bring peace for our people. In exchange, we will pray to the Volcano God and ask her to take you home."

Manu paused, turning to look at the men nearest him, then signaled for one in particular to come close. The chief spoke low, and the young man in black warrior underwear cupped a hand to his ear. They exchanged words, and the old man finally nodded and turned back to Dash.

"The woman will be fertile in four days, maybe five," Manu said, and the men on either side of Dash jabbed elbows into him, one making a clucking sound. The clucker also made a circle with two fingers and tried sliding an index finger in and out, but he was too drunk and kept missing.

Dash reached down and touched the front of his underpants. There'd been no miracle. "What if I can't?"

"You have no choice," said Manu. "You will do it for my people."

"That's not what I mean." Dash's head was spinning from the harsh alcohol. He struggled to find the right words, tongue fumbling in his dry mouth. "What if it doesn't work? What if it's broken? What if I can't do it?"

The men flanking Manu cut him off with angry words in their sing-song language, spittle flying. The clap-clap cup was knocked to the center of the circle by flailing arms, where it spun twice and stopped with its open mouth facing Dash. The chief allowed the men to have their say, then held up both hands. The circle of warriors fell silent, their chests heaving, bloodshot eyes bulging all around.

"If there is no baby, then the cracker goes into the Volcano," said Manu, who reached for the clap-clap cup and gestured to one of the warriors, who filled it. "We feed her with a human sacrifice. She always likes that."

Chapter 12

——

DASH BARELY REMEMBERED stumbling through the tunnel toward his soft airplane seats after the clap-clap was gone. The fresh candle he'd had—one of the fat ones made from a coconut shell—was now bobbing in the tide pool. The seat made the pounding in his head bearable, and the steady sea breeze kept him from being eaten alive. His eyes opened when the seat dipped to accept the weight of Willy's bulk.

"Never been in an airplane before." Willy was shifting his great thighs and buttocks to fit.

Dash coughed, rubbed his temples hard. "You're not in one now."

"Pretty night." Willy raised a hand toward the setting moon. The sky was already lightening in the east. "So there was a little window here to look out? With a shade to open and close?"

"They're going to throw me into the volcano."

"They believe human sacrifice will calm her down. And before you ask if it works, I have no clue. Except maybe if you factor in the power of suggestion. If they truly believe good things are coming, then maybe they will. None of that hocus-pocus on my island."

"You didn't have a volcano."

"That's true," said Willy. "But they wouldn't have done anything so barbaric unless the situation was pretty dire. No luck with your Penis God?"

Dash sighed. "Same old nothing."

"Sorry. The village women are sprucing up your own special love hut. A sacrificial virgin all picked out. A real looker, too."

"That's not funny."

"Maybe it's exactly what the doctor ordered."

A little girl's singing voice came from the jungle path.

"She sounds like a bird," said Willy.

"The soldiers will take her away."

Willy put his hands on the armrest, looked ready to leave, but settled back when Tiki walked through his massive legs and plopped into the middle seat.

The former god snapped his fingers, then waved a hand in front of her, but she didn't flinch. "Just checking," he said.

"The moon is so pretty down here. The smoke in the village makes it fuzzy," She said, tucking her legs to sit sideways. She leaned into Dash across the armrest and put a hand on his forearm. "Can you see it from your house?"

"Yes, sure."

"Does it look the same?"

"I guess," said Dash. "But you should be sleeping."

"Do you think you can see it wherever you go? Even big cities?"

"Everyone can see it. Sometimes it's hard because of tall buildings, but it's still there."

"Maybe it helps people from being homesick."

Dash couldn't read minds, but knew she was talking about her and not him. What if he convinced Manu to fight back, to use two hundred village men armed with spears against a few armed thugs? The soldiers wouldn't expect a rebellion, not after all this time. They'd have the element of surprise.

"They did try." Willy's voice was soft, his bulb glowing dimly.

"The second season the white men came."

"What happened?" Dash asked, and Tiki rubbed her fingers over a small lump on her arm.

"A bitey bug, I guess. A dumb mosquito." She began pulling at Dash's arm hair, plucking out little blond strands. "There were swarms in the jungle. It's better here."

Willy's bulb moved side to side. "The white men opened fire. One of them was hit by a spear in the meaty part of his thigh. It bobbed up and down as he turned his gun where the women and children were hiding in the huts. I suppose they thought they were safe because they couldn't be seen."

"How many dead?"

"I don't kill them. I swish them like this," said Tiki, demonstrating. "I don't like to squish them because they're filled up with people's blood."

"Manu was shot in the arm," said Willy. "The same arm that had speared the bastard. It was an orange-haired man who limped across the compound where Manu was lying in the dirt bleeding, trying to get up. The soldier stood over him, pulled out the spear, and ordered Manu to summon his wife. The chief looked him in the face and told him no, that he would not. The soldier brandished the gun like he was going to strike him with the stock, but then had an idea. He looked around for a good target, saw a boy hiding next to the cistern, and pulled the trigger like it meant nothing."

"I had no idea," said Dash.

"The missioners said mosquitoes bring sickness, but never to our people. Makes us itchy," said Tiki, scratching.

"There were screams from the edge of the jungle, and the man fired at the sounds," said Willy. "Then he stood waiting, tan pants turning dark from his wound. No other words were spoken. No pleading, no more orders. It was as though things happened as they were meant to, like a story that's already been told and can't be changed. Manu's wife stood from a pocket of ferns, had to peel her daughter off like a scared little monkey.

Handed her to a woman huddled with two babies of her own. This is the little monkey, by the way." Willy used his thumb to point at Tiki. "This is Manu's daughter, who was even more of a runt back when her mama walked out of the jungle, chin held high and proud. She knew what the orange hair man wanted, knew she was walking toward pure evil. She strode past the bastard and knelt down to her injured husband. The soldier fired when Manu reached for her, and the shape of her head changed in an awful way."

Tiki's voice was soft. "Are you sleeping?"

"Sorry, I was thinking."

"The soldiers torched the huts, some filled with people. They shot most of the pigs. More than half of the villagers were slaughtered by a few men with guns. When their boat was gone, it took an entire day to carry all the bodies to the sea. Even the gods mourned. The birds did not fly and the insects did not speak. The Volcano didn't exhale her smoke, and the wind was still. The dead drifted away slowly, in silence."

Willy rose from the airplane seat and walked toward the spot where the moon had fallen into the dark ocean. The little girl leaning on Dash's arm began to snore.

Chapter 13

—

T IKI ARRANGED AN armload of tapered candles she'd brought from the village, squeezing the bases into holes in Dash's lava cave wall. He loved the idea of plugging the hiding spots after witnessing a spider the size of his hand crawl into one and not come out. He imagined all the cracks must be filled with awful things, and when he'd taken a candle to investigate with the flame held out for protection, he was certain something hissed.

"Does orange hair feel different? Is it like the fever that made your face orange when you first came here?"

"It's called red hair, not orange," said Dash. "And it's just a different color that's handed down from parents and grandparents. Doesn't mean anything more. Like mine is brown and my fiancée's is blonde, which is kind of like white. It's nothing but color, like a bird's feathers."

"The missioners had black hair. Big bushy eyebrows and hair in their noses. The soldiers all have hair like yours, except one."

He didn't know what she remembered or had been told about her mother's death. He made a mental note to ask Willy if the man who killed her mother was still among those returning for more children.

"My favorite actress has red hair, or at least she did. It was a long time ago," Dash said. He sat on his sleeping mat watching her finish with the candles. She'd also brought the makings for a broom—a length of bamboo and a vine cord to fasten long stiff leaves that had gone brown.

"Actress?"

"It's a woman in a show that's like your ceremonies. Only this actress was in a comedy, where they did funny things."

"What was the show about?"

He tried remembering a storyline from one of the *Gilligan's Island* episodes, but they blurred together, some black and white, some color. He'd grown up with only three lousy channels on their ancient television, his father too stingy for cable or a satellite dish. Dash had been teased for not knowing the important things other kids knew from Nickelodeon and the Cartoon Channel. He knew Mary Ann and Ginger, though, alternating crushes on women from thirty-year-old sitcom reruns. He'd once asked his mom to make a coconut cream pie like the ones they made on the show.

"There was a bad storm that caused a boat full of people to run aground on an island," he said. "They were supposed to be taking a short ride, but I guess the Storm God lost its temper. The boat ended up with a big hole in it on a beach."

"That doesn't sound funny."

"Well, the people did silly things," he said, but couldn't recall a single example.

"Were there people my color?"

"No, no brown people. There was the boat crew, a teacher, a farm girl, and a rich old couple. All my color."

"And the actress you liked."

"Her name was Ginger, and she played a beautiful movie star. A movie is like a show, but much bigger. She always wore fancy long dresses."

"Did Ginger have a kitten at her house? Who would feed it if she got lost on an island?"

"I think she had a roommate back in Hollywood, but she never mentioned a kitten."

"Is that close to Vermont?"

"It's all the way across the country. Most people ride in an airplane if they want to visit."

"Did Ginger make a baby on the island?"

"Nobody made babies."

"If you make a Baby Jesus I won't be able to leave the island," she said, reaching for the broom parts he'd been playing around with but not assembling. "And I'll never get a kitten."

"A Baby Jesus? I don't understand. That's something you know from the missioners?"

She shrugged. "From the books that were mostly burned. There are pictures of the baby that Manu says will make the soldiers stop taking the beautiful girls. The missioners talked about Baby Jesus, said he was the Son of God."

"Everyone loves you here. They're your family. Why do you want to leave so badly?"

"I want a kitten more than anything. And I want to see new places." She looked around the cave while looping the vine over the leaves. She tied a knot, tightening it with her front teeth, then handed him the broom. "The spiders won't build nests if you fill the cracks with sand. Everybody knows that."

"Nests?" He held the new broom in front of his chest, ready for a fight.

"A mama spider can have a hundred babies. Maybe more. They aren't like people. Manu says they're good because they eat bugs that bite."

"Manu is right, but they still scare me."

"Was Ginger scared of spiders, or was she a warrior?"

The question hurt a little, but he went outside to scoop a handful of sand. She was dragging out his sleeping mat when he came back.

"The sun kills eggs," she said as they passed.

He began filling in cracks, then used the broom to usher a trio of baby geckos across the ceiling, toward the mouth of the cave.

"One more moon until your big date, right? How's the plumbing?" Willy was sitting crammed in the spot where Dash had first regained consciousness. His mass made the chamber even smaller.

"My plumbing is unchanged."

"I can't get comfortable in here." Willy flexed his jaw, twitching his fleshy light, which was drawing tiny moth-like insects.

"You've seen all the rats and snakes outside? There are bats that look like they could carry a dog away."

"Don't bats live in caves?"

"You came to give me a hard time?" Dash asked.

"I was just saying."

"And you're welcome to read my mind instead of asking about my broken plumbing."

"You're too worried about the girl," said Willy, who burped a fine puff of white moth wings. "Too much pressure isn't going to help. Or is it that the natives aren't your style?"

"I don't have a style. And I don't want to think about Sarah or ten-year-old sex slaves."

Willy lifted a hand, rubbed under his jaw. "You won't be able to live with yourself if she's taken."

"Maybe they really are trained to be house girls, put to work cleaning. What the hell do we know?"

"Right, friend, pre-teen girls with perfect skin and lustrous hair for wealthy couples wanting to skip the dirty diaper phase. That's a good one. Maybe the buyers are the Howells on your pretend island. Thurston and Lovey collecting pretty young things to circulate cheese trays and deliver vodka martinis and Rob Roys."

"Stop."

"We'll buy three, Lovey." Willy's voice turned into Thurston Howell's, exactly as Dash remembered. "Or what say we make it four? Those splendid little darlings do divine work. Simply divine."

"Knock it off."

"They found easy pickings on islands out here, then figured out the most valuable specimens to grab. How much do you think one of these young beauty queens is worth to a rich pimp? No low-ball figures here. Think of all the years of service girls this age offer."

Dash felt like throwing up.

"Kid thinks she's getting a kitten," said Willy. "Ain't that the sweetest thing? She's right about the fancy clothes. They'll want her dolled up for the things she'll be forced to do."

"We have to do something." Dash dropped the broom, sat hard on the floor. "We have to convince Manu to try again. Anything's better than letting them take the girls. Anything."

"You have a better chance getting your plumbing working," Willy said, then faded away when Tiki came back with two handfuls of sand.

She was singing a made-up song about a kitten named Ginger.

Chapter 14

"GO GET 'EM, tiger. Win one for the Gipper!"

Dash dropped the skipping stones he was collecting by the water and turned toward Willy's voice, but it was Tiki waving from next to the tide pool.

She cupped her hands to her mouth to be heard over the crashing surf. "Manu wants you to come right now."

The blowhole sent a ten-foot geyser that was caught by the wind and turned into rain.

Dash tiptoed across lava, leaving behind a bounty of polished flat stones that would make great hoppers. They were everywhere now that he had other business. He was up to nine skips over the chop, his right throwing arm stronger every day. The pursuit took him to a peaceful place where his useless body parts didn't matter. Now that he'd gotten the angle and timing near perfection, he was being summoned to an impossible task that would lead to his death.

He glanced at the volcano and whispered. "I hope you choke on me."

The wind lifted the girl's hair, teased it in all directions, the last of the sun tinting her skin a rich copper as she stood waiting. She would become a beautiful woman, which was probably why her mother had been chosen as the chief's wife. Dash conjured a picture to save his life. He imagined her mother's long bare legs and high full breasts, hands held lightly over angular hips. Her lips parted in a smile to greet the expert rock skipper back from a new record toss. He paused next to the blowhole, waited for any sign of an impending erection. But the image changed as another burst of water erupted, showering his back and shoulders, plugging his left ear. The ghost's face became something else, graceful jaw line rearranging into a jigsaw puzzle with missing pieces, a hole littered with broken teeth and splintered bone, flesh singed from the soldier's bullet. Dash also saw in that instant that her pride had not weakened—her life was taken without her showing fear.

"God bless us all," the good captain had said.

Tiki was alone again, hopping foot to foot as the sun touched the sea, another nearly endless day relinquishing its heat and light. "Hurry. It's getting late."

He put one hand on her bare shoulder as she led them into the noisy tunnel behind a single tiny flame. The mosquitoes fell on them, Dash swatting at his shoulders and head, digging at his ears and spitting.

"Careful you don't blow on the candle," she said, holding it out in front. "The jungle is different tonight. It's not good to be in the dark when it is so upset."

Night came quickly on the island. It wasn't a place to be caught hiking a jungle path or up the coast without a candle or the torches he'd seen villagers use. Sunsets lasted a few minutes, no hour-long dusk where the sun slipped behind New England mountains. Night was a cellar door closing on rusty hinges. It had twice left him groping with an armload of firewood after becoming preoccupied by washed up junk.

He slapped at his face, stumbled into her.

"Wave, don't squish," she reminded, using two hands to

steady the flame as they came to the end of the path. "Blood makes more come."

The hazy dome was higher, less smothering, and the new cool air changed his spirits. He was a castaway on an exotic island, complete with an active volcano, surrounded by strange gods and people from the pages of a colorful travel magazine. The sweat dripping off him was filled with drowned mosquitoes, but that suddenly didn't matter. And neither did beautiful stoic ghosts or his defunct libido. He raised a mosquito-ravaged chin and headed for the circle of men passing the diesel-flavored booze.

The drinking circle had moved to the mats where communal meals were served, as it had for the pageant of beauty ceremony. Dash was instantly aware of a different mood among the men.

"Come, Cracker, this is a special night." Manu made room, patted the ground. From the tame voices, Dash guessed the cup hadn't been passed for long. When he dropped to his butt, the circle changed shape. Those with backs to the stage turned and became the first row of the audience, dusting their hands and getting comfortable behind a row of flickering shell candles. A full cup was pressed into his hand.

"Cheers," said Manu, his face in a smile so wide his eyes disappeared.

"Eat," said the man on his other side, offering a bowl of blackened wings and legs.

Dash passed the bowl on, then took a sip to prime his body. His second drink was longer, two gulps of the hellish liquid before spitting into the cup and holding out to the chief. "Smooth like silk," he said, gasping.

Manu drank and then clapped his hands, barking orders that brought the rest of the villagers from their huts or whatever tasks they'd been doing to complete the day. Drummers rolled out their instruments and made a few thumps. *Sound checks*, Dash thought, then checked to see how far the cup had traveled. He searched for Tiki's face in the crowd gathered at each end of the mat but didn't find her in the dim light. He saw no children.

The cup returned, and he drank and spit. "Like silk," he repeated, then hiccupped. Manu clapped him hard and took the cup.

The drums banged for real when six fully naked women slipped out through the frond curtain onto the dusty stage. They formed a row behind the candles, oiled and glistening, brown skin a landscape of dangerous places Dash couldn't help but explore with wide eyes. The women swayed in unison, hips tilting, sweeping hands reaching to tell a story. All but one appeared to be in some stage of pregnancy.

Manu jabbed a bony elbow. "Better than America." He pointed a crooked finger, clucked his tongue.

Each was lovely in her own way. Two were tall and thin, while the women on the ends were short and thick, with large breasts jutting into the night. All twelve nipples had been stained bright red, perhaps to honor the volcano.

The cup returned, and the drumming went fast and then slowed, dancers matching the pace. Their arms were snakes, sometimes lifting high to represent the sun or moon, he guessed. He compared their areolas, picking the roundest pair that held the tiniest bulls-eye bumps. He wondered how the red nubs would feel between his thumb and index finger, and if the oil coating the silky mounds would taste like coconut or some tangy fruit.

The women turned their backs, a dozen cheeks jiggling in a frantic drum solo. Maybe it was the clap-clap, but Dash saw the lovely rumps blur together, become a single wave of flesh, and was reminded of the chocolate fountain Sarah had picked out for their wedding reception for an extra three hundred bucks. The salesman switched it on and handed them each a pineapple slice they dipped into the cascading chocolate. Sarah grabbed his wrist before he could take a bite, looked into his eyes, hers big and bluish green, and brought his hand to her mouth. She licked the pineapple and then sucked each of his fingers clean while the salesman stood there making asthmatic breathing sounds.

The drumming slowed and hips became butter churns, the women still displaying their rear ends. The hula-style dance morphed into something completely different when the women covered their shining butt cheeks with both hands and bent at the waist to display all sorts of new dark niches. Dash thought of the spiders' hiding spots in his lava cave and shivered.

Manu elbowed him again as the women lifted back up and turned to face the audience. The drumming halted and the dancers huddled close, suddenly shy, crossing their legs to hide their lower parts. The villagers at each end of the mats clapped. The tall dancer with the small nipples Dash had admired left the group, stepping between the candles and up to where he sat, trying not to look at her triangle of sparkling pubic hair. Sarah had always waxed everything away, only once missing a single hair that had managed to grow more than an inch. During an especially intimate moment, he had unfurled it from its home above and to the right of where he was supposed to be paying attention. He'd felt bad for the hair, knew it was doomed, was even tempted to pluck it out of its misery and let it revel in the brief pain its removal would cause its harsh owner.

"What are you doing?" Sarah had asked.

He had let the hair live one more day. "Sorry," he'd whispered, ever the coward.

"Come."

Dash was startled, for an instant believing the mass of looming pubic hair had spoken. He accepted the young woman's slick hand and stood, woozy from alcohol and the heady smell of coconut oil. He followed her away from men speaking in low, conspiratorial voices and women giggling, down a strip of bare earth covered in white flower petals. The woman's undulating rear end led the way, its surface picking up the light of the candles, abandoned cooking fires, and maybe even a few rays from the newly risen moon.

She herded him up three stone steps and into a grass hut and made him lie face down onto a thick sleeping mat in the center of the room. Small candles were already lit, and more petals competed with her floral-scented flesh. He lifted his hips when she leaned down to tug away his underpants. She lowered herself onto his naked butt, pinning him, her flesh warm and slick. He felt her reaching, and then a liquid trickle between his shoulder blades that ran down the middle of his back. He could also feel the crinkle of her pubic hair, and he had the urge to roll over, but her strong thighs were clamped tight, had him trapped. His face still tingled from the clap-clap as he tried to relax. Her fingers began kneading muscles, made designs over his skin. Her hands pushed up from his lower back, then out and down his arms, squeezing and twisting his fingers before repeating the heavenly maneuvers.

He nearly fell asleep twice, jerking back awake, and she tugged under his right armpit when she finally wanted him to roll onto his back. He kept his eyes shut, breathing in the heavenly smells, hardly caring there was no door on this or any of the huts. He might even have heard voices, more giggles, but oil was dripped in the sign of the cross and firm fingers made tantalizing shapes around his own hard nipples. He heard the distant drumbeat over low whispers as if he were a champion golfer lining up a putt on the eighteenth green.

The hips over his waist shifted and the crinkly hair found a different spot. There was wetness in a new place and the sensation was beyond glorious. He took a deep, even breath, as any golfer would when the trophy was on the line. Even the crowd went perfectly silent, drummers paused in mid-beat, everyone waiting to explode at the sound of the ball dropping into the cup, to see the victor raise a pumping fist.

"What's the matter with you, Cracker?"

The silence was broken, his concentration lost mid-golf

stroke. He opened his eyes to the sight of the exotic young woman straddling him, her eyebrows furrowed, her lips pursed. Her perfect nipples cast sideways shadows across chocolate breasts. From a million miles away he could feel pressure on his penis, prodding fingers that were surely warm, wonderful, and full of knowledge.

"Your battle knife feels like dead lizard," said the woman, and he could hear the words repeated by the nearby gallery.

He closed his eyes again, imagined falling backward from the edge of the hungry volcano, failed putter in one hand, a single curling pubic hair from his cheating fiancée pinched between two fingers of the other.

Chapter 15

Tiki knelt over Dash's bedroll, gently tapping a finger on his pounding forehead, while a single flame did a slow dance at the bottom of a coconut shell. He could still taste the vomit, and nearly retched again. His body was oily and coated in a dusty film and bits of grass. He smelled like suntan lotion after a long day at the beach.

He reached a greasy hand and touched her elbow. "I didn't do so good."

"I don't want you to die," she said in a whisper.

He couldn't see her face in the shadows, but felt the tears on his chest. "Manu might change his mind," he said.

"It's not Manu's choice. The Volcano will drown our village with her blood if we do not please her." Tiki's head shook side to side, hair brushing across his face. "He's afraid for our people. Only your god can change her mind."

"I don't have a god," he said. "Not anymore. I gave up when my dad died, but never really believed. It wasn't part of my life."

"Then you have to come right now." She tugged at his arm, but her hands slid free in the gritty leftover oil, and she fell back on her rump. Now he could see she was crying. "I heard them talk. It will happen in the next balance, when the moon's face is half black and half bright. Your god has to come convince the Volcano."

✝

THERE WAS NO path where Tiki ducked into the thick vegetation, only a vertical black slit she crawled through like a reverse birth. It was Alice's plunge down the rabbit hole, only one filled with snakes and spiders that attacked birds, and giant prehistoric lizards with foot-long tongues. The most dangerous animal he'd encountered in Vermont was a black bear struck dead by a propane delivery truck. He'd been sent by his editor to get a quote from the driver and game warden. *Are there more bears than years past? Can residents expect a rash of such unfortunate accidents? Is this the first bear you've crashed into?*

"Don't grab the vines," Tiki warned, and must have seen the puzzled look on his face. "They might be something that bites."

"I won't touch anything."

They maneuvered through a maze of deadfall for the first hundred yards. The sound level rose with each step—birds angry at the intrusion, and darting tree creatures that whooped and howled, some stopping to hurl broken twigs.

"It's not too much farther," she said, allowing him to catch his breath. Even she was coated in sweat, little dead bugs dotting her body like black pepper. She squatted with elbows on her knees, while he swatted the air.

The jungle continued moving when you stood still. Every inch of plant and rock surface had an ant or beetle-like insect performing choreographed labor. The more dangerous creatures, the brightly colored spiders with hinged legs perhaps designed for jumping, lurked higher up, building sticky webs at a white man's eye level. The ground was carpeted with spotted leaves and ancient ferns, all hosting colonies of smaller life forms. Exploring bamboo shoots were alien fingers pointing the way home.

"Come."

She led them deeper into the interior, slashing with bare feet and tiny hands. She climbed over the sturdy vines and plowed through the weak. The ground tilted upward as they neared the base of the volcano's cone, glimpses of sun on its brown face appearing through breaks in the canopy.

They came to a spot that had once been cleared, trees chopped to stumps, broken lava stacked knee high in a perimeter wall. He brushed bugs from a log and risked sitting, breathing air so thick it was practically warm liquid. The flying swarms were scarcer here, and he assumed it was due to the pungent flowering bushes left to flourish within the black wall.

"This is what you wanted me to see?" He tried to make sense of the manmade landscape. In front of them was a raised area topped with a flat rock the shape and size of a twin mattress. It was a stage of sorts, probably something to do with religion and gods. Dash had a vision of a more hands-on brand of human sacrifice, and the savages who chanted for the blood to hurry up and flow.

"It's where the missioners explained how there is only one god. They named it God's House. There was a path to the village." She pointed to a solid wall of greenery, then began rooting through an old pile of cut bamboo shafts at her feet. She chose a pair of fat, foot-long sections and held one out. "The Volcano covered the path with rocks to block the way. Manu said it was a warning for our people not to come here. The missioners were angry."

He took the bamboo, held it like a knife. "It's pretty spooky, but so are the churches back home." He looked through the treetops to where the volcano continued spewing a line of smoke.

"Our gods like it here. You can feel them close by, especially during the black face moon. And sometimes you hear a voice which sounds like all the people from a hundred villages speaking at once. I was scared the first time. Help me dig." She knelt below the stone altar and jabbed the bamboo into the soft earth, as he came beside her. "It's not deep, but the roots will try to hold on."

He dug in, easily pulling away the rich dirt for the first few inches, but then struck the network of subterranean bamboo runners. "What are we looking for?"

"A box." She maneuvered her stick as a crowbar against the stubborn roots. "It's right here."

He tugged tendrils that came free like buried rope. She dropped her tool to scoop the dirt from the top of a metal container the size of a cigar box, lifting it from the shallow hole. She wiped her hands on the sides of her underpants and worked the latch, forcing hinges that made a sound like one of the jungle birds. Inside was a lump of clear plastic she began carefully unraveling. Protected from moisture was a small leather-bound book, maybe four inches tall and about half as thick. She brushed bits of dirt and her own sweat from the cover that read Holy Bible.

Dash was deflated. He sat back, realizing he'd been hoping for some sort of magic weapon. A glowing lightsaber, perhaps, or a Harry Potter wand. The hole had been too small for a time machine, but if only Gollum's precious ring had been buried here to protect one heathen from a miserable, fiery end. He looked up at the canopy, a torn green tent fed by death and decay. Birds zipped from side to side, and giant white moths flew in slow meandering paths.

"It's only a Bible," he finally said.

She held the small book out with both dirty hands. "The missioners said it saved people. It can save *you*, let your god know where you are, and that you need help."

"It's only paper and ink. It has a fancy cover with nothing but words inside."

"They used it to baptize our people. They talked to your god, prayed to him every day. They said being saved meant you were delivered from sin and death." She lowered her voice to a whisper. "If it keeps you safe from the devil, then it will protect you from the Volcano."

He shook his head. "It's not a magic book. And they needed water to baptize people. Lots of water. Maybe even a river. There's no water here, Tiki. There's just sweat and blood. Were missioners on the island when the soldiers took girls?"

"Sometimes, but the missioners never interfered. They came here to be with their god until the soldiers left. They said the soldiers were punishment for our sins." She paused to get her words right. "God didn't cause Mama to be killed, sinning did. And not being saved. I think having one god makes things more complicated."

She reached out and pressed the Bible into his hands. "Hold this until I'm ready."

"What are you doing?"

"You must be quiet and not move. Sit here." She stood and patted the first chiseled step that led to the altar, then climbed up onto the huge flat rock and swept away dead leaves and brown, skeleton-like fronds. She sat and brushed her hands, then took a few deep breaths. She held out one hand and wiggled her fingers at him.

"What?"

"The Bible."

He put the book in her hand, and she clutched it to her chest. She made the sign of the cross, then put the same index finger to her lips to keep him quiet. She lowered onto her back and dropped both arms to her sides, the Bible lying there as if weighing her down.

He listened to the birds talk and small animals rattle through the undergrowth. He watched the pretty little girl's chest rise and fall under the leather-bound book, her brown eyes fluttering closed just as a dragonfly came in for a closer look and then zoomed away. Minutes passed, and he had to stifle a yawn, thinking she might have fallen asleep. The girl seemed at peace, a child in a comfortable place about to dream.

The leaves scattered about the stone's perimeter began to move. And as if Tiki knew he was about to call or reach out to her, she slowly raised one hand to him, waved her fingers for him to stop. The swarm of a million tiny creatures, black spiders no bigger than grains of rice, emerged from every direction and scrambled over themselves to reach her smooth skin. The spiders came up from the heels of her feet and from her pointy elbows. They surged along the tops of her fingers, tumbling over her knuckles, sprinting past her wrist for the long stretch of her forearm. Her hair began to sway and shift as if it had come to life, the tight curls a twisting roller-coaster path for countless scurrying legs. A palpitating black shade was lowered over her face; a wriggling mask out of some fever-induced nightmare.

Dash wanted to go to her, brush them away, but he held back because this is what she'd wanted him to see. In only two or three minutes, nearly every bit on her skin was coated in a throbbing layer of tiny spiders that seemed to be turning in circles, searching for something once they'd found their place on her body. Even her underpants had gone black as they raced across and under the thin material. The Bible had also come alive; it moved and swayed, threatened to slide off her body as though balanced on ball bearings.

A few more minutes and the process reversed course. Sections of Tiki's skin reappeared as the spiders finished their crazy waltz and flooded back down her arms and legs. The spiders rushed from her chest and face, poured from her hair out onto the stone, where they disappeared into the carpet of leaves. Under the dappled sunlight, he could see the girl's skin had been left perfectly clean. The specs of dead flies, the sweat-streaked mud, and every bit of oil in her hair had been consumed by the swarm that streamed off her fingertips and down her ankles like black sludge.

She opened her eyes and sat up, smiling. She brushed her hands together. "It's kind of icky when they go up your nose." She shook out her hair, then rubbed her face. She turned and looked at him closely. "Now it's your turn to be saved."

Chapter 16

———

THEY'D BEEN SCAVENGING the eastern beach for an hour when Tiki let out a squeal that chased a hundred birds from a cluster of nearby trees, the brown-winged creatures careening through the air as though navigating an invisible maze. She hopped up and down, bird-like herself, and waved a pink toothbrush above her head.

She stopped to hold it out, turning it over in her hands. "Can you believe it? It's so pretty. I wished for one like this."

"It looks brand new."

"The missioners gave us ugly black ones." She ran a finger through the bristles. "The hair was no good and fell out. This is special."

She smiled, then stepped up on the crown of a large rock and began brushing her teeth, turning a slow circle to scan for more goodies.

It was morning, and Tiki had pulled him away from a dream in which he stood poised at the very end of a diving board, toes curled over the edge, judges in all-white off to one side with score cards at the ready. The Olympic-size pool was filled with millions of tiny spiders instead of water, but they weren't his concern. Spiders were a good thing, in fact, since they didn't cause a splash even with a less than perfect entry. It was the chanting crowd that was making him sweat. "Burn up slow, burn up slow," they sang with increasing fervor. And the dreaming Dash knew they meant for him to suffer a long, agonizing death in the volcano. They were willing him to miss the fire, land among the scorched rocks to languish in a slow broil. He'd woken with the image of the cards held high over the judges' heads, and he quickly tried adding the numbers before they dropped their hands. He was certain his score was how many days he had to live.

He held his bucket half-filled with pieces of civilization that might have traveled from cities for which the girl was destined when the soldiers returned. He'd hoped for containers to store water, recalling the bleak news reports of islands made up of plastic bottles floating across the Pacific, slowly disintegrating into pieces small enough for aquatic life to eat and thus becoming part of the food chain. But the bottles he found were torn and useless, except as souvenirs. He picked up each fragment, brushed away the sand. If only their labels—with numbers and weights and words—had survived, perhaps some generic warning to prove he was worth keeping alive.

Tiki scoured the rocky beach, head down, picking at tangled seaweed clumps. "I want to find a special decoration for tonight, something better than a toothbrush or coral. All the kids find stupid coral."

She squealed again before he could ask what she was decorating. She dropped the pieces she'd found and ran, feet kicking a spray of sand. He followed, stealing a glance in the opposite direction, half expecting a ghost, or maybe a giant man with a fish where its head should be.

She stopped and fell to her knees, allowing him to catch up to her. "What is it?"

"A little woman," she said, her voice awe filled and breathless. "A fairy princess."

He watched her carefully lift a blonde Barbie doll that was missing both legs, but otherwise intact. It had blue eyes, and lips the same color as the nipples of last night's dancers.

"It's Barbie," he said.

"I get to name her," she snapped. "I found her."

She smoothed the doll's hair with her palm, licked her thumb and cleaned smudges from the mounds of its bare chest.

Dash stood, not wanting to argue. She also got to her feet, held the doll out by its tiny hands. He could see her thinking hard then break into a smile.

"Her name is Sarah, like the girl you wanted to marry. She'll be my decoration."

He laughed. "Sarah would love that. It's a wonderful tribute."

"What's a tribute?"

He scratched his head. "It's doing something to show respect for someone."

Tiki nodded that she understood. "Like how Manu is giving you to the Volcano?"

Joy from the treasure hunt drained away. "Are we done now?"

"It'll be the best decoration ever," she said. "What jewelry did Ginger have on her island? The movie star woman."

He tried remembering. The rich old lady had strings of pearls, but he couldn't picture a necklace accenting any of the Hollywood starlet's low cut evening gowns. "Earrings, I think. She sometimes wore diamond earrings."

"Okay, let's find diamond earrings. Then we're done." Tiki tiptoed across the round rocks to deposit the doll in his bucket. "I can wear them when the soldiers come."

"Stop saying that stuff. You can't go with them," he said, but she acted like she didn't hear, or didn't care, walking out to where the water splashed the lava rocks to continue her search.

The east side of the island was leeward facing and had no reef. The black earth dropped immediately away at water's edge, the ocean steadily undulating rather than forming waves.

"That's where Mama went." She pointed out over the water. "Her body, anyway. It's where the dead start their journey. They put them right here, then the Sea God swallows them when they float out a little."

"What if I build a boat? One like the fishermen have, or a bamboo raft. You could help me. You tie better knots than I ever could."

"To go to Vermont?"

"We could make it to the shipping lanes, where a bigger boat would take us to Vermont. You could ride in an airplane."

She looked at the sky, shaking her head. "Manu would know."

"It would be a secret. We'd hide it until it was ready to go."

"You see all the birds? They watch. They see everything."

Dash looked back at the jungle. The treetops were again filled with small birds that hopped and preened. Seagulls picked at things along the tide line, patrolled the sky above.

"If the Bird God didn't tell him, then another god would," she whispered.

He thought for a minute. "We'd leave when it's darkest. There's more than a week until the new moon."

"The black face moon," she corrected.

"Most birds will be asleep. And the others won't be able to see us. What if you could have beautiful clothes and a kitten in Vermont? You'd see the same moon and stars from your bed every night."

She squatted, picked a broken clam shell from between the rocks. "I'd be too lonely in Vermont, even with a kitten."

"No, you'd be with me. I'll take care of you. You'll be in a safe place where no one will hurt you. You'll go to a real school and have new friends. I'll sign you up for soccer. You'll play just like here."

She shook her head as she dropped the shell into his bucket. "You already asked your god to be saved. Everything will be okay."

"I'm about to be pushed into the volcano and you're going

to be taken from your people. No little book is going to stop it from happening."

"You need to have faith," she said. "Like I have faith I'll be chosen as pretty enough."

He stooped to pick up another toothbrush that had also survived an overseas journey, although sun-bleached and missing half its bristles. He dropped it into the bucket. "You aren't going with them. We'll figure something out."

Tiki lifted a dead crab, held it out and jiggled it to make its legs dance. "I'm going to name my kitten Ginger, even if she isn't orange."

Chapter 17

—

Tiki BEGGED HIM to return to the village with her, something to do with the legless doll she'd found. She remained cryptic, and he couldn't handle surprises. Every noise made him jump. They would come for him soon if he didn't find a way out. Thatching together a raft was a thing of stories, not something a sane man considered when sitting on a beach at eye level to the open ocean. It was suicide.

"They will be kinder," she promised, and took four of his fingers to squeeze. "You are needed. You will save them. Manu warned that anybody who hurts you will also be given to the Volcano God."

Misery loves company.

"I will protect you," she told the man who'd already lost a fight with an unarmed little boy, the man who'd scurried away in the dark, a drunken eunuch with soiled underwear balled in one hand.

"It's important to me," she said, and the coward relented.

Tiki pulled free when they reached the edge of the compound, sprinting to a tree that had appeared out of nowhere. As he warily followed, he saw the tree was adorned with shells and chunks of coral, but was currently overlooked by villagers going about late day chores. It was a relief to also be unnoticed.

He walked slowly around the tree while Tiki searched out a spot to put her ornament. She pulled down a piece of vine being used for a garland and spliced it into a thin strip to fashion a noose. She hung the Barbie torso from the highest empty spot within reach, then stepped back and turned to him with an enormous grin.

He nodded. "It's perfect."

The tree was a twenty-foot bamboo pole plunged into the earth in the village center. Smaller shoots had been driven through the upright tube every foot or so, similar to the artificial Christmas tree Dash's father had kept year 'round in his store. Ferns were woven into each level of branches, adding girth, and delicate flower petals were strung and looped from top to bottom. Ornaments were hung by woven grass blades, their weight pulling at the branches, making them droop.

White shells the size of dinner plates were scattered beneath. Shiny new ones at the perimeter, nearest their feet; older, dull shells, some badly chipped, were at the center. Tiki knelt and began lifting the half shells, shaking her head each time until she found the one she was seeking. She handed it to Dash, who tilted its concave interior toward the fire. An image of a woman's face was scratched into the surface.

"Mama," was all she said before taking it back.

"Is this Christmas?"

"It's Yule," she said, stepping back and turning her face to him. "It comes on the same night every year."

Instead of a star, the tree was topped by what first appeared to be a chunk of bleached driftwood. But when a nearby cook fire flared, he could see the bleached eye sockets and nasal cavity. The human skull was missing its lower jaw.

"Who is it?"

She frowned, as though the answer was obvious. "It's Jesus."

"Who told you that?"

She only shrugged, and before he could press her, a woman came up from behind and put a torch to the first of four wood piles set in vertical, teepee shapes. By the time she reached the last, the entire population had converged around the tree, shadows cast down over the shell memorials. Tiki crowded him as the heat rose, flames licking into the night sky.

Rising panic and claustrophobia grew nearly unbearable. He wanted to bolt, make a break for the tunnel, but the circle was at least ten souls deep, a mass of brown flesh and flashing eyes and teeth. The fire crackled, threw sparks into the night. He would be dead soon, murdered by these savages. Their eyes were everywhere, boring into him through gaps in the tree, drilling into his temples from each side, into the back of his head.

He wanted to scream, and for a brief instant believed the high-pitched sound was coming from inside his own frail body. It was the women's voices first, and then the children's, a song in tribal language from a hundred mouths. The tune was familiar, a Christmas carol.

His heart slowed, and Tiki again took hold of his fingers, watching him from the shadows.

"Pa rumpa pump um," she sang along, and the men joined in with gusto, their voices so deep the words seemed to vibrate.

The second song was an unknown mishmash, but "Let It Snow" was definitely third. And then the villagers with their backs to the volcano slowly turned, heads rising, voices lifting toward the orange eye reflecting in the low clouds. When the eye blinked, some of the carolers lost their place.

The people swayed, clapping in rhythm, although Dash didn't feel there was much joy until it began snowing. Voices reached higher pitches as the space between the first wafting flakes began to fill in. His eyes began tearing and then burning, and he rubbed hard with his free hand, a horrible bitter taste on his tongue. He closed his mouth when he realized it was ash. It was accumulating on the Yule tree, pushing down the already burdened branches; the coating on top of Jesus' skull was a gray toupee.

Tiki tugged his fingers, pulled him through the crowd now performing "Winter Wonderland" in their own language, squeezing sideways out into the cool air toward the unmarried women's huts. Except for the end units, all shared outside walls. *Row houses*, he thought, as they left the light of the fires. She took him to the farthest structure, where the odor from the outhouse and pig corral mixed with the low hanging smoke. She let his hand go and ran inside. He could see his feet had turned gray when she emerged from her small home with a fat candle in one hand, a cup in the other.

"Men can't go inside the girl huts or they have to get married. It's a silly rule." She carefully placed the candle on the ground between them to brush ash from two sitting logs. "Here's some water. The ash burns your throat."

"I thought it was snowing."

He drank half and handed back the cup.

"Stay here while I find something."

She ducked back inside, and he listened to her rummage in the dark. The ash made his body itch, had attached itself to his oiliest spots. He thought how good a plunge in the swimming hole would feel, but resisted any temptation at the thought of all the terrible things gliding through the ebony water.

He could see her smiling face when she came through the opening with hands cupped together, eyes bright from the distant flames, hair frosted from ash. Sweat ran from her collar bones down to her belly in shiny lines.

"What is it?"

"Something I made." She held out her hands. "It's a Yule present for you."

"I'm so sorry. I should have found you something." He looked down at his empty hands, then guiltily at hers. He was almost crying and didn't know why. "I would have made you a gift. I would have found diamond earrings."

"It doesn't matter." She rocked from foot to foot, anxious for him to take the gift.

"Thank you." He lifted a hand and she let the present drop into his palm, then covered her mouth to stifle a squeal.

It was the size and shape of a quarter, and he took it between his thumb and index finger to hold it near the flickering candle. The molded amber disk, probably formed from tree sap, was translucent against the flame. Trapped inside were a dozen white crescent moons.

"That's me," she whispered. "I got the idea from the missioners. They made us eat the body of Christ, but it was only little pieces of stale bread. Eating people is bad, even if the person is a god."

"It's beautiful."

"Those are my fingernails inside."

"I thought so."

She sat next to him and leaned hard, as they listened to the carolers' version of "I'll Be Home for Christmas." She yawned and covered her mouth.

He rubbed the smooth disk with his fingertips. "I'll keep it forever."

Chapter 18

———

DASH SAT RUBBING the smooth disk, the sun setting on another day with no escape plan. Willy hummed a Christmas carol from the window seat.

"There's never a ship out there," Dash said.

Willy began drumming his fingers. "Only takes one, right? Gotta look at the glass half full."

"I'm a lonely man with malfunctioning parts. A man in the blue Pacific without a whole lot of options."

"These seats are sublime."

Dash turned to look at him. "You just stole that out of my head. It was a word Sarah used all the time. She said it about everything, even about dopey things, like ice cream."

"I love ice cream."

"You've never eaten ice cream," said Dash.

"No, but I know it's sublime. What's your point?"

Dash shrugged. "The girl thinks I'm protected from the Volcano God, delivered from sin with a baptism by spiders. They'll throw me in to save her people, and I'll swim out of the fire and brush myself off."

"Kids, nowadays." Willy lifted one giant foot at a time into the tide pool. Tiny trapped creatures fled to the far side. He reached up and pushed an imaginary button for the reading light, his own flesh bulb brightening.

"Really, Willy?" He felt violated by Willy's mind reading, which produced a physical sensation that ran across the inside of his skull. A tickling, as though a feather lightly stroked his brain's gray matter. It was unnerving, and a little stomach turning. Dash scratched his forehead. "You know that was my father's favorite phrase. 'Kids, nowadays.' The antique business doesn't have a place for kids. Tourists would come into the shop and their kids would head straight for anything fragile, or at least that's how he saw it. They'd flick lamps on and off, and he'd go crazy."

"Kids were the best part of my job," said Willy. "They had just as many worries as adults, but were much easier to calm down. Sometimes I didn't even need words. You know how mothers sing lullabies? It was like that."

"You miss the kids."

Willy's head tilted, mouth full of pointed teeth opening and closing slowly, bulb pulsing dimmer. "My island went underwater. There was no safe place, no ground high enough. A volcano would have at least saved them from drowning. But the waves rolled across the backs of other waves, and more waves rode across those until the rich soil was covered from west to east. I know because even though I'd blacked out from all the alcohol, I felt the panic somewhere deep. I heard the prayers in my sleep, dreamed the death of each of my people."

"Willy …."

"The storm came and went, took what it wanted. The day after, the sky was deep blue, the sun high and strong. I stood on the beach facing the ocean, my back to what had happened. The sea and heavens were unchanged, the same as they'd always been. The storm only scarred things behind me. It wasn't so bad standing there, not as long as I didn't turn around. I wanted to keep looking at that peaceful scene, the pictures you see all over postcard racks in your world. The sun, water, and sand were all the mixings for a tropical paradise. Give me a piña colada with a little umbrella, a beach chair, and some heavy duty lotion."

Dash waited for him to continue, but the big man didn't. "You had to turn around," said Dash.

"It was like those old black and white movies you watched when you were a kid," Willy said. "It was London during the Great Plague, men pulling carts through mud streets, calling for people to bring out their dead. Only I didn't have a cart, and I was doing all the bringing out. I carried them two at a time, one broken body over each shoulder. People I loved, and people who had loved me. People who believed in me enough to make me a god. Believed I'd take care of them."

"No survivors?"

Willy's light blinked a little brighter. "One thing lived. A small dog with big ears and sad eyes. Mutt wouldn't leave me alone, kept right on my heels, back and forth as I carried the bodies to what had been the growing fields. The ground was soft there, the bamboo roots cut away for taro. I suppose I found the kid who'd taken care of the dog, a boy younger than Tiki. I pulled him from the crook of a tree, set him among the rest. It was the only time the dog left me. He hopped around and yipped, started licking the boy's crooked face. He climbed across his chest, nuzzling and licking some more. I stood watching, maybe hoping something would happen, half expecting a miracle to come from all that love. I mean, how could it not? But the dog finally gave up, came moping back to me with his tail curled beneath his legs. I can't hear most animal thoughts, but knew he was asking me to make the boy better, to fix him. The dog begged me to wake him."

Willy was shaking his head.

"I went back to work until I had them all lined up. The ones who hadn't washed out to sea. The fish took care of those, which was fine because that's what they're supposed to do. I started digging holes, one by one. Not deep like the ones your people make, but deep enough to keep the birds away. And it'll be a good long while before rats find their way back to the island."

"How long did it take to bury them?'

Willy gave a long exhale. "I don't know. More than three hundred graves. Four days, maybe. Five. That little mutt never again left my side, though he whined like crazy when I covered up his boy. Started digging real fast, dirt flying up from between his legs. I slapped my hands together, told him 'no, bad dog.' When I tamped down the last grave, I sat in the middle of the field, surrounded by my people. It should have been noisy, the air filled up with the chatter of a thousand thoughts. It should have been like standing in the middle of a busy marketplace on a Saturday morning."

Willy paused again.

"Even the insects had washed away?"

"Yes, the insects were gone," said Willy. "And not a single dirty seagull was in the air. It was dead silent, not one soul left to pray. Stupid little dog jumped in my lap, all starved looking, shadows between each rib. He hadn't eaten because there was nothing left. I tried listening for his thoughts, but those had gone quiet, too. The thing he most cared about was buried, like a bone to dig up later."

"What happened to the dog?" Dash asked, but Willy only dropped his strange chin to his chest. "Did you leave him alone on the island?"

Willy's mouth opened slowly, the sound of air rushing in and out of his massive chest the only noise for quite a while. He finally raised his head and cleared his throat, took another deep breath.

"I picked him up in my arms and rocked him. It was nice.

I'd never held a dog before, but could tell right away what all the hullabaloo was about," said Willy. "I held him real tight. I guess I held him too tight, because I ended up having to dig another hole."

Chapter 19

—

D ASH FOUND THE cave opening by starlight after Willy slipped back into the sea. He fumbled with the striker over coconut husks, then touched a wick to the flame. Stashing Tiki's gift with other finds, he drank straight from his bucket, pouring the last of the water over his face and chest. He stepped out of his wet underpants and draped them across one of the knobs protruding from the wall. He shook hidden bugs from his sleeping matt, then grabbed the candle and went around the room touching the flame to all the others.

"Deck the fucking halls," he sang, and dropped onto his matt. His useless member stared up at him with one black eye.

Numb genitals hadn't been an issue with Sarah. She'd repeatedly crushed his heart while questioning his spine, but even the darkest times would find him skulking away with a semi-erection.

On the final Christmas break from school, he'd tucked a heavily flawed diamond engagement ring into his front pocket. It was the beginning of an ice storm, a light rain falling and freezing to everything, a sugary coating that caused tree limbs to reach toward the dead grass. The ice tested power lines along the empty roads as he drove to Sarah's apartment building, where she didn't answer the buzzer. He would have given up and gone home around midnight, but his nearly bald tires were no match for the lousy weather, spinning in place until he cut the engine. The power blinked off an hour later, and his car ran out of gas a little past three while he tried to keep warm.

He plodded back up the walkway to the heavy lobby door and pressed the buzzer again, but it made no sound. A yellow emergency light in the foyer cast long shadows. His own black image divided the icy landing, a weary ghost locked from its haunt. He hammered on the door until his knuckles were sore. A man pushed open a second floor window as he turned away, told him to stop the racket or he'd call the cops. Dash sat on the stoop and watched the ice thicken, his coat turning stiff, until there was a crunching sound each time he shifted his ass on the cement.

He huddled and eventually dozed, hair freezing to the brick wall, fingers and toes aching from the icy dampness, even in his dream.

There would be a girl and a boy, close in age, with Sarah's blonde hair. They would be three explorers roaming the paths of his lonely childhood, holding hands when there was room. He'd show why he'd brought sheets of construction paper when they reached the grassy patch next to the stream. Dash blew on his hands, despite the summer heat, then went about folding and creasing paper the exact way his mother had made hats for her porcelain babies at play time.

"What are you making?"

"Can mine be green?"

"I want the red."

"It's a hat!"

Dash shook his head, smiled, and began work on the sheet of green.

These hats would be boats made to sail away from little

fingers, occasioning nervous gasps when they went out of reach, then glee when approaching the rapids, four feet spinning and scurrying along the bank to play catch-up.

"Mine is faster!"

"Mine will sail forever."

Wet sneakers and muddy pants. Miniature clothing covered miniature body parts.

"Be careful."

The explorers would go as far as thorn bushes allowed, boats driven by fearless captains finally dipping into dark channels between mossy rocks.

Everything disappeared.

A truck with a flashing yellow dome over the cab rolled up the street, pushing a wave of dirty ice over the curb. Brakes squealed at the end of the apartment walkway. The truck's salt spreader cast pellets in a shimmering arc.

The driver's face was in profile, lit by dashboard instruments and plow lights reflecting from the giant blade. Tommy Chambers was behind the wheel, eyes closed and head tilted up, cigarette dangling from his lips. Tommy was rocking in his seat, a slight but steady motion as if the truck was rolling over a cobblestone street. Dash first thought he was moving to music, but that wasn't it. Not the way his back arched, the way his head lolled. What else could it be? The local tough guy, too cool for school, or any boss for more than a few weeks, was bopping his bologna along a public street in the heart of an ice storm, had pulled over to masturbate while his truck continued flinging salt against the grill of a parked Chevy.

Dash could feel the smirk draw across his own cold face, the slew of snide comments bubbling forth. You gonna buy that hand dinner, Tommy? Hey, Tommy, you bowl righty and beat it lefty? You wanna polish my car when you're done polishing your knob?

It was just too good to disturb. The great and awesome Tommy Chambers spanking his monkey in a town plow truck, face now scrunched up as if it hurt, orange tip of his butt so low it should be burning his greasy chin whiskers. Dash half-expected some cowboy to yahoo when he finished, but Tommy only went limp, head drooping forward. Tommy took a deep drag that made his face glow, blinked and rubbed his eyes as if he'd just woken up.

Dash was flush with superiority for the first time in his life. There he sat, suffering through a brutal night while waiting for the love of his life to return, a man right off the pages of a romance novel. So what if he was actually stranded, and that Sarah had been wise enough to stay off the roads, probably spending the night with her folks? It had turned out to be a good night, priceless even, despite his freezing extremities.

When Sarah sat up in the truck cab next to Tommy and wiped the back of a hand across her mouth, Dash discovered the rain had somehow gotten inside his body to turn the rest of him to ice. His frozen lungs could draw no more breaths, and his rigid heart could no longer beat.

Time stopped, or at least hesitated. The spinning salt spreader went still. The truck's exhaust hung in a cloud that did not drift. The turning dome light over the cab paused on the same tree and the same porch across the street.

Tommy didn't climb out and open Sarah's door. He let her push it open, step down from the high seat into the slushy mess without help. Dash knew Tommy was thinking, *Fuck it, she'll be back. They love it when you treat them like shit. They eat it up.* Dash could see her brown boots under the truck's belly. The door slammed and the boots turned and disappeared around the plow blade. Tommy revved the engine and Sarah skipped back into view, in and out of the blazing headlights. Dash imagined himself behind the wheel, dropping the transmission into gear and popping the clutch when she was in the center of the massive blade. Here, let me wipe your mouth, I've got something to get rid of what Tommy left on your lips, and I'll toss some road salt on it for good measure.

Sarah was pulling her white knit hat down over her ears when she looked up and found Dash. Her stride didn't flinch when Tommy blasted the horn and ground the gears.

"What are you doing here?" Sarah was smiling, lips shining from the cherry lip balm she always used.

"I'm cold," was all he could manage.

Sarah dug through the pockets of her puffy winter coat, coins and keys jingling. "The power's off all over town," she said, and he wondered if it was something she'd seen for herself, or if Tommy had given her a play by play while she was bent over his lap. Had it been cold in there? *Did you keep your coat zipped when you were tugging down his fly? Did he feel warm in your hands? Was the red check-engine light on, flickering in your silver hoop earrings while you went to work under the steering wheel? Were your eyes closed? Did you think of me?*

"I brought you something." He found the ring in his pocket, held it out in his palm. Sarah squinted, her door key pointing at the tiny diamond.

"It's a diamond ring," Sarah said, looking up at him. The whites of her eyes were yellow from the emergency light.

He nodded and shrugged, his hand shaking.

"It looks like an engagement ring," she said.

He nodded again, cupped hand turning pink from the bitter air. Icy rain droplets, each bigger than the diamond, collected on his bare skin.

"Of course I'll marry you!" Sarah lunged at him, and he squeezed his hand closed just in time. She covered his face in cherry-scented kisses, her lips soft and damp on his cold skin and warm tears. Sarah pulled open her coat to share her warmth, nuzzling into his neck, whispering things about love and happiness. He trembled as she pressed her whole body against him, nearly suffocating him with the residue of Tommy's Old Spice cologne.

DASH AWOKE SHIVERING in the stifling cave, feeling the ghost of Sarah's embrace. He tried holding onto the dream, grasping it tight to make it stay despite the truth. Loneliness made him want to retain all her smells, even the ones that cut his heart into pieces.

He grabbed his underwear and stumbled into the sunshine. He walked the path along the coast, toward the cove where the villagers did their laundry and bathed, and the fishermen tied their skiffs. He had an urgent need to be near people, to be close to them without being seen. They hated him, wanted him burned to death because he'd failed. Did they really believe throwing him into the volcano would calm their god?

Ducking low when he heard voices, he crept forward to squat behind a screen of sticker bushes with twisted barbwire arms. Noise carried farther here, the healthy reef slicing apart the waves, sapping most of their energy. Scavenging birds took their complaints away from the shoreline, more intent on silver flashes among the coral and tumbling whitewater. A wedge of quiet space between jungle insects and ocean was left for human voices.

Three women faced one other in mid-thigh water. They chattered while scrubbing small pieces of clothing they pulled one by one from a floating basket. The clean clothes went into a woven sack strung from one woman's shoulder. A trail of gray water bled from them in a narrow river that led back down the coast. Dash had smelled the soap while sitting by his tide pool on still days.

All were naked, two with small pregnant bellies, the third showed only her backside as she wrung out underpants and sports bras, tucking each item into her sack. They worked slowly, spoke with hands that danced and sprayed droplets. He imagined the women in a coin-op Laundromat back home, meeting once a week at the same time, catching up on gossip, family news. Two would have been friends since middle school, married high school sweethearts, turned up pregnant within a month of each other. The newcomer was young, brought dating stories to the group that the others ate up. He imagined she'd recently struck out on her own, moving into a tiny efficiency, paid for from her salary as an insurance company secretary. She could type like the wind, which was another reason the pregnant homemakers embraced her. It was a skill, something more exotic than their last two years of meatloaves and Lemon Pledge shines.

The women were living artwork and Dash was powerless to look away. He yearned to be a part of their painting, but there would never be a place for someone like him, even if the brushes were still at work. He'd be the lurking shadow, would ruin the composition. He would corrupt the story of loving friendship, expose tension, or introduce dread. The artist would fill his skinny arms with rank chum he couldn't hold, a few flicks of a talented wrist bringing sharks to the scent.

Dash craved everything he'd lost, then realized he'd never experienced anything like what these women seemed to happily take for granted. His mother had promised he'd find good friends; they just hadn't met each other yet. But she was wrong. School was miserable, and summers worse. Summers brought solitary confinement where he suffered the demands and eccentricities of his father.

One woman laughed, put a wet hand on another's shoulder, and pointed an index finger, a soapy bra dangling from her fist. The woman with her back to him turned.

She was as dark and beautiful as when she'd slid over his body in the love hut. Younger under the sun, her eyes wide at first, curious as she followed her friend's words to where he crouched on the shore. He remained frozen among the thorny plants while her eyes explored the landscape and found him. She took three slow steps away from the others, allowed the strap to fall from her shoulder, the half-filled sack set adrift. Dash searched for words, an apology, anything that would make her come closer, come touch him. He would learn her language to share anything she wanted to know about mountains not filled with fire or pillows made of feathers. He had nothing, but still had so much to give.

He read lips that formed the word *cracker*, and held his breath, praying for those lips to curve into a smile. She jostled in the water to spread her feet, pushing her hips forward. He tried to look away when she reached down and snatched fists of coarse hair and screamed two words at him, then repeated the message each time she thrust her hips.

"*Nova oom*," he heard himself repeat, recognizing the words Tiki sometimes used.

"*Nova oom*," shouted the woman, pulling at her hair, rocking her hips. *My daughter is nine*, she called out with two sing-song words that to Dash sounded like a moan at end of the world. And he knew her daughter must have the same fine bones and unmarked skin, and was incubating under the sun for her turn with evil.

Dash ran away, bare feet slapping down on things hard and sharp, not stopping until he was curled up alone in his dark cave, surrounded by spiders.

Chapter 20

Thunder rattled the cave, shook dust from the ceiling and sent startled spiders scrambling for their holes. Dash rolled from his mat to hobble down the rocks and splash cold water on his chest. He washed his gritty feet and picked thorns from a callused heel, thick skin that was the color and texture of a worn sandal. He should be building a boat rather than moping, but standing there alone made him feel every god was against him. The storm had gathered to the southeast, with soaring clouds flashing lightning deep inside their purple guts, wind lifting spray from whitecaps. He could never build something capable of withstanding such power.

He took one step forward to feel the energy of the rushing tide push against him, foamy water riding up his shins and cascading off bony knees. Another step and he felt the energy begin to shift, as if deciding it might want to take him with it. He barely existed on this island, as if there really had been no survivors. The plane and all its beings who mattered were at the bottom of the sea. It wouldn't be a sin to keep walking, if only he possessed the courage.

Had Sarah bothered attending his funeral? Did she stand

next to his crying mother whose useful life had already ended? His throat tightened at the thought of his mother's image. As pale and fragile as the tea cups his father kept on the highest shelves, away from the grubby hands of youth.

Tommy Chambers was good with heavy equipment; perhaps his latest job had been at the cemetery. Tommy in the excavator cab, cigarette dangling, as on the night he'd given Sarah a ride in the plow truck. Good old Tommy, waiting for the last person to leave so he could sling some dirt, looking forward to sharing a good laugh with his drinking buddies about the assholes who paid cold hard cash to bury an empty coffin.

Dash turned from the sea, trudged back up to where Willy lounged in his favorite window seat.

"A real fairy tale story," Willy said, fingers from both hands working to prop a three-inch plastic Snoopy doll on his muscular abdomen. The toy had been deposited in the tide pool the day before, along with two baby eels currently doing laps, probing the walls for a way out.

Dash sat to watch the waves roll over the black lava. The wind blew from the north, pushing at the storm as an invisible barrier, piling the clouds taller. "I lost my job because of that bastard. My fiancée and my job. Everything."

"You have your health," Willy said, then glanced down at Dash's crotch and made a wet clicking sound with his mouth. "Oh, sorry."

"That's for the girl." Dash pointed at the Snoopy. "She expects the soldiers to give her a kitten. Nice clothes and a kitten."

"Do they really have nine lives?"

"I won't let her go. I need to figure out how to build a boat, and keep the birds from ratting me out. Who knew birds took sides?"

"This was made in China." Willy held the toy upside down for Dash to see the stamped letters. "Imagine it coming so far. If the girl doesn't know you found it, we should put it back in the ocean and let it keep going."

"I should have died in the crash with everyone else."

Willy made the clicking sound again, which was followed by a bright flash and rolling thunder Dash felt through the seat.

"You're a bundle of joy," said Willy. "You survived for a reason, my friend. She knocked the plane out of the sky and let you live. You might have been singled out as the best baby-making prospect, but she didn't figure on you throwing a wrench into your delicate mechanism."

Dash leaned forward, turned to look up at the monstrosity spewing wispy puffs of smoke into the gray scud. From where they sat, it looked too steep to climb. There had to be a path on a hidden side, chiseled steps in the stone face making easy access for sending innocent castaways to their deaths. He imagined a lovable, bumbling Gilligan with his trademark white cap gone, his red shirt and white pants in bloody tatters, being prodded to the edge of the volcano by sharpened spears, the villagers humming the sitcom theme song.

"You're bumming me out with this shit," Willy said, obviously reading his thoughts. "Think of something cheerful, will ya? Tell me the story about your bride-to-be and the snow plow driver. That was a good one."

"You can be a real jerk."

"How'd the guy get you fired?"

Dash reached across the middle seat and plucked the Snoopy from Willy's cavernous belly button. "I really do want to give this to Tiki."

"Suit yourself. How'd he get you shit-canned?"

"Tommy worked the counter at his old man's bowling alley when he wasn't driving a plow. You know anything about bowling?"

Willy tilted his fish head at him, bulb at the end of the dorsal spine flickering. "I know whatever you know about bowling. You'd order a couple of light beers and try to impress your girl with an awesome follow-through."

"Okay, okay, so we'd either catch a movie or bowl a few

games on Saturday nights. It was the winter after graduation, and I'd started writing for the newspaper. Not a whole lot to do in northern Vermont once the sun goes down."

"You spent your time bowling even though your penis worked? Must be a very satisfying game."

Dash ignored the sarcasm. "I started noticing some of the people who'd come into the bowling alley. They'd hang around the front counter where Tommy chain-smoked behind the register and sprayed disinfectant into rental shoes."

Willy lifted a huge bare foot and wiggled his toes. "Never owned a pair of shoes in my life."

"I recognized a lot of these guys, mostly local business owners. One had a third-generation sandwich shop, another owned a Hallmark franchise. An insurance guy, a tax preparer, all pillar-of-the-community types. I also knew their faces because they'd stop in to shoot the breeze with our ad reps at the paper, or go to lunch with my managing editor. But what the heck were they doing at the bowling alley with this lowlife Chambers? A few times they rolled a couple of frames, but some didn't even switch out of their street shoes."

"Bad for the lanes, right? Scuffs them up."

"Yeah, I guess. You're supposed to wear special shoes," said Dash, who owned his own pair, kept them tucked away in a hall closet. Only now they were either boxed up in his mother's basement or had been donated to charity. He'd kept them next to the used bowling ball he'd found on Craigslist for fifteen bucks. "Sarah complained that we stopped going to movies because I planned on trying out for the Olympics."

"No kidding? Bowling is an Olympic sport?"

"Jesus, I don't know. Something was going on between Tommy and the business owners. I started a list of who was coming and going. There was a story buried there some place, and I was determined to dig it up. It involved a whole lot of important people in town."

"You sound like a lousy date." Willy made more clicking

sounds with his mouth. "Your girl didn't know what you were up to?"

"I couldn't trust her to keep it secret. She was still going out drinking with her friends on nights I had late assignments."

"You were a lucky guy to land such a princess."

"Anyway, I figured it all out by accident. I was headed to the snack shop for two more beers, but detoured toward the men's room. By coincidence, Tommy was walking down the hall ahead of me and pulled his wallet from a back pocket. It was one of those set-ups with a chain attached to one corner that connects to a belt loop."

"Biker style," said Willy. "Wicked chic."

"When he goes for his wallet, I see a little square packet pop out and land on the carpet. I was real smooth, scooping it up and slipping it into my pocket without missing a beat. Then I stood right next to the fucker at the urinal while we both took a piss. He had a dangling cigarette, acted like I was invisible. He zips up, hits the handle, and doesn't even pretend to wash his hands."

"To be fair, you said he was spraying disinfectant."

"Can I finish?"

"I'm listening," said Willy.

"I had all the answers practically burning a hole in my pocket. I knew before looking that it was cocaine he was dealing."

"Bingo!" Willy clapped his hands just as a lightning bolt crashed down and touched the ocean surface a few hundred yards away. The white flash spread out like a wave in all directions. "Front page story, right?"

"I needed proof. I had to get it on video. I could report what I'd seen, plus I had the little package of coke, but it wasn't enough. Without video, it was my word against his. And what had I really seen? I needed to show money exchanging hands, then confront one of the buyers away from the bowling alley where he'd have to take me up on my offer. I'd promise to keep his name out of the paper in exchange for everything he knew."

"You were a man with a plan," Willy said. "Very impressive."

"I pictured the story getting picked up by all the dailies in the state, the Associated Press including it in its regional and maybe even national feed if any councilmen had their hands in it. They really get off on that stuff. Local bowling alley owner's son is narcotics supplier to downtown business bigwigs."

"How'd your boss feel about your investigative reporting?"

Dash used his big toe to draw a wavy line in the black sand. "Not anything like I expected. He threatened to fire my ass and make certain I never worked at another paper in the state. The ad revenue from the people I'd be destroying was the lifeblood of the newspaper. If he found out I so much as took one more note or asked one more question, my career was over."

"But you couldn't leave it alone," said Willy.

"I borrowed a video camera from a friend, cut a hole in an old gym bag for the lens. I asked for lane eight or nine, the ones with a good view of the front counter, said they were lucky for me. I set the camera to record while we bowled."

"What made you take Sarah to that joint in the first place? It had to be pure hell being around some guy you were pretty sure had hooked up with your girl."

Dash drew more lines in the sand. "You already know."

"You're telling the story. I'm just sitting here listening."

"The night we got engaged kept coming back. I did everything I could to pretend I hadn't seen what happened, what she'd done in the truck. But it got into my dreams and was harder and harder to push out of my head."

Willy was nodding. "You wanted to hurt him bad."

"I wanted to *kill* him. It's why I took Sarah bowling in the first place. I couldn't hide from it anymore, so I faced it the only way I knew. The story was dumb luck. But even after I knew something shady was going down, I followed him to the bathroom to confront him. I'd started losing it big time. I was fantasizing non-stop about murdering him, had a hundred different ways of doing it running through my head. Dropping the coke saved the fucker's life. I would have smashed his head into the tile wall while he was pissing. Grabbed him by the neck and just kept smashing and smashing."

"You had him in a different way. One that kept you from rotting in prison for the rest of your life."

"I had video of a dozen bedrock citizens buying drugs from Tommy Chambers." Dash paused and took a deep breath of salty ozone. "Or at least appearing to buy little square packages that may or may not contain drugs. So I kept to my original plan and picked the guy most likely to roll over on the rest. He owned a new shoe store, was married and had two young kids. It was also the one guy I didn't want to see ruined. I wasn't trying to judge people for buying coke. I was caught up in doing a real story for the first time in my shitty career."

"And you wanted to take Tommy down."

"The next best thing to bashing in his head."

"So you took the guy a copy of the tape?"

Dash nodded. "I walked into his store around lunch time. His name was Bob, and damn if he didn't have a smear of white powder under one nostril while I was trying to explain my offer. But he was hyper as hell, sniffing and rubbing at his nose, scared shitless that I was some kind of blackmailer. I tried calming him down, but he was amped up. 'I don't have money,' he tells me, and goes on about two mortgages and twenty grand worth of Buster Browns nobody was buying. So I tell him again what I need, and something seems to finally click in his head. He bends over the glass counter, looks down at the knickknacks lined up in the case as if they have the answer, and starts talking. Tells me everything I needed to know. Gives me Tommy's prices, who turned him on to the operation, and who he suspected was Tommy's supplier."

"Hot damn. Signed, sealed, and delivered. You were a helluva reporter after all."

"Bob went home and hung himself in the garage," said Dash. "Did I mention his two little girls? And would you believe his wife had just found out she was pregnant again? Not many people have the sort of life insurance that covers self-inflicted rope wounds."

Willy reached across and patted Dash's hand. "Funny how things work out."

"I went ahead and wrote the story, but didn't give it to my editor. I sent it right to the wire service, and reporters from all over the state were on the phone looking to fill in some blanks or add quotes from me. My boss wrote a retraction of the story the minute he found out, sent it over the wires marked urgent, saying a former reporter had fabricated the entire piece as an act of retribution. He claimed I'd gone crazy, was trying to pull off some sort of sick stunt that caused an innocent man's suicide."

"Boy, oh boy." Willy squeezed Dash's hand, held it. "What a story that made, huh? Husband and loving father driven to suicide by crazed journalist. Talk about front page news."

"I made the front page, for sure."

"I really like that Snoopy," Willy said, pointing to the figure on Dash's lap. "I like things you can touch and not worry about killing."

Dash handed him the toy.

"Thanks." Willy propped Snoopy back in his belly button. "You have some time before the big weenie roast. Seems like a waste, grinding on things you can't fix. Try spending your time with something productive, maybe work on your stone skipping."

Dash watched the storm as it was pushed farther to the south. The village fishermen were headed home through the heavy surf, making the last turn at the southern tip of the reef. One waved to Dash, who lifted his hand from habit. Maybe becoming a human sacrifice was exactly what he deserved.

Chapter 21

———

Dᴀꜱʜ ꜱᴋɪᴘᴘᴇᴅ ꜱᴛᴏɴᴇꜱ across the rolling wave tops. The wind had died down when the thunderheads disappeared, the sea as calm as it ever got south of the reef. Foam spilled over the rocks, gulls squawking and battling for air space. They chased the flat stones, were frustrated when the tempting objects dug in and sank out of sight. Tiki laughed, gathered more for him to throw.

"Come, I wanna teach you." He held a stone with his curled index finger and thumb.

"Did you have happy times with her?"

"Who do you mean?"

"You and Sarah."

He backed away from the meager surf, stone still in his right hand. He sat next to Tiki as she stacked her collection into a pyramid.

"Was she a good cook? Did she make you clothes?"

He would never admit the only successful aspect of their relationship to a ten-year-old girl. He had, come to think of it, once blurted out to Sarah that she was like a pro when it came to certain endeavors. She bopped him in the head for that one.

They were in bed, still panting, when the words slipped out. She stormed from the sweaty covers into the bathroom, locking the door. He knew she'd sit on the toilet for an hour, reading magazines and smoking from a stale pack of Marlboros she kept stashed in the medicine cabinet. He'd been forced to pee in the kitchen sink.

"She seemed to really like my mom," he finally said. "And my mom sure loved her. She thought Sarah was the best thing in the world for me. My mom was a sucker for a good love story, maybe because hers had turned out so sad."

"Did your mama tell Sarah stories?"

"Is that what loving mothers do?" he asked, knowing the answer. "I guess she would have if they'd spent more time together. My mom wanted a grandchild almost too much."

He'd worried about his mother, how she'd grown increasingly distant from friends, doing things that crossed the line into full-fledged eccentricity. The store had looked less and less like an antique shop, and more like a stage set for a large, Victorian-era family. One with eight babies roughly the same age.

While her home was cluttered with trash bags spilling from the kitchen out onto the front porch, the shop was immaculate in the years following her husband's death. White candles burned in each window. A fresh wreath hung on the front door year-round. The enormous dining room table had been cleared of inexpensive bric-a-brac, replaced with a fourteen-person China set, gold-plated silverware, hundred-year-old serving plates, and elegant stemware. Eight chairs held hand-crafted booster seats and porcelain baby dolls with fine linen bibs.

The dolls were her babies, and she showed them off to her friends when they came to the shop for tea. The women had smiled when his mother brought out an album, photos of the same babies in the same chairs. He'd been lugging boxes past the heartbreaking scene, wanted to interrupt his mother, make some excuse for her. But he allowed it to continue, letting her dote over the dolls while serving cookies and finger sandwiches to her uncomfortable lady friends who would soon stop their visits. Reputations slid fast in a small town, and he heard snippets regarding the poor widow who'd been getting loonier and loonier since the nasty business with her husband.

"Sarah said she wanted to get to know my mom. We were invited to dinner at the shop right after we were engaged." Dash recalled the snowy roads on the way out to the store, how the town plow driver had seriously slacked off. "Every window was lit by a dancing flame, and even the old gas lamp at the end of the walkway burned. There was an antique sled with a green silk ribbon propped by the door. Mom had decorated the Christmas tree, hung evergreen wreathes across the doorways and mantle. It was beautiful."

"It sounds like magic."

"It was magic," he said.

"A Christmas tree is the same as our Yule tree, but yours is named after Baby Jesus. I know that from the burned books."

"That's right. It's the most important holiday in our culture, or at least used to be. It was once all about religion, but now it's mostly about buying gifts."

"Can kittens be gifts?"

"I'm sure lots of kids want a kitten for Christmas."

"Did your mother give Sarah a kitten?"

"No, we were only there for dinner, the three of us and Mom's eight baby dolls."

"Baby dolls can eat?"

"You can pretend to feed them. Dolls are toys for little girls to practice being mothers."

"I want a baby doll and a kitten."

"My mom gave us an envelope." Dash closed his eyes and saw the red paper with a card tucked inside. "It contained plane tickets, which were to be a wedding gift. Tickets for the airplane that brought me here."

"She didn't know the Volcano was going to make it crash,"

Tiki said, reaching to touch his hand.

"My mom was wearing white makeup all over her face." He remembered now what he'd dismissed at the time, mostly because Sarah had seemed to find it all so charming and normal, "and a hat with a stuffed parrot on top."

"A stuffed parrot? You mean it was dead?" She looked back over her shoulder to where the small green birds darted among tree tops.

"The women from long ago wore hats with flowers and big feathers stuck into them. Some of the expensive ones had dead birds that had been cut open and filled with sawdust."

Tiki scrunched up her face.

"Yeah, no kidding, but they eventually stopped doing it. My mom also wore a dress with puffy sleeves and a huge bustle in back. That's bunched-up material."

"To make it soft when she sat down," she said, nodding.

"Sure, maybe. Sarah went around to each doll, asking its name and where it had come from. And my mother poured tea and went on and on about each of her precious babies. She had a harrowing story for each, how it had been orphaned by war or terrible famine."

"It sounds nice. Scary, but nice."

"They were just made-up stories, none of them true, of course. The dolls were nothing but playthings made out of baked clay and cotton stuffing. But Sarah kept asking questions, kept urging my mother on about this baby and the next. The more she asked, the more fantastic the stories became. I began to see how my mother had gotten totally lost in these possessions, the dresses, the furniture, the dolls."

"Her friends shouldn't have stopped liking her."

"I should have stayed to take care of her," he said. "Anyway, Mom finally announced it was time for dinner, went sweeping off into the kitchen in her grand dress, then came back with an empty serving platter. She dipped an invisible ladle into invisible bowls of nothing, and filled our plates with make-believe food. Sarah was all cooing and full of smiles, while I watched my poor crazy mother spoon-feed her children."

"Your mother believed everything was real."

"She was lonely. My father had left her alone and she couldn't deal with it."

Tiki's eyes were wide as she fiddled with the stack of flat rocks. "I know what that's like."

"On the car ride home, Sarah told me she'd never go back, that my mother should be put in an asylum. Better yet, she should be put out of her misery, maybe stuffed and displayed on her front porch like one of her freak-show parrots."

"When you go back home you should give your mom a Christmas present that will keep her from being lonely."

Dash laughed. He snatched one of the bottom row stones that toppled her pyramid, and then got to his feet. "Let me guess what you have in mind. Something that meows and chases balls of yarn?"

"No," said Tiki. "You should give her a kitten."

Chapter 22

———

"MY MAMA WOULD have been nice to yours. She would have stayed friends if their huts were close."

They were trudging back up to the village side by side, Tiki full of chatter and wearing the water bucket as a hat.

"You call it a house," she said. "Hut and house start with the same letter. In my language the word is *tabu*, and that's almost the same as *tabua*, but means something really different."

She turned and pulled her upper lip back to show her teeth. "A *tabua* is a whale tooth. I can teach you all our words. The missioners said our language came from the animals, so we should learn English."

"That was a rotten thing for them to say. Your language is music, even when I'm getting yelled at."

"Books are in your language, so they were probably right. I want to make books with pictures of my favorite things. I'll write stories about my pictures, but not like in the Bible. The Bible is too scary. And a lot of the words were hard even for missioners. Sometimes we asked what a word meant and they pretended not to hear."

Dash used the back of his hand to wipe the sweat streaming

over his brow and stinging his eyes. They were in the tunnel's final stretch; the opening was a white-hot, lopsided circle directly ahead.

"I need more candles," he said, chest heaving as though he'd been sprinting.

"The missioners said heathens live in darkness. That's why they taught us to make them."

Tiki had pulled ahead, was talking over her shoulder as they emerged into the blinding sun. He followed with his chin to his chest, trying not to be seen. He'd been using the ocean for his business instead of the outhouse, but couldn't survive without fresh water. She didn't stop to dip the bucket at the cistern, kept walking through a group of women busy weaving the palm fronds used for walls and the open lean-tos for hanging fish over smoky fires to make their leathery jerky.

They continued down an open path behind the chief's hut and into a clearing he hadn't known existed. Beyond was a lush field of taro.

"The missioners said welcoming Jesus into your heart was lifting a heavy shade. But I don't understood how shade can be heavy. I try to pick it up but it makes you part of it."

"I suppose they meant light was knowledge," said Dash. "And you were in the dark until you saw things their way. I've also heard that sermon from teachers."

"They built these so we would have light." She stepped aside for him to see the four paint-chipped, wooden bee boxes standing on low stone piles. She skipped over to a woman tending a metal pot over smoldering coals and threw her arms across her shoulders for a hug from behind. The woman was pushing and pulling a bamboo stick to stir heavy liquid. She paused to listen to the girl, and then nodded. He peeked over the rim of another pot to see a smaller pot inside, three quarters filled with a simmering brown mixture that smelled of warm honey.

Tiki danced back to where he was relishing the sweet scent.

"The water boils in the big pot. It heats the smaller one that holds the wax. It gets hot enough to melt, but not burn. I know all about it," she said.

Candles hung in pairs by uncut wicks, suspended over thin vines tied into a maze in branches of a heavily pruned puka tree. A second woman was recycling the fancier coconut shell candles, scraping out the remaining singed wax and polishing the interiors.

"Come see." Tiki led him to one of the bee boxes swarming with busy workers. A steady stream flew in from over his shoulders, buzzing past his face to land on the box and scurry inside. He guessed they were back from collecting pollen.

"It's pretty cool." He watched her lift a metal handle to slide a wooden frame section from the top of the box. Attached was a perfect honeycomb manned by hundreds of bees, golden honey dripping back into the open slot. She caught some of the thick cascade in her other palm, took a taste, and replaced the frame. The box hummed with the sound of their collaboration.

"Are there bees at your house?"

"I'm pretty sure bees are everywhere. But I've never seen a bee box up close. Our neighbors made syrup rather than raise honey bees. Syrup is from a tree, the same as what you used to make my Yule present."

"Is it sweet?"

"A different kind of sweet, but used in the same ways."

"Do they make candles?"

"No, just the syrup. They drill a small hole in the tree and it slowly drips into a bucket. Then it gets boiled down until it's really thick."

"The honeycombs are what make the candles." She pointed to a grass mat stacked with tiny connected hexagons. "Mama was a candle maker before she was killed. I was little, but I remember washing the honeycombs with her. The bees make them to hold honey and also their eggs. She let me dip the candles until they got too heavy."

"Families in Vermont make candles together, too. I've seen the wax in stores, big blocks to melt in kitchen pots."

"But you have lights that turn on without fire. And the metal tubes you hold and point."

"Flashlights."

"The missioners had them to find the outhouse at night. The also had them on their boats, but took them away when they left."

"People like my mother burn candles because they're pretty. And they come in handy when your batteries wear out. We get storms called nor'easters that knock over trees and bring snow that's almost as deep as you are tall. Our lights stop working for days after those storms."

"Maybe there will be storms like that where I go."

He brushed at a bee that tried landing on his face. "You aren't going anywhere."

She lifted some of the empty honeycombs and dropped them into a bucket half-filled with water. She squatted and rubbed at the combs one by one, picking out and flicking away dead bees that floated to the surface.

"I'll turn on every light when I'm in the city," she said. "I'll make it like daytime. I won't want candles."

He watched bees circle the girl's thick hair. Some landed on her bare shoulder and she chased them with a shrug. "I'll still like honey, though," she said, grabbing more honeycombs to scrub.

Dash felt a tickle on top of his ear, the buzz of a bee exploring his own waxy cavity.

"Don't swat them," she said, just as he began to swat. "They get mad really easy."

"Hey!"

He weaved and ducked, was a boxer avoiding a roundhouse punch from an invisible opponent. Then there was something electric—a sharp pain that took his breath. It froze him for a moment and gave the bees an easy place to land. The first sting was on his neck, beneath the hinge of his jaw. The second was at the top of his scalp, and the third was in the middle of his back, where his hands couldn't reach. He slapped and slapped as the swarm fell on him, Tiki's voice drowned out by their angry noise. He remembered old instructions he'd gotten as a kid about stopping, dropping, and rolling when you caught on fire. And the sudden burning pain all over his body sure felt like fire. The screaming hadn't been part of the lesson, was his addition to the emergency drill. He'd been a Cub Scout in a blue uniform and yellow scarf, laughing with his friends as his den mother made them take turns extinguishing an imaginary fire by rolling around on her living room carpet.

It went quiet when his throat closed. Instead of screaming, he used the energy trying to pull air into his lungs through an impossibly tiny slit. The bees were in his nose and mouth, plugging both ears, and some even tried burrowing under his eyelids. He swiped at his eyes with hands that had become fat clubs, useless for any more swatting. Every movement became an enormous effort, his muscles numbing from poison, the Earth's gravity tripling. The ground turned slow circles as he lay spent on his back, chest heaving as he gasped for breath.

There were worried female voices, and Tiki was crying. But at least the bees had begun their victorious retreat. He tried spitting out the ones that had turned his tongue into a useless lump, but they weren't leaving until they were good and ready, emerging from between swollen lips to take flight one by one. Did honey bees die after using their stingers? He hoped so, and he made a mental note to tell Tiki that syrup making was a thousand times safer than this honey and candle stuff. Sure, maybe a maple tree fell on your house in one of those nor'easters, but there was none of this crawling up your nose and trying to sting your brains shit.

His vision went black as he willed himself toward a dark place, away from the burning stingers and the lingerers burrowed in his tangled hair, delivering final volleys. He was stirred back when he was lifted by his wrists and ankles, tried twisting free in a sudden panic, certain the bees had returned with burlier reinforcements.

"Looks like a pig," said one of the bees attached to a wrist. "Pink skin all fat, like it gonna pop."

Another bee laughed, made its own joke in the island language, then grunted when it latched onto his ankles and worked for a solid hold on his greasy skin.

He surrendered and managed to relax in their grip. He allowed himself to be carried away with no further fight, dreamed he was a balloon swaying on the wind over a forest of sharp tree limbs.

✠

THE BEES WERE back. He tried getting up, to move from the noise, only to bang his head. He lifted a hand to the rock wall, reached down to the familiar mat beneath his thighs. Something was wrong with his fingers, as though he'd stuck them in a pair of boxing gloves. His thumbs seemed to wiggle, but the other fingers were squeezed together, so bloated there was no separation. He touched his face, but it was a distant feeling, pins and needles, as though his fingers and face had fallen asleep.

The swarm raged. Their anger was carried by the onshore breeze that occasionally caused the flame of his candles to flinch. He listened, lying trapped in his cave with no hiding spots for anything larger than a spider. There was a bubbling to the drone, and he remembered the bees wanting into his mouth, his inability to spit them out. Now his mouth was dry, tongue a solid block against the back of his teeth.

He waited for their arrival, for them to round the corner into his dark home to finish him off. Heat radiated from his core, a pulsing fever that brought flashes of red to his black world, but he was otherwise numb. More stings wouldn't hurt, at least not as bad. One last flourish of barbs would take him away, would save him.

The droning sound veered, changed pitch, as if the bees had suddenly zeroed in on someone or something else. He felt regret for their new target, hoped it had speedy legs or wings. But doubt blossomed, made him wonder if it really was the sound of a hunting swarm. There was something mechanical about the noise, something familiar, as though it came from Dash's world and not from some jungle clearing. Maybe it was a motor, the kind attached to a boat. And it made sense of the wet bubbling and lowered pitch, a craft swinging around the tip of the reef, powering down to maneuver in the shallow water. A boat meant he was going home, that his rescuers had arrived to deliver him from this hell on earth. Adrenaline rushed through his body, tensed his muscles, and stirred the poison in his blood.

"Help," he tried saying, but his tongue was too far gone. The fever swept away his consciousness, took him to a place without dreams.

DASH WAS WRENCHED from sleep when the word 'help' was repeated, a plaintive cry from a voice he knew.

He tried calling Tiki's name, but not enough healing time had passed since the motor sound. It might take days or weeks, or maybe his tongue would never work again, as forever numb and useless as his penis. His bones ached from shivering, the fever wicking the last of his liquid through burning skin. His lips felt like they were turned inside out.

"My eyes," he tried saying, touching a bloated hand to his swollen brow. The bees had gotten into the softest parts, had jabbed their barbed weapons into the most fragile surfaces.

The girl's voice returned in a scream, not far away, but the cave's acoustics made it difficult to judge. He rolled from his mat, crawled on hands and knees toward the sound, toward Tiki and whatever had her.

He knew it was something to do with the motor. The soldiers were back, had gotten hold of the child and were hurting her. He scrambled blindly, reaching the cave's opening on his knees, knowing it was day from the sun's heat. He lifted his chin, eyes swollen completely shut, and gently pawed at the puffy mess with one hand. He reached out to the wall at the cave's mouth and pushed his way up, getting first one and then the second wobbling foot under him.

He listened for more cries, and it was a minute before her voice came again. More screams, and maybe she called his name. He stumbled forward on bent legs, hands out in front, forming a picture of the tunnel-like pathway toward the village. Up and over a slight knoll carpeted with broken shells, and then into the humid air as the vegetation closed around him. The sound of insects grew tenfold as he crept forward, vines ensnaring his feet and sharp things drawing blood from probing hands. A man's laughter and more screams, but not from the direction of the village. Tiki had been caught, pulled inside the jungle by a monster, and Dash was feebler than ever, blind and stumbling, because he hadn't heeded her simple advice not to swat the bees.

Twenty more steps and the insect noise was maddening, blood pulsing in his ears as he collapsed to his knees and felt for the opening that led toward her last scream. It was the clearing with the stone altar she must have been taken to, hopefully biting and scratching. God's House, the missionaries had named it. He tore at the vines, cutting his hands on the prickly bushes, his knees becoming pincushions. He stopped prodding the thick wall of low growth to pull out a finger-length thorn sticking from the top of his left thigh. He fingered the needle in his clumsy hands, touched the tip to one wrist to test its strength, where it slid easily through his skin and found muscle.

He could feel the jungle vibrate as he brought the thorn to his left eyelid and slipped the point into his puss-filled flesh. The skin burst like a volcanic pimple, and he carefully kneaded the inflamed tissue with his bulbous knuckles. He wiped the mess away with his sweaty forearm, then switched hands and slowly plunged the thorn into his other bloated eyelid. He plunged twice this time, pressing and kneading. He could once again blink, could see forms in the dark jungle—the yellow leaf plants and white flowering vines giving texture to black satin shadows. The world looked hazy, as if deep under water.

The opening through which Tiki once led him was five paces beyond, and he got back to his feet and lunged forward. He could hear her cries over the insect noise, as well as her captor's mocking voice. Or maybe it was his imagination that kept her alive, his desperate hope that her throat hadn't been slit on the sacrificial altar. He stumbled over rotted tree stumps and through tangles of bushes that claimed pieces of flesh. He flung his body forward, falling and clawing to his feet, his panicked mind driving him to her rescue. Nothing in his disappointing life had ever mattered as much as getting to her, as stopping whatever the monster was doing.

Dash tumbled into the circle of piled stones beneath the leaf-covered altar. His breath was gone, blackness threatening to take away the vision he'd recovered. He searched the shadows for a uniform, although he'd only imagined what the soldiers wore. He'd pictured them in Australian outback clothing—tan uniforms suitable for the harshest bush. He rose, stood tall with his fists out in front, ready for a battle to the death.

But there was nothing to fight, only a small slumped figure on the wide stone where the countless spiders had saved their souls. When he reached for the whimpering child, she made a choked noise and pulled away. Her underpants lay in a lump next to her, a bloody handprint on the outside of her thigh. He dropped his forehead to the wet stone, let his eyes close until night took firm hold.

Chapter 23

———

THE TINY, CAREENING spiders stayed hidden, maybe because they'd failed, or maybe because they didn't exist. Dash leaned over the massive stone, watching the empty leaves, the only movement caused by Tiki's occasional fits of shivering. It was hours before she stopped pulling away from his touch. He slid his hands beneath her dirty knees and fragile neck, gently scooping her up and holding her as steadily as his own frail body allowed. He carried her through the jungle and delivered her to the sea without resting, cradling her in the protected water until she said she was clean. The soldiers' boat was gone, with only a single aluminum can left bobbing, trash captured in a lazy vortex within the reef's bony tip.

She spent two days and nights in the cave, Dash sleeping restlessly under the Pacific sky in an aisle seat, his own toxins drifting away on the wind.

He dreamed of thousands of spiders spinning their frantic circles, him standing over them in judgment. He lifted a bare foot and brought it down over their soft bodies, smearing them in a short arc in one direction and then the other. The blood and guts looked like the two strokes a child's crayon might make when drawing a seagull.

He checked on her before heading up the east coast to gather driftwood for a signal fire. She'd been sound asleep on his grass mat, but halfway up the beach he noticed her following his footsteps in the sand. He slowed for her to catch up.

They made it all the way to where waves swept across dead coral shallows at the island's northern tip. It was a foreboding panorama, bleak and windy, stinking of things rotting in salt. But maybe if he'd first woken here, had spent weeks and months staring out over this landscape, it would all be as familiar and comfortable as the southern end.

Wood was plentiful, caught in bleached tangles like smashed ribcages over the rocky terrain. He picked the driest pieces, snapped them into similar lengths.

"They took one of my sisters," she whispered, her voice forced through a too small space, as if she was still being choked. "We need longer vines."

It broke his heart some more as he watched her tie a perfect knot in a green strip to secure one bundle. She walked to the edge of the jungle and disappeared without hesitation, barefoot and determined. Her fearlessness made him feel pathetic. Not in a million years would he dare wander into the thick growth that was infested with snakes and colorful giant spiders with hinged legs. And maybe white men filled with even worse poison.

He didn't explain the expedition, and she helped without question. A signal fire would bring rescue, make everything right. Safely away, he'd convey the plight of the villagers to anyone who'd listen. The pirate raids to steal children would cause outrage, bring protection after years of misery and loss. Salvation was achieved from one's self, not a god who may or may not understand words amid the raucous chorus. His escape was the only chance for her people, not his murder or suicide. Not his persecution.

She touched his arm with a vine lasso for his bundle of sticks. He hoisted the wood across his shoulders, sharp parts digging into sunburned flesh. She pulled her package lengthwise from a cord around her waist, the back end bumping over rocks and sand, a wavering claw-mark trail left behind.

The fire's purpose was the first lie. He told her he wanted to cook his own last meals, even if he had to ask for handouts from the passing fishermen. She would only need to bring his water, and he'd have no trips at all to the village. He was ashamed to be playing on her sympathy, but he knew she expected him to follow Manu's vision into the volcano's mouth. Perhaps if Dash had rescued her, she would have understood him wanting to rescue himself.

They lugged the wood across the lava to a spot near the airplane seats, where she picked at the knots. They arranged the wood in a log cabin stack that rose just above her shoulders. He filled the hollow center with the driest foliage he could scavenge. The sun would bake out any remaining moisture in one afternoon. They pulled giant banana leaves into a pile next to the tinder chimney. He would use the leaves to shelter the wood if rain threatened, but their main purpose was to create smoke once the stack was burning. The green leaves would become the signal, white smoke against black lava and the brown volcano behind.

They stepped back to look at their work.

He heard skepticism in her choked voice. "You can't cook with this. It'll get too hot, burn up too fast. The wood will be wasted."

His heart broke some more.

"It's for coals." It was his second lie, but he still felt a sense of accomplishment. He looked beyond the structure to the glimmering sea, dotted with whitecaps in the late afternoon breeze, each spec on the horizon a potential ship. And help for these people, too, he reasoned, looking down at the girl who was watching him, her eyes filled with emotions he didn't recognize.

She returned to the village alone, but her face came back to Dash when he was lying on his sleeping mat under a single candle's yellow glow. He again saw her eyes, and recognized the emotions as sadness and betrayal.

When he walked down to the tide pool in the morning light, he wasn't surprised to find his chimney of wood gone. Each stick and every last twig had vanished, probably cast back out into the water to drift another thousand miles.

He stood with his arms at his sides, the breeze cold on the open sores left by the stings, his only company a thirty foot shadow of a lonely man. He turned his back to the sun and raised his arms to change the shadow into a cross. Then he spread his legs and dropped his hands to form a triangle that might also be a volcano. He hooked his thumbs and made a shadow puppet bird, then turned it into two mouths that talked.

"I'll go to a movie."

"A Coke with ice would hit the spot."

"And sit in the first row."

"Let the light and colors fall over me."

"Laugh at things not funny."

"Or cry."

"A double feature if they still have them."

"Hope for a happy ending."

"There are no happy endings."

"What makes them believe the almighty Volcano won't spit you back up to where the big planes fly?"

"Before drowning them in melted rock."

"Blood, the girl calls it."

"The girl dragged into the jungle, violated and left on an altar, while one less tempting was snatched away forever."

"Left *at* the altar."

"You're their savior."

"Their last hope."

"There are no happy endings."

His arms were tired when he dropped his hands. The sun burned his still shoulders, his skinny neck. He scanned the ocean beyond the coral reef and decided to follow the driftwood.

Chapter 24

———

THE BIRDS WERE watching, one gull circling like a vulture, head tilting a dead eye wherever he went. Small brown things with probing beaks were tucked into low bushes where they didn't belong, out of tree tops and vulnerable to snakes, no longer performing high-pitched songs. The sound of wings came at night while he squatted to relieve himself in the ocean, the snapping leather noise of feeding bats. But would bat radar work on a man slinking up a path? Would the gods trust something blind? Was the blind thing only a myth?

He waited two nights for solid cloud cover, using the time scouting the spot where the fishermen beached their skiffs at day's end. The gull rode the air above, but Dash walked like he had no plan, picked up stones and slung them out into the flat water. He had a fair idea of the layout near the lagoon's crescent mouth, and it was a simple hike along the shoreline, the unused path marked by toenail slashes, tiny marks from rats or mice. The jungle was kept at bay by the high tides that overpowered hopeful vines and left a salt coating to bake in the sun.

The cove's southern edge was where women did their

washing and bathed with the children, and where he'd been spotted spying on his love hut girl. Below the lagoon were flat stones set in the sand for gutting the daily catch. The area was desolate after sundown except for the birds swooping in to explore the scent of entrails pulled toward the open sea by the current. He imagined the underwater creatures drawn by the gore, swimming upstream with mouths open, gills pumping.

He followed a single candle flame for his escape. He lugged a half dozen coconuts packed inside his sleeping mat, a bucket of fresh water held steady against his side. Tightly rolled rice balls in folded banana leaves were tucked between the coconuts, along with his last three candles and the magnesium bar and striker. He also slipped the amber disk Tiki made for him into the top of the bundle, wedging it next to a finger-shaped stone he'd use for opening coconuts.

His stomach was queasy with the prospect of going out into the open water. He hoped Willy would make an appearance, assure him everything would be okay. He'd been alone since discovering the vandalized rescue fire. He hoped Tiki found the comfort she needed from the village women. Maybe Willy could somehow let her know how much he would miss her.

Dropping his mat into the bow of the nearest skiff, he pinched out the candle and stowed it with the supplies. It took a moment for some gray light to give depth and texture to the darkness, and it was enough to allow him to carefully set the water bucket into the skiff's flat midsection, anchoring it against his bundled mat. He followed the rope to the mooring tree and worked the knot with shaking fingers. He slid the heavy craft through the sand, sending it into the still water in reverse. It was a longer and fatter wood version of the canoes he'd rowed in the quiet ponds near his home. Hopping in, he grabbed the paddle and was successfully away.

It took ten minutes to reach the end of the reef, the bow more difficult to control as the chop increased. The skiff was longer than two men, always wanting to overcorrect, but he managed the turn into the deeper water, his trio of empty airplane seats left directly behind. He felt propelled as the current took over for the first hour. The wind remained still, and the prevailing flow allowed him the cut through the black water at a decent clip with easy strokes.

Freedom replaced apprehension, and a nagging feeling of being followed slipped away as his muscles warmed and then began to ache. He paddled blindly, pulling the oar twice on one side, then switching to the other, hoping for a straight course.

His hands were bleeding when the sky lightened and began its color change. Blisters had formed in the dark like mushrooms and then burst. When he finally dropped the slick handle and reached for the bucket to drink, he noticed Willy slumped behind on the stern bench, his enormous body translucent.

"Welcome aboard, old pal," Dash mumbled, lifting a leg and turning to straddle the bench. The volcano over Willy's shoulder rose out of a low haze that hid the island. "How far, ya think? Four miles? Ten?"

Dash took a deep breath and exhaled noisily, waited for the sick feeling of pins and needles to leave his wrists and elbows. He licked his cracked lips. "You're looking a little see-through. Not sure you wanna be here? Or is it that I can't decide if you're real?"

Willy's fish head lay sideways across one shoulder, gills pulling deep and hard, bulb dark. Dash leaned to pull the water bucket close with the heels of his hands, joints cracking and lower back muscles a balled knot. He drank until his belly ached, then waited for any sign of returning energy, a second or third wind, or whatever number he was up to.

"You just came along for the ride, huh? Cat got your tongue?"

Dash turned back to face the bow. He held his breath when he took the paddle in his hands. It was a glowing iron from a blacksmith's fire, but he held his grip, lifting the pear-shaped blade over one side of the hull and pulling a long stroke. *A few million more and I'm in New Zealand, or maybe Australia.*

"How many licks does it take to get to the center of a Tootsie Pop?" Dash asked through clenched teeth and then made a strangled chuckling sound that turned into a coughing fit.

"If I don't know, then you probably don't either," he said after catching his breath.

He resumed his strokes, but glanced back and noticed one of Willy's arms extended out over the water, fingers skimming at first, but then cutting deeper into the surface. The fingers infuriated Dash. They were slowing the momentum, creating drag that was responsible for his bleeding hands and the brutal throbbing in his shoulders. It was Willy's fault his body was turning into one big infected tooth. Dash fought an impulse to turn and smash him with the paddle, make him pay for his suffering. But he kept pulling the long strokes, sometimes keeping count, then losing his place. He paddled into a morning fog that echoed back his grunts, as though some other sorry bastard was in the same predicament, just out of view, grimy feet half submerged in briny water turning red as his life also drained away.

He took a final stroke when the sun reached its apex, a merciless prison spotlight with no shadows. The sea was gray and nearly still, and there seemed to be no birds. When he looked behind, Willy was almost clear, his body leaning so far back that his head touched the sea, bulb submerged. The bow should be high in the air with all the weight so far aft, but then Dash realized Willy probably weighed no more than a bad dream.

"You could have saved her," Dash hissed, drooling despite his thirst and ruined lips. He wished for the strength to push the former god overboard. "You did nothing. I made you up, and now I'm done with you."

He let the paddle slide from his hands, quarter-size bits of skin attached like barnacles. He half-rose, then lunged forward to the short bow seat and grabbed at his sleeping mat. The bristled edges sent lightning bolts across his vision, the pain so raw and unbelievable because nothing could possibly hurt so much. He swooned, his world going dark for seconds or maybe minutes, his own animal panting the first thing he was conscious of when his senses returned. He dropped from the bench to his knees, then curled against the side of the hull. Using only his fingertips, he tugged the mat over himself to hide from the sun.

HE SLEPT FOR hours. The sun dropped enough to throw shadows over half the skiff. The volcano smoked on the horizon, creating a vertical line that combined with the island to form an exclamation mark, although a high-altitude wind would eventually bend it into a question. He examined the mess he'd made of hands that now involuntarily pulled into claws. He tried shielding his palms from the sun, then leaned over the side of the skiff and plunged them into the cool seawater. The first seconds were bliss, the immaculate relief of soothing salve. Then he heard the shrieks—of someone or something, a pig caught in a leg hold trap, a siren stuck in the on position with a broken switch. Dash screamed his throat raw, holding his damaged hands out in front as the minutes passed.

Willy came back. He was nearly solid, head cocked in sympathy, body leaning forward as if to deliver comforting words. Through the searing pain, Dash sensed he'd summoned Willy, the fire in his hands and fingers causing his mind to seek out anything that might alleviate his suffering. Dash silently begged for mercy, an unspoken plea to heal his wounds or slice off his hands and take them far away. Either would be an acceptable solution.

The more the pain ebbed, the more he believed that although Willy was nothing like a flesh and bone creature, neither was he a mere ghost from his imagination. The diminishing pain left space to truly imagine the misery Willy had absorbed from the thousands of souls he'd had to bury. Willy had come as a beacon, an energy form to accept Dash's agony, a man-shaped sponge to take on the hurt. Human torment made Willy whole.

Dash leaned forward, elbows on his knees, limp and useless hands dangling in front. A bead of drool dropped from his lower lip on a thin line toward the bloody water. "Maybe you're real," he whispered, and then mouthed the word *sorry*.

Willy's dangerous mouth, with its horrible spiked teeth, became a lopsided smile. "You never had to be afraid," he said in a familiar woman's voice.

Dash's mother had taught him to believe in things he could not see or touch. Her bedtime stories ranged from rainbows that ended at pots of gold, to magic bunnies that hid chocolate eggs for children who cleaned their rooms without being asked. His father had provided the skepticism, and would come sit on the edge of his young son's bed in the spot still warm from his mother.

"Your mother told you about Good Rabbit?" his father would ask, and Dash would nod, eyes wide as he inched the blanket higher for protection, knowing the story to come. "But she doesn't tell you anything about Bad Rabbit. That's the bunny a boy's really got to know about."

Dash had barely started school when the more graphic tales had begun, and they'd lasted for years. He suspected they only ended because he stopped showing fear, stopped believing they might be true. Or maybe they ended when scaring a child stopped being entertainment for his father.

"Bad Rabbit sneaks into a child's room late at night, and there's nothing anyone can do to stop him from coming. Even if there are no windows, he knows a magic entrance, just like Santa Claus. Once inside, he crawls right in with the unsuspecting bed owner," his father would say, patting Dash's blanket where the interloper would take refuge. "The child is safe from any real harm because Bad Rabbit isn't interested in biting them. Of course, your sheet and blanket, and even your favorite pillow, will turn awful from an odor so foul that no amount of detergent will make them right."

His father spread his hands out over the bed. "All this will have to be set afire come daylight. Everything will need to go right into the burn barrel, lest the odors get into the walls."

"But kids can be washed, right?" Dash pictured being rolled up in his bedding and stuffed inside the rusty old drum down by the brook that cut through their property.

"Well, I've never heard of a child having to be burned." His father would pause, removing his metal frame glasses to polish on his shirt. "But I don't think parents would want that sort of thing in the news. It's very bad form to admit you've torched your child for smelling bad. Might even bring the law."

Dash nodded, trying to recall the worst thing he'd ever smelled, something so bad that his parents wouldn't want him anymore if it got on him. There had been a raccoon killed on the road near their house early that summer, maybe too close to their neighbor's driveway for the vultures to get at. The coon had gotten fatter and fatter, and his father had explained it was because of the gases forming inside, just like a party balloon. It gave Dash the notion to sneak out by the road with a stick to see if it was true, thinking somehow that if he poked a little, the raccoon might lift up off the ground and drift away on the summer breeze. But the coon was heavy, all muscle and hair. His father had lied. It was nothing like a balloon. He jabbed hard, trying to push it off the gravel and into the grass when it made a wet thump and began to deflate.

"Pay attention, son," his father warned. "Bad Rabbit goes for the easy pickings first, so you should listen close."

Young Dash would peer up at the black rectangle of glass on the far wall. "The window," he whispered, smelling the memory of the coon.

His father would follow his gaze, nodding slowly. "Easy as pie. Bad Rabbit would use his front paws to raise the wood frame, get his long nails underneath and push. Then he'd slip his fat belly over the sill and drop to the floor like a sack of butcher's meat."

"What does he want?" Dash knew the story, but felt compelled to repeat the questions he'd asked the first time. It was his part in the telling.

"Like your mother says, a bunny comes to deliver a chocolate egg."

"He has a basket?"

"No, Bad Rabbit has a special place where he carries an egg," his father would say, an unpleasant smile on his face, like maybe he was smelling the dead raccoon, too. "You see, he's twice the size of most children, although shaped very much like your average bunny, with the fleshy pink color of a baby hamster."

"My hamster had babies."

Dash's father frowned while he nodded. "So you know the color. It's a color that looks like it might be fragile, don't you think? And his fur is handsome in some places, smooth to the touch. It might even tempt you to stroke Bad Rabbit in those spots."

Dash shook his head that he wouldn't, not in a million years.

"But the rest of him is matted with burs and chewing gum, and other bits of garbage."

"Where does he keep the chocolate egg?"

"Oh, yes, the egg is tucked up inside his rolls of fat, right about here." Dash's father would pat his own flat stomach, where there was no place to hide an egg. "It is all those layers of fat which cause the most unpleasant feature of Bad Rabbit."

"Even worse than his smell?"

"Worse because when he sneaks into your bed and curls next to you, he begins to sweat. Not the kind of perspiration you get from lifting boxes and running around out back on the hottest of days. It is a sweat that leaks out of every part of him, so much that a child wakes up and begins to cry, believing they've done number one."

Dash knew he would cry, too, because he'd peed his bed right up until the second week of pre-K. The accidents had stopped when the new life in school became routine.

"But Bad Rabbit's badness is much worse for a grownup. If a parent was to check on a child late at night, sit on the edge of a bed where he lay hidden, Bad Rabbit would lash out with his long rabbit teeth and bite down hard, right through the blanket. He would not let go until the parent was also in tears."

"What happens to the chocolate egg?"

"Oh, Bad Rabbit always leaves it. That's his job, after all. He tucks it under a sweaty pillow with his filthy paws, arranges it on its side just right. Children expect their treats and would be disappointed."

Dash's father had no idea of the nightmares he caused his son. Or maybe he did. As an adult, Dash rationalized that his father had only wanted to balance what he considered his wife's obsession with things made-up. His father could not tolerate people who were gullible, who would flock to church to hear a mortal human being justify their existence. What man could know the thoughts of any creature able to create the universe? What muttonhead would sit there and listen? The Bible was ink and paper to his father, no different than any self-help book hawked on late night infomercials. But after his father died, Dash began believing the stories had all been for the man's enjoyment, his desire for control. Not every fragile antique could be put out of the children's reach, but his own son was easy pickings for both him and Bad Rabbit.

"The pain is a little better?" Willy's voice sounded like it came from another room.

Dash looked down at his hands and mistook the awful mess for a melted chocolate egg.

Chapter 25

——

A THUD JARRED the skiff to one side hard enough for cold water to splash over Dash. He banged the top of his head in the dark as he came awake, confused and shielding himself with both arms. He pushed free of the mat, used his elbows to lift onto the bench, and then searched the cocoon of blackness. It had to be a ship. There were no crashing waves, no squawk of night birds. There was no smell of too-sweet flowers or decaying jungle. But there was also no sound of men talking, no radio static, no creak from a giant wooden stern or metallic squeal of shifting steel. A ship would have lights, and here it was pitch black, no moon or stars. There was nothing but a few dull plunks from rain drops.

"Willy?" No one answered his raspy whisper. "Willy?"

There was only the sound of water against wood, teasing slaps and lazy trickles. He crept over the middle bench and reached out, needing not to be alone, but terrified of touching a dead god. Willy's hollow form had at least offered comfort, as much as did an old family photograph hung too many years in the sun.

A new jolt knocked Dash back into the narrow bow. His

head struck the flooded bottom, and when his hands with their raw wounds found the paddle blade, white flashes crossed his vision. The next impact turned the skiff, forcing him to grab one side or go overboard. He balanced on all fours until the motion settled, then he turned and lowered himself onto his crumpled mat.

A slit opened in the clouds, was pulled wider as if the Storm God had something for him to see. Enough light showered down to display the weak crests of the stirred ocean, the nearest stars returning dimension to his perilous new world. A gleaming dorsal fin slid through the water like a prowling submarine. The shark was longer than his meager boat, easily measured when it streamed past on a parallel course, its wake nearly enough to roll the skiff and begin the feeding.

He used his forearms to scramble up against the pinched bow, adrenaline the only fuel for his spent muscles. He faced a pale outline with a hovering green speck, what might be the last fleeting glow of a squashed firefly.

"Can you hear me? You believe this shit? They sicced a shark on me, Willy. A goddamn shark of all things." He turned to the water, his voice giddy, nearly hysterical as he began shouting, "I saw this fucking movie as a kid. Shark eats man, aliens not friendly, dinosaurs chase kids. Bring on the flesh-eating zombies, motherfuckers!"

He collapsed back, out of breath. Heart pumping as if it wanted out, he looked up at Willy's slumped figure. "Sorry about the zombie thing, buddy boy. You can't help what you look like."

It was a head-on strike that lifted the skiff under Dash's ass and sent him weightless. The keel slapped down hard, wood splintering. At least two precious coconuts were sent airborne and splashed into the ocean with solid kerplunks. Something larger also went overboard, and at first he thought it might be what remained of Willy. Pushing back up, he could see the floating paddle forever out of reach. Not that his hands would ever heal enough to put it back to use, having rowed himself into the questionable mercy of gods he didn't know.

He braced for the final assault, with the regret of not having fashioned a spear for his escape into shark territory. He imagined the satisfaction of returning some of the pain with a mighty jab, a sudden epiphany over what went on in the heads of killers who stabbed their victims a hundred times. Once you'd started, why stop? He might have been Custer of the Sea, making a glorious last stand in this primitive craft, weapon at the ready to track the canny man-eater. He'd sound a battle cry before putting out one of his assailant's eyes with a bulls-eye throw before being swallowed whole. The idea of bravery made him laugh, and then made him weep. He was a raging coward who ran from trouble in the real world—left innocent, motherless girls to suffer murderous devils alone.

Minutes passed, and then an hour or more. The clouds broke farther apart and the stars changed positions. The shark did not come again. Maybe it had grown bored, or maybe frustrated enough to move on. Perhaps it would return later for another go.

Dash reached for the leaning bucket with his fingertips and righted it. He touched the moist interior and brought the dampness to his lips. He sat with his legs folded, elbows on the seat behind. The amber disk Tiki had given him sat on its edge, leaning against his right foot. As he took it between his fingers and rubbed the smooth surface, the guilt for leaving her was almost too much to bear. He tucked her gift into his underwear.

The stern seemed empty, but not quite. Not when he looked real hard. He could discern Willy's beefy torso that reflected some of the light from the heavens. "Talk to me, Willy. Are you pissed that I blamed you for the girl getting hurt? So what if she didn't believe in you? I needed you to help her."

There was no response, no flicker from his bulb.

"She was just a kid. Becoming a god after the fact, after rotten things happen, is bullshit. It's all backwards. That girl and her people would have good reason to hate you if they knew you existed. Christ, the only thing more useless than talking to a god is listening to one."

Dash's head rolled with the waves, a loose coconut bumping his knee in the sloshing water. He was tired and alone, and needed this to end. It wasn't possible to live another day by himself.

"You lied," he said, wanting to provoke a response. "My plane wasn't knocked out of the sky by some crazy Volcano bitch. I felt what happened. We ran out of fucking gas, or some tube fell out of the carburetor. It wasn't any more magic than you are. It was one of those shit happens things."

Dash tilted his head toward the egg-shaped opening in the clouds. Stars twinkled from a fast moving low scud, perhaps the same stars he'd taken for granted back in Vermont. Stars were meant for real sailors and for people in love. They were for children to make wishes that sometimes came true. Watching the flickering light, he made his own wish that he would die easily, without much pain. He also wished there to be no afterlife with judgmental gods hanging around to keep score, only an instantaneous transition from all this loneliness to perfect nothingness.

The skiff rocked him into a sleep where he dreamed about birds that flew at night.

HE WOKE WITH the sun warm on his face, a wood box floating at his feet, probably dislodged from the old netting stuffed under the middle bench. It was about a foot across and three fingers tall. He lifted it with his knuckles and balanced it on his thigh. The surface was polished, with tiny intricate hinges engraved in fine designs. It was constructed some place far away. He pushed open the metal latch and lifted the lid to expose a dozen crude bone hooks, a small square mirror, and a Western-style serrated knife with a brown stain running the blade's length. He set the box next to him, flexed his right hand to stretch the skin being pulled tight by fledgling scabs. The wounds itched and burned, but were bearable. He gripped the knife's wood handle. The brown stuff was rust, or maybe fish blood.

"Look." He held his find up to Willy, whose eyes appeared to move, face muscles to twitch. Hard to be certain, since the sky behind him was nearly the same brightness as his translucent head.

Dash sniffed the blade, stuck his tongue out over cracked lips to taste the steel.

"Don't."

Dash jerked, nearly sliced his tongue, heart thumping.

"What the hell, Willy?" It hurt his throat to speak above a whisper. "I was seeing if it was blood."

The outline of Willy's slumped body filled in and became a little more real. Dash could see his light pulsing.

"How old were you?" Willy asked.

Dash ignored the question. Maybe he also had the power to read minds, because he knew what Willy had returned to ask.

"It's just an old fishing knife."

"Were you alone when you found him?" Willy's voice came from one of those tin can phone set-ups you put together as a kid, running a string from one can to the other, smelling chicken soup the whole time. It was as if Willy was in a nearby boat, rather than sucking breath through a grotesque fish mouth two seats away and hurling accusing questions.

"You want to know about my father."

"Yes, that's what I'm asking," said Willy, who'd come fully back. "We're on a sea cruise, could use a little entertainment, but I'm all talked out. Time for a story from my last friend in the world."

Dash remembered seeing his breath in the house, and his mother worrying that the oil truck hadn't delivered even though she'd called and left dire messages. The entire winter he'd turned fifteen was miserable, felt like it would never end. Spring came on the calendar, but the snow pack remained a solid five feet. There hadn't been a whole lot of big nor'easters, but there hadn't been the usual thaws. Snow built up in layers, reflecting back the good warm sun. The cold had gotten inside their home, had invaded their family.

"I was fifteen, a sophomore in high school." Dash pinched the blade between his fingers, then drew it along slowly. It came clean in spots, flashing bright when it caught the sun. He wiped the brown stuff on his thigh.

"Not a whole lot of friends?"

"No," said Dash. "I worked in my folk's store when I wasn't at school. Helped in the summers, too. Not a lot of kids wanted to hang around a dusty old antique shop. I sure as hell didn't."

"Your clothes smelled like the store when you went to school."

Dash remembered the girl in math class. He had a crush on her and she didn't know he was alive. He practiced a hundred ways of talking to her. *Those are pretty earrings*, he'd tell her in algebra class. *Did you get that bracelet for Christmas? That drawing is great, you should be an artist.* He imagined Lisa Pederson would smile, perfect white teeth flashing just for him. And she'd say thank you, it was nice of him to say. Dash also secretly noticed the strain between the third and fourth buttons of her blouse, the little gap that showed her tan bra. *Skin color*, he'd thought after his first peek. *Lisa Pederson wears a skin-color bra.*

And they had finally spoken. Actually, she'd spoken to him when she leaned across the narrow aisle where she sat to his right. He flinched away at first, thinking maybe she dropped her number two pencil, didn't want to be the guy who head-butted her like a total dork. But she hadn't bent over, just moved in so her face was real close to his. He could smell her perfume or body wash, or whatever girls splashed themselves with to smell so awesome. He could feel his dopey smile, waiting for her to crack a joke about Mrs. Harbough's blooming pit stains, ready to snicker along. It was going to be great, until he saw Lisa's nose wrinkle, and her beautiful lips pucker as if she'd tasted something sour.

She sniffed twice, then cocked her head sideways. "You smell like mildew." Lisa's voice was loud enough for other kids to turn and look at the kid with the funny odor.

"I would have gotten an instant nickname if she'd used a different word," said Dash. "At least she used a word that wasn't catchy. So I was Mildew Boy for a couple days, but no big deal. It would have been worse if she said I smelled like moldy cheese or a dirty jock strap. How's it goin', Stinky Cheese? That would have lasted."

"Not a great crowd to help get you through your dad's death, huh?"

Dash shook his head. "I knew two other kids who lost a parent. Danny's mom died of cancer, and Jenna's old man was killed in a car wreck. That was a drunk driving thing. Don't know if her dad was drunk, or if it was the other driver. Not that it mattered, right? Same result."

"Both kids were treated differently than you."

Dash was quiet for a minute. He remembered going to church services for each family, and it seemed like the entire town had turned out. It was a rare time when kids hung with parents instead of collecting in their own groups and moving off to find something more interesting. You had the feeling some cosmic balance was off, and being with your folks was safer. Men were bawling their eyes out. Men who wore greasy work shirts and dark blue uniform pants during the day were filling up handkerchiefs with snot and tears, and didn't seem the least bit embarrassed. It made teenagers cling to their parents seeing that. You could look down into a coffin at somebody's dead mom easier than you could look at a grown man cry.

"There were those big yellow chrysanthemums at the service for Danny's mom. I remember ladies saying they were her favorite. The whole church had that smell. I don't know how anyone could think it was good. Made the air so thick that I had to work to keep from gagging."

"They didn't come when your dad died," Willy said. "Not most of them."

Dash had looked back over his shoulder in the church, his suit coat two sizes too small, but who could blame his mom for not being in a shopping mood after her husband cut open both his wrists? By that time, Lisa Pederson had pointed out he smelled like mildew, and sure enough, that was exactly the odor coming off his old suit. The smell was probably worse than all his other clothes combined, but Lisa had been the first to point it out, to show her disgust by crinkling her nose.

"At least I didn't smell like those fucking chrysanthemums," Dash told Willy, who was slowly shaking his big fish head, light a steady glow.

"They weren't just cuts on your father's wrists, though, were they?"

Dash took a deep breath, tapped the flat part of the blade on his thigh. "Christ, it was like he took it all out on himself with a steak knife. He hacked away with one hand, then was able to switch up and do a pretty equal job on the other wrist. It was like something you read off the metro wire at the paper. Something some kid on crack or meth might do."

"Why'd he do it?"

"You can read my mind. You already know everything."

"We're friends talking. It's good to get it out, it helps."

"That was the big joke. Mildew Boy's crooked father slit his wrists because of an old table. Let me try and remember." Dash paused, looked up at the clear sky. "Technically, it was known as a French carved-oak barley-twist center table. But an old table is just an old table when there's a good piece of gossip to share around."

"What was it about the table?"

"It was a fake, just like all the other crap in the shop. He'd sold it for something like three grand to a guy and his wife supposedly up from Manhattan. A month later, my dad gets a visit from two police detectives. It had been a setup, some kind of sting by the state cops. The paper ate it up, too. My dad had told the undercover couple the table was from an estate sale in the Loire Valley of Central France."

"Made in China, huh?"

"Hong Kong. Same place all the big ticket inventory came from, the stuff that paid the bills, kept the place open over the years. The stuff that opened up the fat wallets of New York and Boston tourists, and put heating oil in the tank."

"What did his note say?" Willy asked, and Dash noticed the outline of his wide shoulders begin to waver, and the colors of his hulking body to fade.

"What note?"

"Tell me what his suicide note said. Details keep the plot juicy, make the story sing."

Dash could see an image of his father's sweeping script, the feminine handwriting that a few of his teachers commented on when he turned in school notes. He also knew Willy could see the writing, including the red line where blood had run across the middle, cutting in half the oddly formal signature. The note began with an apology to his wife, garbage about how much he loved her and how she'd been his entire world. The last line had been for his teenage son.

Dash leaned back to look at the sky. There were no birds or clouds, no sign of high-flying jets. The volcano was gone, or maybe it was behind him. He didn't care enough to turn. He cleared his throat, remembering his father's final message. " 'I should have played catch with you,' " he said.

They drifted without talking, the water lapping against the hull. Dash wondered how far from land they must be for there not to be a single bird. He'd seen gulls flock around fishing boats like a shaken snow globe, but did they follow tankers along shipping lanes?

"Willy, you ever see a snow globe?"

Willy flashed a pincushion smile, gills opening and closing. "We're in the globe, my friend," he said. "We're in the globe."

They were quiet again, at the mercy of the current, water making the only noise until Dash spoke.

"On the plane, right before it crashed," he began, then coughed to clear his throat, "there was a voice on the intercom calling for someone."

"Cindy," Willy said, and gooseflesh broke out across Dash's damaged skin.

"Right. The voice kept calling for Cindy. I don't think it was the captain."

But Willy was shaking his head even before Dash could ask. "Maybe you imagined it," he said. "Or maybe it was another lonely person who knew he was about to die. You can relate to that, right?"

The silence between them came back and stayed.

Dash tossed the knife overboard when the sun began dipping into the horizon. The blade caught the orange and yellow rays twice as it rotated through the air, winking at him before slicing into the dark surface. Dash knew for certain he'd carve the same brutal grooves in his own wrists if he didn't get rid of it before spending another night alone.

Chapter 26

———

THE CURRENT REVERSED track and began pulling the skiff into its own wake. Dash watched the cloudless sky rotate, head forced to one side, the remaining coconuts sloshing against his legs. Seagulls had found them. They clamored, flapping filthy wings, shitting in bursts and then swooping down to investigate what each had deposited on the waves. *Idiots*, he thought, hating the smug bastards who had spied on him for the volcanic shrew who'd surely sent the shark. He was consumed by conspiracy, surrounded by those writing his ticket to martyrdom.

"Valelailai," he whispered, remembering the day he'd met the wobbly old chief. It was what the whites christened the island, but had it been the soldiers or the missionaries using the word 'toilet' to rename what he'd first seen as paradise? No big deal, Manu told him. One name is as good as any. "Then I'll call it Hell," Dash now said in a hoarse croak. "I'm going to Hell." His laughter stopped when he coughed a bloody spray across his sunburned chest. He smeared the blistered pad of his right index finger and drew a red smiley face on his gaunt stomach.

The boat drifted, bumping and swaying across the

undulating surf. It sometimes strayed, veering either north or south, but eventually it was tugged back on course, just as an errant pupil is chastised into behaving when finally noticed by the distracted teacher.

Willy was silent. Sometimes he was as real as the smooth coconuts at his giant feet; sometimes nothing but wisps of gossamer silk. Out beyond his changing form, another god spewed angry smoke, and had grown fatter around the middle, her rock and dirt waist bulging, threatening to explode in all directions.

"She sent the shark." Dash looked out over the moving water, knowing the animal wouldn't return, its job done. He hadn't been in any danger, could have leaned over and rammed his head into its mouth, and would have been spit out like a dented license plate. It was the Volcano who wanted to eat him.

Willy's eyes were yellow marbles, his jaw opening and closing only once every half minute or so. His body rocked with the boat's motion as though he was dead weight, and he showed no sign of hearing Dash's voice or thoughts.

"Simon says touch your nose," Dash said. "Simon says take us to Tahiti." Dash turned his head side to side, looking out over the water. "I guess you're out, Willy. Take a seat at the end of the boat and pretend you're dying."

The skiff continued slow rotations as it was summoned. The brown monolith grew larger, its white smoke more vivid. Dash mostly slept, welcoming even the worst dreams as escape. In one, he married Sarah and they had a baby girl with brown skin. "Love her now," Sarah told him. "Love her while you can because they are coming to take her away." And he probably cried out in his sleep, asking who was coming, and why he couldn't keep his daughter. He held her little body in his arms, determined not to let her go. But then he must have held her too tightly, because she stopped breathing and no amount of shaking could wake her. And then Dash was on his knees in a wide field under a pale sky filled with a scorching sun.

A thousand seagulls made lazy circles, and he watched their shadows with wings that were too sharp, bat-like and evil. He could see their heads turn as they passed closer and closer, shadows jerking as their eyes hunted. Dash began pulling at the dirt, scooping and flinging it between his legs like a dog with a bone, his lifeless daughter growing cold in the sweltering heat.

It was in one of these dreams that he realized his daughter's name was Cindy.

THEY DRIFTED THREE days, not a single cloud blotting the sun for even a second. It was his punishment, one he accepted and endured with blistering lips and a blazing fever. He sprawled on the skiff's smooth floor; the few inches of salt water he lay in had turned hot—a soup of blood, puss, and what little urine had trickled from his emaciated body. The smiley face he'd made on his stomach was mostly washed away; only part of one eye and the corner of its smile remained.

As they got closer, Dash pictured the volcano as a steam locomotive, heard the chugging engine strain against metal brakes, and he was going to be late. He found himself wanting to hurry back, willing the waves to pull faster. Inside the volcano would be dark and blessedly full of shade. He couldn't imagine ever thinking anything different; couldn't imagine not wanting to be out of the sun, tucked away inside something so willing to envelop his body and end his suffering.

Willy had been jostled to an odd position, legs up and ankles crossed on one side of the hull. The bottoms of his feet, which had lost color from days of soaking, were puffy and lined with deep cracks.

A yellow flash near those huge feet caught Dash's attention, and he had to blink his crusty eyes to focus on the small bird perched on Willy's pinky toe. The bird preened, stretched its delicate wings, and then froze with its head cocked toward Willy's face. Another flash of yellow and the bird landed on the fantastic creature's brawny shoulder, head tilted to inspect the dangling appendage in front of those awesome teeth. The bird was tantalized by the lure's herky-jerky motion, and the fleshy bulb pulsed brighter, as though Willy was working all the angles to draw the creature in. The bird made sideways steps, edging toward the bands of iron neck tendons for a better shot at the mesmerizing prey. It was the hunter being hunted, as the bird coiled its toothpick legs and tensed for attack. The bird flung itself upward, legs unsprung, wings beating in a bright flourish.

Willy's mouth snapped open and shut. The bird was simply no more. Dash watched the muscles in Willy's neck work, might have heard bones crunch.

"Dinner is served," Dash told the air where the bird had been. Perhaps the god, if he was one, cracked a smile.

The water bucket was long dry and Dash didn't bother with the remaining coconuts. He hadn't seen the stone he brought to pry them open, assumed it went overboard with the paddle. He only watched the billowing smoke until the southern tip of the island was visible over newly sprouted whitecaps. The heavenly airplane seats were there behind his tide pool, and good old Manu had brought a greeting party of four strapping young warriors. The five brown men in funny underpants waited patiently. No one shifted from foot to foot. No one pulled a pocket watch from a dirty waistband to frown and shake his head. They were all on the Volcano God's time, knew Dash would arrive soon enough.

Someone will have to go for a paddle if they want to get this thing back to the lagoon, he thought guiltily. The one he'd lost probably took days to carve, and even though he hadn't summoned the shark, it was his fault for stealing the boat in the first place.

And then Dash saw Willy's mighty hands squeeze hard, as if bracing for impact. Willy's knuckles turned the same color as the skiff's bleached wood when the bottom struck the rocky shelf, spinning sideways in the surf. The next wave was larger, the sun suddenly eclipsed by Dash's scrawny legs as the skiff rolled. He watched Tiki's little amber disk go airborne and tumble into the foam.

The noise of the locomotive was overwhelming as the train dragged him down and ran him over.

Chapter 27

DASH TUMBLED ACROSS the jagged lava, spinning and rolling with the rushing water. Wave after wave pushed and pulled, and he barely managed gulps of air. He heard shouting over the thunder, and glimpsed muscular brown legs beating against the tide. Strong hands under his armpits lifted and then lugged his limp body, the tops of his feet bumping along. His shins burned and blood ran from his elbows. The other men charged past, probably to recover the skiff.

He was carried to Manu, where they set him down on bruised knees. Salt water released from his sinuses, gushing over his mouth and off his chin. He coughed hard and spit bloody foam onto the rocks.

"Ocean is bad place for you, Cracker. She keeps chewing you up, spitting you out. Maybe you taste bad."

Dash tried swallowing, wanted to tell Manu that you didn't have to be a drunken old chief to be visited by a Volcano God. Hell, he'd even gotten up close and personal with one of her bootlicking minions dressed in a shark suit.

Fuck you, he wanted to say more than anything.

"Every man must strive for freedom. So many of my people

died because I did not understand where real freedom lives." Manu put a hand on his bony chest and tapped. "I did not know to listen to the gods. To respect their will. To accept sacrifice with an open heart."

Dash mouthed the word 'sacrifice' and wanted to laugh. His father used the word a thousand times. At least it wasn't part of his final letter. That would have been a little too rich. Manu squinted, leathery face filling with deep wrinkles, perhaps mistaking Dash's disgust for revelation. The old man rubbed his chin and nodded.

"Sacrifice," said Manu. "Sacrifice brings freedom. I give my blood every time the white soldiers come. My flesh and blood leaves on their boat."

The skiff skidded across the rocks behind, and Dash craned his neck to see if Willy was still aboard. He no longer wanted inside the volcano, but to curl up alone in his spider-infested cave. Sulfur was heavy in the air, the blue haze even here where the steady breeze kept mosquitoes at bay. He tried twisting from the iron grip of the men clamped to each shoulder, but they held him down with ease.

Manu spoke in his native tongue, waved an arm for them all to head back up the path Dash had crept along under cover of darkness. The two men walking at his sides were now his guards. Dehydrated and trickling blood from dozens of small cuts, he imagined making a break for it. Unable to get away in a boat, he'd tackle one of those big birds that nested in underground burrows. Surely he was sufficiently emaciated for a piggy-back ride to the nearest cargo ship bound for civilization. Wouldn't a man riding a bird be a more difficult target for rocks slung from a volcano? Those bastard sharks could circle and snap their jaws all they wanted while he prodded the bird with imaginary spurs. The birds owed him, after all.

He was out of breath when the path opened to the mouth of the lagoon, his heart pounding, chest heaving. The guards allowed him to bend and grab his bloody knees. The skiff was lowered onto the narrow strip of sand and given a once-over, four hands running along the inner and outer surface. The men, who found plenty to complain about, grumbled to each other and the chief.

Dash noticed Willy lurking in the protected water up to his thighs, twenty yards from where two women were fishing with circular throwing nets. Willy was only half solid, the breakers out beyond the reef visible through his upper torso. Willy eyed the women at work, his muscular arms flexing, hands making wide, sweeping motions. The women stood back to back, at a slight angle, casting the nets out in identical spinning arcs. It took Dash a moment to understand Willy's strange, traffic cop motions, as he was now signaling with his entire body, looking down over the clear water. Willy was directing schools of silvery fish toward the women's outspread nets.

Manu handed Dash a six-inch section of bamboo plugged at both ends and motioned for him to drink. The water was hot from sitting in a sunny patch next to a pile of spare paddles, but he opened and drained the container in two gulps.

Manu led the group along a jungle path Dash had never seen. It was slightly uphill, even more cave-like than the one connecting the village to the island's southern tip. No light penetrated and the heat was stifling. Dash could hear dozens of low voices when they approached the bright opening of the compound, as if an important meeting was going on instead of the usual busy work of preparing food and fixing broken things. The children weren't screaming or laughing, or out of breath from chasing balls.

The fresh air struck Dash's sweat-drenched body like a bucket of ice water, as Manu led them to the center of the village where the entire population was gathered. They walked to the spot where the Yule tree had been the night Tiki had given him his gift. Dash frantically patted his mostly naked body, as though trying to find car keys in a winter coat. His hands froze, and again he saw the smooth amber disk disappear into the foam and the surge that must have drawn it straight out to sea. Some fish would bolt from the deep and swallow it whole, or a fucking bird would snatch it in its talons to feed its young.

The guards had fallen back, and it was only Dash and Manu who were enveloped by the hushed mass of brown flesh. Dash briefly wondered if this was where the boat thief would be set upon, torn apart by people who'd endured years of murder and kidnapping by people whose skin matched his. Their faces gave nothing away. There were no tight lips or furrowed brows, and no smiles either. They weren't his enemies, but he might very well be theirs. Manu stood close, shoulder to shoulder, while Dash looked from face to face, seeing the people, fifteen deep in places. Children in the outer perimeter were jumping up and down for a glimpse, little faces appearing and disappearing as if they were riding pogo sticks. So many faces, all with calm expressions, bright white eyes shifting from him to Manu, waiting for the chief's next order as the old man seemed to gather his thoughts.

The volcano spoke first with a low growl, the sound of a dog's bad dream. Then a gassy hiss from high above followed, and a few heads turned for a peek. The smoke drifted sideways from the mountain, turned the haze a deeper blue, the stink of rotten eggs ten times worse. The volcano had its own stash of hidden eggs, Dash thought, smiling as he recalled his dead father's bedtime story. Several people flashed toothy grins in return, but only for a second.

The ground shivered and a flock of small birds took flight from trees on one side of the village clearing. They zigged and zagged with one mind, soaring over the crowd and then finding safety in an identical tree on the opposite side. *Not nearly far enough*, Dash could have told them, as he watched a few stragglers join the rest. You'll need to find a good warm wind, one leading to a place that'll hold together through a storm or two and keep you out of the mouths of sharks and away from dancing bait.

Manu cleared his throat for attention, and Dash could feel the circle collapse farther inward. He could close his eyes and count the people by heat and smell.

"There will be no white baby to offer the soldiers." Manu's voice was strong and convincing, commanding respect, like that of an old-time news anchor, back when television was black and white. No wonder he was chief. You didn't question that voice, just waited for the next order, prepared to act without hesitation. It was the voice of a jetliner captain.

The people pressed into Dash to hear the plan, the volcano shaking their footing, ruffling the walls of their homes. Hanging metal pots swung over cooking fires; the pigs in their corral squealing for food or a chance to outrun the volcano. The birds had vanished from the tree top, and Dash wondered if they'd taken his advice.

"The Volcano God speaks clearly of her desire for sacrifice," said Manu. "And she will protect us as she has since our fathers were summoned to her shadow. We will present her gift the night the moon is in balance and shows half its face."

Dash felt something creep along his injured right hand with the probing legs of a spider. His three middle fingers were encircled by Tiki's small moist hand. He looked down to see her tear-streaked face tilted up to the crowding villagers. Dash was confused when Manu's speech resumed—the words scrambled, nonsensical—and then realized the chief had switched to his native language. Heads nodded all around as Manu spoke faster, words less measured. The crowd murmured, Dash sensing instructions were being given and agreed to by the people.

Dash's fingers were squeezed tighter when the surrounding faces turned downward at Tiki and cast accusing eyes at her doomed soul.

"The Volcano wants me, too," she whispered up to him, as if reading his mind.

Chapter 28

—

A SLIVER OF moon arced across the cruddy sky, nearly invisible until the dull sun dropped below the treetops. Dash knew it was a waning crescent from an intro to astronomy course, knew it had been up there all day, leading the sun across the sky's dome even though it couldn't be seen most of the time. He never suspected the lesson would come to bear so much weight on his existence.

The countdown would begin for real when the moon rose in full shadow to follow the sun, then make a tandem plunge into the western sea. It would mark seven days until its white and black faces came into balance—what his professor called a first quarter moon—and send him and the girl off a cliff and into the volcano's fire. He dared to hope another crescent would rise that dawn, allow more time for a miracle, if only for the girl's sake.

He sat up in the former love hut, watching the burly backs of two men guarding the opening. He'd listened to the village sounds as days and nights dragged by. The casual, workaday vibe changed, anxiety hanging in the air heavy as the foul stench. Mothers scolded roughhousing soccer players in sharper tones; the men developed short tempers, back from fishing or tending the taro with chips on their shoulders, ready for a fight.

He listened to scuffles, the sounds of slapping skin and animal grunts, and feet shuffling in the dirt for leverage. The confrontations started and ended quickly, and he decided these people were more comfortable being a society of victims than fighters. Going to battle would never be in their blood. But the bickering increased, regular arguments in sing-song words, as the volcano kept the village shrouded in putrid fog.

Healing hands itched in a way he could not scratch, and sunburned skin peeled in fat strips over scabby blisters on his shoulders and back. His beard, long enough to see if he pulled it from his chin, had turned blond from the salt and sun, or maybe fear had made it white. He ate bowls of tasteless fish and rice twice a day, drank watered-down clap-clap from a tall jug. He huddled on death row in a cell made of bamboo, grass, and woven fronds, waiting for Tiki to come, but fearing the news she might bring, that the moon's orbit had sped up, a mighty shove given by a volcano impatient to feast.

He thought about his mother, had developed a new kind of empathy for her craziness. She'd had her finely crafted baby dolls to confer with, while he now spoke to half empty bowls, usually when the jug was spent. Sarah had ridiculed her for believing the dolls were alive, but how many movies had they sat through with his fiancée wiping away tears? Sarah, caught up in fiction, wept for imaginary things, laughing and jeering at villains and heroes who were all phony. She'd squeezed his hand, braced for death or survival that was nothing but light and shade cast upon a painted white screen. Any cheating fiancée should be sentenced to nights in a black cave filled with spiders and watched over by cynical gods. Perhaps it would soften a few heartless souls.

Dash fell out of love on a sleeping mat still scented with oils from a failed night of sex. "You can have her," he told the backs of his guards. "You hear me, Curly? You got that, Moe? Don't leave her alone with that Tommy guy, and you'll be hunky dory, live happily ever after." They ignored his offer, but he didn't care.

The pregnant woman who brought his food lingered while he picked at the burned fish. She knelt with her arms folded across her belly, as if wanting to speak, or maybe only to observe a condemned man up close. She watched him eat, then spoke slowly, telling him that Manu wanted him at the drinking circle when he was finished. But she hesitated, had something more to say.

He sipped bitter water, offered her the empty cup when she took his uneaten food.

"It's wrong for you to die," she finally whispered, then got to her feet and walked out. She paused for a brief exchange with the guards, who let Dash pass a few minutes later.

THE CLAP-CLAP CIRCLE was aglow. Every other man held a coconut candle in front, eerie shadows cast on their haggard faces. Dash was woozy after one round, but grateful to see Willy amble up and seem to sit on top of two men to his right. His semi-translucent body settled over their spots, seemed to possess both until one of the men sneezed, and then wiped his nose on his forearm. It was clear the three were simply sharing the space, Willy with his own cup and jug, one in each hand, apparently off the wagon.

The man on Dash's left drank and spit. He held the cup out, and Dash raised it in a toast. "Long live the fish!" He sipped and spit, then passed it on as Willy chugged his own private stash. The two men trapped inside Willy's aura were more fidgety than the others. They kept looking back over their shoulders, rubbing at their ears as though they were plugged with water.

"I thought you quit drinking," Dash asked the former god, and the men on either side of Willy shrugged and looked toward their chief.

"Our ancestors came to this island from a distant land." Manu's voice silenced the boozy murmurs, although Willy hummed and poured a refill. "They traveled beneath mighty sails, in boats wide and flat, to carry the pigs and goats, all their possessions."

"My mother came from a fish tank," said Willy, who was double the size of the man next to him but had a voice much smaller than the chief's.

"The journey took two cycles of the moon," said Manu. "They left their homeland under a black face moon to show faith in their gods. They knew they would be taken care of, that their gods were closest when the moon was hidden."

"My mother was a special attraction on a passenger steam ship sailing under a British flag," said Willy, draining another cup. "On board were a hundred children of wealthy aristocrats being sent overseas to study. Couple of young bucks snuck into the dining room late one night, when it was dark like this. Thought it would be a hoot to steal my mother from the tank over the bar, put her in their girlfriends' wash basin as a practical joke. Imagine turning on the light and finding something like this?" Willy tapped a finger to his head, the fleshy bulb pulsing to illuminate his sharp teeth.

The men inside Willy looked up at the sky, then rubbed their eyes hard.

"Twenty-eight brave explorers on two boats," Manu continued. "They fished and collected rainwater, and might have traveled ten more moons had the Storm God not made herself known."

"Girls screamed bloody murder when they found her," said Willy. "Dropped their toothbrushes and bolted out of the crapper. Somebody in the hall pulled the fire alarm, put the entire ship into a frenzy. The boys knew they were up shit's creek if the crew found the stolen fish. They grabbed my mother and wrapped her in a bath towel. Bastards ran out onto the main deck with the other passengers, who were half asleep, stumbling around in pajamas."

"One boat was lost in the current and never seen again," said Manu. "But seven men and seven women were summoned to these shores by the Volcano's orange eye on the black horizon."

"They threw her overboard in the middle of nowhere," said Willy, slamming an open palm into the dirt. Some of the men felt the impact and watched the rising plume. "Imagine living your whole life in a glass case, fed all the juicy shrimp you can eat, water changed every month. And then to be dropped twenty meters into the wide-open ocean by some pinhead teenagers."

The cup came around to Dash, and Willy held his own out to him. They mimicked clinking them together, both mouthing the word 'cheers.'

"We owe everything we are and everything we will become to the Volcano God," said Manu, who glanced up into the dark.

"One of the men on the lost boat caught my mother on a hook baited with a dead grasshopper. She would have been starving by then, as were the humans. But as hungry as they were, they didn't eat her. She was like no fish they'd ever seen, and they took her as a sign from a god they didn't know. They filled a bucket with seawater and fed her the remaining bait. I never told you how much I look like her. And my father, too." Willy pointed to the lump on his jaw that had a small tail growing from it.

"The Volcano is the mightiest of gods, and accepts our sacrifice as a sign of faith. The stronger the belief, the more powerful is the god," said Manu, voice booming.

"The lost ship beached on a beautiful island three days later," said Willy. "Rich soil as black as coal, and fresh water springs that trickled down from rolling hills. They set my mother free in a crystal lagoon, where I was born a few months later."

"The Volcano God has provided the soil to grow a bounty to feed our people," said Manu.

"Our soil sprouted withered seed from a thousand mile journey, was as fertile as the women who brought a half-dozen babies that first year," said Willy, digging his fingers into the hard ground next to his thigh. "Not like this dust. She doesn't care for her people. No loving god would spit poison ash, tolerate earth like this. The storm slaughtered my people, but not because I didn't provide. I showed my soul through things I gave." Willy's voice trailed off as he refilled his cup. There was silence around the circle before he resumed speaking. "And I planted the dead like they'd planted tubers to grow their taro."

Dash rubbed his scabs, the clap-clap masking the constant itch.

"You hope good things grow in their place." Willy's voice was low, as though not to disturb the men he'd consumed, the two small brown bodies now moving in slow motion, hands out in front to explore the surface of an invisible wall, eyes glued to a dangling light. "Not just weeds and more vines, but something special," said Willy.

"No more stolen children, no more violations. I have the Volcano God's promise that we will be free," said Manu, and the circle nodded and muttered, bodies rocking, all of them drunk. "Peace will rain down when the moon is right and her belly is full."

Willy turned to the chief, whose trembling hands were busy with the cup. "You have it wrong, old man," said Willy, jerking a thumb toward Dash. "You might as well be praying to this guy's sweaty rabbit for a chocolate egg."

The men inside Willy's body were clinging to each another, reciting the same muffled sing-song phrase over and over, when a sudden burst of wind blew out the candles around the circle. The captive pair found themselves free, and began rubbing dust from tearing eyes.

Willy was gone.

Chapter 29

Dash longed for his cushiony airplane seat and the tide pool where the sea delivered surprises twice daily. He was allowed onto his front steps, a pair of stone slabs that were uncomfortable under his boney ass. When the breeze flooded his hut with sour air, he sat outside picking scabs from both palms, missing his dark cave and even the elusive spiders and old urine stink.

The four young men who'd pulled him from the waves were his constant chaperones, although they mostly sat bored in the hut's shadow. They never used English, always traditional words in shorts bursts, as if everything they spoke was a command. Dash assumed they addressed him that way for the same reason that their eyes were filled with resentment and the muscles at the back of their jaws flexed when they looked at him. Dash knew that after killing him slowly they would eat his heart, delivering justice for every crime his color had committed.

"Good for you, Moe," Dash would say when he caught one staring. "Good for you. I'd hate me just as much."

When he needed the outhouse, one escort would get up and

trudge behind. If he lingered near the compound's wild green perimeter, the guard would cross his arms as if tempting him to try something stupid. Dash wished for the mettle to use the element of surprise, maybe shout a few lines of AC/DC lyrics and leap for the nearest tree, swinging from vine to vine, away and free.

"I bet you miss fishing," he told the guard. "I bet your girlfriend is skinny dipping in the lagoon with some handsome new boy toy right about now. You think you know her, but I can tell you plenty of stories."

The guards remained stoic, but there was no mistaking the fire in their eyes.

"Hey, Tarzan, maybe I can talk the Chief into throwing you in with me," Dash told the tallest of the group, who was also the surliest. He had pockmarked cheeks and a small scar across his upper lip that gave him a look of perpetual contempt. "Synchronized diving is an Olympic sport. We only get one shot at a medal, but no guts no glory."

The guard only grunted as he followed Dash to the cut where the six pigs were fenced. Dash had smuggled a piece of fish from his dinner, tossed it to the smallest pig, a gray runt always on the outside of food scrums. The smaller pig hesitated, sniffed the morsel first as if it couldn't believe its fortune or didn't trust who'd thrown it. One of the other pigs snatched it away and gobbled it down, demanded more as the rest of them converged, ramming one another, snouts first.

"You'd get a real charge out of stomping me into the ground and tossing me in there." Dash poked a thumb at the pigs still jockeying for position, greedily licking the mud where the fish had bounced, "but at least I tried to do something. I didn't sit on my ass while my loved ones were dragged into this jungle and raped. How many sisters have they taken? How many nieces and cousins have you watched disappear on their boat? Did you wave goodbye, you bastard?"

The guard, his black underpants even dingier than the rest,

hair tied with grass rope, did not move, but stood with his hands at his sides. Dash suddenly couldn't take his eyes off the scar—a one-inch white slash that drew the man's upper lip away from his teeth ever so slightly. Rage welled, burned in his joints and flooded his wasted muscles. Other than acne, it was the only mark his huge body had sustained, one insignificant nick while he'd allowed the girls to be devastated, kidnapped into the worst of all worlds.

"You fucker," he hissed, but only the pigs answered. Dash took one lunging step forward, right hand balled into a loose fist, injured skin allowing for nothing more. He swung a looping roundhouse blow that connected with the scar and teeth behind. Dash lost balance and stumbled to the hard earth that smelled of pig shit and spoiled food, scraping open the wounds on his knees. The guard's dusty feet were the same dark brown as the rest of his skin, but Dash noticed a distinct line of contrasting shades that extended from toe to heel. The man's hidden flesh was much lighter, almost white on the bottom. And then the feet turned and walked away, flashing Dash with every step.

Tiki was waiting in his hut. She sat folded up in the back corner as if hiding. Her voice was tiny. "I'm sorry for ruining your pile of wood."

He shuffled across the bamboo floor hunched from the low roof to sit facing her. Her hair had been chopped off in spots, a lopsided cut that looked self-inflicted. "I'm sorry I left you."

"I wasn't pretty enough to go with the soldiers. I was only pretty enough to be hurt."

"Being pretty had nothing to do with it. Those men are monsters. Evil." It killed him to look at her. She'd been crying, mud-stained tears tracing vertical lines down her cheeks. He wanted to touch her face, but his hands were a mess. He put them palm up on her knees, and she reached down to feel his damaged skin. She drew soft outlines with the tip of one index finger, sketching paths over the rough texture. He could feel her wounds through that finger, but only the very surface.

"I think I want to die," she said.

And then he was weeping, taking back his hands to hide his face. "I wish I could make everything better," he said. "I tried to find help because I didn't know what else to do. I couldn't protect you. I lost your gift. It fell in the water."

She tugged his hands back down and held on. "When I dream that I'm with Mama and then wake up, I get mad at the gods. I get so mad that I scream how much I hate them. Sometimes it's hard to believe in anything."

He leaned forward and she let go of his wrists, then practically knocked him over, throwing her arms around his neck and clinging. He hugged her back, careful not to squeeze too hard. They rocked that way until her body stopped hitching. He let her go, and she sat back to wipe her face.

"Maybe we can each half-believe," he said. "Together, it'll be like a single person who's one of those Holy-Rolling Bible thumpers."

She smiled. "What's a bible thumper?"

He had to pause. "Someone who believes so hard that they don't tolerate anyone who thinks differently."

"Like the missioners," she said, "and like Manu, I guess."

Dash didn't say that murdering your child put you right at the top of the zealot category, whether you were on a remote South Pacific island or on some cult ranch in rural Texas.

"It's one more night until the black face moon," she said, looking beyond him to the hut's opening.

He quickly counted the eight days they had to live. "We just call it a 'new' moon. It's the opposite of a full moon."

"New moon," she repeated. "That sounds nice. Things are new because the moon goes black?"

"I learned it in school, but don't remember. It means the moon's phase is starting over, or maybe just ended."

"We call it a black face moon because everything is hidden in the dark, and you can't see a face, even if you are looking right at it. It's when they come to be near us."

"Who comes?"

"The gods," she said. "They walk in the jungle all around, but only when it's darkest. They want to be close to us and feel our love. But they know how scared we'd be if we could see them."

He thought of Willy's encounter with the boys along the shoreline. "That doesn't sound like something Manu told you."

"No, Mama told me when I was little. I remember, though. I remember everything she told me, even though I was a baby. You're lucky to still have a mama. You don't have a papa, though."

"No, he died when I was in school."

"How did he die?"

"His heart was sick. One minute he was alive, and then he wasn't."

"Were you sad, too? I cried until the village was flooded by little girl tears when Mama was killed. That's what the grownups said."

"I was sad for my mom, but I was mostly sad about things that never happened. And when he died there was no chance for them to ever happen. Does that make sense?"

"I guess."

"My father didn't play with me. I was jealous of boys whose dads would kick balls with them and throw a football in their yard. Or go skiing with them."

"Skiing?"

"It's like sledding from the Yule songs, only you stand on plastic boards and slide down a mountain on snow."

"I love snow," she said, nodding, and he thought of the ash that fell on their ceremony once a year.

"Me too."

"I still want Mama to brush my hair, and put it in braids." She fingered her curls. "What did your papa do instead of playing?"

"He worked in his antique shop. That's a place that sells old furniture and things. He worked every day, all day long, even in the slow season when my mother could manage by herself. He went to flea markets and garage sales on weekends. That's where people put old belongings they don't want out in front of their houses to sell."

"Your papa took their garbage?"

"Yeah, pretty much."

"I'd rather play with a ball than garbage."

"It was a treasure hunt," he said. "Like when we hunted for things on the beach. He always talked about finding a painting from a famous artist. Or coming across priceless jewelry."

"Things people put in their garbage by mistake?"

"Yes, that's right."

"You shouldn't keep stuff like that. You should tell the people what they did wrong. They'd be happy that you found it and gave it back."

"You're right," he said. "Things are different where I'm from. Some are worse, some are better."

She looked up at him. "Your people would never throw anybody into a volcano."

"There aren't volcanoes anywhere near where I'm from," he said, but figured there were plenty of gangs and mobsters who would happily take advantage of any volcanoes popping up near metro hubs. "Most of my people believe in very different things."

She shook her head. "But you stopped believing in anything."

He smiled, thinking again of Willy and the boys he'd frightened so badly. "My father used to say that seeing is believing. It's why he didn't believe in God."

"Okay," she said. "Then I have something to show you. But you're going to have to be really, really quiet, or they won't come."

Chapter 30

━━━

Dash woke from a dream of oiled dancing women when something began tapping his forehead and then squeezed his nostrils shut.

"Shhhh." Tiki let her fingers slide from his face. "Don't make noise. We have to be more quiet than ever."

As he rose to his feet, the wooden floor creaked as he'd never heard, the thatched grass asking questions when it brushed his hair. The stone slabs rocked the earth with tiny landslides that might have filled the mouths of snoring guards curled up on their mats. They tiptoed over crushed shells and through ash, swept into piles. The last coal from a dying fire blinked twice and stayed black.

She led him away without fire or moon for light, the stars no longer able to penetrate the volcanic fog. The only sound was the whispered counting of her steps in the pitch-black darkness, something she'd practiced in daylight. He held her hand, trusted where she took him despite his fear of what might be inches away.

She brought them toward a point of light hovering low to the ground. She pulled the candle from its shallow resting place and tugged him along a path. The flame was held high, a beacon dripping wax over her wrist. They skirted the edge of the clearing where the bees slept, Dash walking extra softly to avoid crushing any scouts and provoking a new attack. They pressed on, into the wide taro field, stalks too narrow to support elephant ear leaves that were perked up to hear distant lions.

They ducked beneath leaning trees and hurried through silky webs that ignited in bursts, and the flame worried him. The farther they made their way along what was more an animal trail than human path, the more trapped they'd be if the candle went out.

He sensed the expedition's vital nature and didn't want to spoil her secret mission with his worries, even though he could barely take his eyes from the fragile flame.

She handed him the candle when necessary. When she needed both hands to climb over a set of downed palms, the rotted wood teeming with shiny black bugs, some flashing oversized pincers resembling the letter C. He carefully returned the candle and followed, mindful of where he put each bare hand and foot. They startled dozens of rats, which meant the biggest snakes would be out hunting.

Tiki hesitated beyond a small patch of open jungle where newly fallen trees had pulled down a tangle of vines, had a hard time deciding which way the path continued. The fog was thinner, allowing a blue glow to wash over the scene. Lit by stars, the landscape might have been an animal burial ground for enormous creatures, a maze of twisted rib bones and lifeless tails.

"Is there an easier way?" he asked.

"Yes, but it's much longer." She walked on, the candle lighting the trail of bent weeds and tracks of much smaller animals than what would have been ancestors to the decaying skeletons they climbed through. "This is a shortcut."

He followed her back under the canopy, into a shroud of fat

leaves and wispy hanging creepers.

"How much longer?" He knew he sounded like a child in the backseat of a car on a road trip, but the scabs on his legs had torn and the candle lit almost nothing. The darkness was dizzying, the uneven ground hard on his knees and back.

"Shhhh." She reached back to tug him forward. The air was hot and noisy, and he could feel them gaining elevation. "No more talk. We're getting close."

"We're going up the volcano?" he whispered, but she didn't answer.

Another fifty paces and she stopped and turned, the flame under her face casting stark shadows. He worried about the drip of sweat on her chin, whether it was big enough to douse their only light. "Just a little more, but they won't come if they hear you. This is our last chance to see them."

He wanted to ask who *they* were, wanted to tell her he had no interest in meeting anyone or anything out here in the jungle, but she began pulling him along like a toy wagon on rusty wheels. *I have one week to live, and don't want to be stranded chest deep in quicksand listening to hungry growls and circling footsteps.*

The air cooled when she led them through an opening and back into the open air. They stood breathing hard at the foot of an enormous mound of glistening black shards that reminded him of a quarry back home. She led them up the hill at an angle, using one hand for balance. The lava here had been pulverized and deposited by a violent geologic event. When they were above the treetops and had more useful starlight, he could make sense of what might have happened. The volcano's hip had sprung a leak, spilling out tons of small black stones that contrasted with its own brown body. The rocks made tinkling, shell-like sounds when they tumbled away beneath them.

"Is this it?" he asked, but she again grunted for his silence.

She took them to a plateau on the volcano itself, a spot where the ground was level because the earth had collapsed when the stones had fallen out. They would climb five times as high in seven days. Or maybe it was ten times. They would climb until there was no more climbing to do.

She pulled him down to the dirt next to her, and he nearly cried out when he saw her blow the flame dead.

"It's okay," she whispered in a voice so soft that he mostly read her lips. "We can go the long way back. It's under the stars."

He would have sat right there until daylight before returning to the jungle with no candle. There hadn't been the usual swarming mosquitoes, but the air was filled with a symphony of restless legs and wings. He imagined the infinite tiny scenes of fighting and mating going on all around.

She leaned into him. "No more talk. They will be here soon."

He tried to relax, allowed his eyes to adjust. He blinked, then kept them open wide and focused on the lighter spots of the canopy. They had a view all the way to the sea, a black semicircle across the horizon, ocean darker than the land except where the waves broke and boiled. The air was chilly for the first time since he'd been washed up. The stars were an endless carpet of twinkling dots, and he could make out the trail of smoke from the volcano.

The jungle went silent, as though a switch had been flicked. The vibrating bodies, hoots and squeals, and the beating wings became still all at once. She squeezed his hand, and he could see her white teeth as if she were smiling wide. There was gooseflesh across her naked shoulder and her body shook. She snuggled in closer, and he wrapped an arm around her, trying to give some warmth.

Looking out into the dark, he imagined this must be what it was like taking your daughter to a movie—a daughter who is mostly naked and covered in cold sweat and dirt because she hasn't been recently cleaned by a legion of dancing spiders. This was a daughter not worried about too much homework, or a boy who likes her on the bus. She was child who had never tasted a blueberry Pop-Tart, but had already been violated by a stranger and sentenced to die by her father. She was a little girl who mostly wanted a kitten. He squeezed her again, but not too hard. He wished they were thousands of miles away, closer to his world rather than sitting with their backs turned to a not-so-restful volcano.

More details emerged as his eyes continued to adjust. Their view was out over a rounded clearing, maybe half the size of a football field. It was a wide bowl, with dark sides and a lighter bottom. Strewn across it were downed trees lying crisscrossed, with black smudges he recognized as humps of lava rock. What looked at first like fog was actually low brush, or maybe stray taro brought by thieving rodents that chewed the sweet parts and left pieces to grow and multiply.

Tiki suddenly flinched as if she'd touched an electric wire, and he heard her suck in a breath but not exhale. One hand pulled free and she pointed, and although he couldn't see what excited her, wind seemed to rattle the leaves at the left edge of the bowl, a few drooping vines swaying. The clearing was empty, but he watched her eyes follow something from one side to the other. Her eyes were huge, unblinking, and when a patch of jungle was disturbed on the right side, she quickly looked back to the other edge.

"What do you see?"

"She was so beautiful. Her hair was like mine, but she was prettier."

"Who?"

She shook her head, calmed her breathing to whisper. "She looked like Mama."

"I don't understand."

"They become almost like us. Almost, but not quite. They have bodies like ours to understand how easy it is to fall with only two legs. Stomachs like us to feel hunger and thirst. They have our hearts to know how simple they are to break."

"Who, Tiki? I don't understand."

She half turned and spoke slowly, reaching to put a hand flat against his chest, directly over his heart. "The Volcano God came as Mama, wore her eyes and her smile. She put on Mama's face to be near me."

"I couldn't see her."

He heard a sharp sound, a snapping limb, maybe, and both looked toward the field. She patted his chest once, and then clasped her hands together as if to pray. "Another is coming," she whispered through her fingers. "Look!"

But he saw only more vines being made to sway, and then shrubs that seemed to flatten, and spots of soft earth that compressed and filled with new shadows. The swirling breeze carried the scent of tropical flowers and salty fish, as well as the distant sound of jumbled voices, as though a radio dial was slowly turned across a hundred stations on a clear summer night.

She covered her mouth as if to stifle a cry, wide eyes again following the path of something spectacular.

"I hear them," he said, and she gave a quick nod.

"Look!" She pointed to where two palm trees leaned apart and dropped fruit with hollow thuds. "Maybe the sea, or maybe the sun. It's a giant god, but she has a disguise."

"What is she wearing?" he asked, but wasn't answered.

They sat silently watching the invisible procession of three more gods, as the breeze came up stronger and the chill crept deeper. By the time the insects resumed their conversations, Tiki was making little snoring sounds against his shoulder. A flock of birds took off from a shadowy corner of the clearing, and Dash squinted at a moving shape in a spot he hadn't noticed. There was another of the black lumps where lava had pushed up through the ground, maybe a hundred or a thousand years earlier. This stone bulge was wider, had formed a bench similar to the one he used before the airplane seats washed up.

A mostly human figure was sitting, had watched the parade of gods from a vantage not risked by mortals. Dash could tell the man-like creature had huge shoulders that slumped forward from unbearable sadness. The figure that was neither human nor godly slowly rose and turned from where Dash huddled with the girl. In a lumbering motion, the giant man took four long strides and stepped inside the thick jungle. Dash caught a glimpse of the tiny dangling light hanging over Willy's forehead before he disappeared.

Chapter 31

DASH WAS JARRED awake by the ground rumbling and the heavens answering. Lightning scored the roiling clouds beyond the hut's entryway, made white-hot lines in imperfect seams as if tasting the grass walls. His sleeping mat bucked and slid as the earth tilted hard. He dismounted, crawled to the threshold on unsteady boards, waved down at the four guards huddled on their own collection of mats in the scrub grass and dirt. The expressions of the strapping young men were bewildered; they were apparently still drunk and making no attempt to test their balance.

Villagers emerged from their own sleep, the sky creating a strobe effect on brown bodies stretching and hands rubbing upturned faces. Feet shuffled forward a step or two and then back, some moving side to side, a dance with their god they might have done before. Children were the first to be fully awake, finding their ball and dividing into teams out on the field. A lightning bolt connecting clouds to the tops of trees somewhere out in the jungle went unnoticed by the screaming players, was seen as nothing special. Men scratched their backs and pissed into the ferns next to their huts. Women began stoking cooking fires as on any other day, Dash in awe of their dispassion toward the pending apocalypse.

Clouds turned slow rotations over the volcano's peak, and Dash could make out the bird flocks gliding on the heated wind over the crater. There was thunder, but most of the noise came from the children, a happy game that took priority over end-of-times declarations from an attention-hungry god. He watched the boys and girls give chase and tumble, sometimes having to pause for the next bolt to show them where the ball rolled in past the jungle's edge.

Tiki came to him, stepping over the guards and wiggling into the narrow space next to where he watched the world as he'd never seen it.

He shook his head and looked down at her. "What does it mean?"

"Nothing. It's not time for us." She leaned into him and put an arm across his bony knee to rest her chin. "Manu wants to know if you're hungry."

"I couldn't eat." He leaned back against his hands, enjoying a perfect view of the volcano and sky.

"It's a hard climb," she said. "So many steps."

"You've been up there?"

"An older boy claimed this wasn't an island. He tried making us believe we were on the tip of a great land, and that Manu and the missioners lied to keep children from wandering off to places with buildings that touch the clouds. He said any kids who hiked the entire shore became confused, would see a river and not the sea, and that a bridge of dry earth would let us walk to the other side of the world. I climbed the Volcano to be sure."

"What did you see?"

She looked up, eyebrows scrunched. "It's an island. And it's smaller than I thought it would be."

His voice became a whisper. "Have you seen people thrown into the volcano?"

She was quiet for a moment, and then shook her head. She made crying sounds, and he felt her warm tears wander down his shins. "Only the grownups went to the top. But Manu says it's important for the whole village to witness our sacrifice. Even the kids."

Dash was startled by Willy's voice from behind. "People bounce and then roll down the steep interior. There are loose rocks and ash mounds, but they come to a fast stop against the boulders. They are hurt and bleeding, but most are still conscious. They've fallen two or three hundred feet, broken many bones. Sometimes they are screaming, and sometimes they are praying. It all depends. But you hear them because of the acoustics. It's a funnel shape, and voices rise on the heated air. And that's what gets them. The heat. No plunge into fire, no instant death. They slow roast like pigs over coals. It might be twenty minutes before their hair begins to smoke, and forty before it catches fire. The human body has good fuels inside, and the people looking down from the rim stay until the fire is burned out, until they know the Volcano has been satisfied."

Dash waited to see if Willy was done. He listened to the thunder and the shouting children, the sharp claps that followed the brightest flashes.

"I could hear your god talking," Tiki said, sniffling. "I couldn't understand what he was saying, but I could hear his voice."

Dash stroked her hair, touched the places where she must have tried hacking it away while he was drifting at sea. "He's not really my god. He's more of a friend, I think."

She turned her head to look up at him. "That's the best kind of god."

∽⋉

THE GUARDS CAME fully alert when a pack of kids ran across them, chasing their ball, one washboard stomach used as a launch pad, a perfect ashen footprint left as a temporary brand. The men cursed in their own language, looked up at Dash and cursed him, too. When Tiki lifted her head and glared down, the men looked embarrassed, got to their knees and seemed to become aware of the hullabaloo going on all around. The largest barked orders that sent one scurrying toward the chief's hut, while the other two sauntered off and cut to the front of the outhouse line.

Tiki sat up, but still leaned heavily. Her skin was cool in the humid air, eyes perfectly white despite all the tears. "Manu says the soldiers will be back soon."

"Did the volcano tell him?"

"She tells him everything. He says our sacrifice will send them away. But he calls it 'his sacrifice' because of me. Did you ever want children?"

"Yes, someday."

The tone of her voice altered, turned bitter. "If I had children I would keep them safe instead of killing them."

The vent's billowing smoke changed color, went from orange to red in a swirling vortex. Lightning flashed over the expanding mass in super-heated tunnels, fat arteries and a mesh of tiny capillaries. It wanted to grow a heart, Dash realized, wanted to come to life in a way it didn't yet understand. Perhaps a lack of any soul kept it an angry mountain, limited it to brief monthly visits in a masked human form.

Dash knew how to mix vinegar and baking soda for science class projects, but was clueless about the stages of eruption, or even if there were stages. Maybe each volcano behaved differently, the important workings deep inside the earth, somewhere in its distant brain. But the abrupt shifting of the ground made it feel close to something big, its remaining fibers poised to snap. The low haze had gone from amber to a deep shade of yellow, the odor sharper, a spoiled food smell beyond the stench of rotten eggs.

"Brimstone," he said.

"Who's that?"

"Not a person," he said. "It's a stone that burns. Someone I knew used to say it a lot."

"Sarah?"

"No, it was actually someone on television who was more like a missioner. She was on late at night, and my college friends played a game where you took a sip of booze, of clap-clap, every time she said the word."

"The men here would play that game."

The real draw to the cable-access show was the lovely preacher's gothic looks, which half the guys argued was unintended. Jet black hair that fell to her ass, heavy boots that nearly reached a knee-length skirt, leaving flashes of pale skin that drove everyone nuts. She used the same middle finger knuckle on her right hand to push up librarian-style glasses on a silver chain. She pounded the lectern and shook a fist in the air. There was an old-fashioned blackboard with the message of the day written in thick script as a backdrop.

"Brimstone!" she would herald, head thrown back, long fragile throat exposed above a white rectangle.

"Drink!" they'd sing, tipping shot glasses all at once, and then slamming them down for refills. Victory to the last man standing.

She was a caged animal stalking the stage, spitting scripture for venom, Bible clasped as a weapon or shield.

"Brimstone!"

"Drink!"

"Brimstone!"

Sarah was missing in action the week after they'd met. Everyone claimed to have just seen her, but nobody knew where she was. Check this guy's room, or maybe she's with that guy. Give her time, buddy, she's gotta come up for air sooner or later. Dash was alone and already drunk when the preacher came on that night. He sat with a bottle half empty, microwave chirping that his burrito was done.

The word 'suicide' was written in the preacher's harried strokes, slashed across the blackboard in lowercase script.

The preacher ranted about the evils of the unforgivably selfish act of taking one's own life. He forgot his food, remembered the private family room's smell, where the funeral home director had led him and his mom before his father's viewing. It was an escape from well-meaning mourners, a place to rest your ears more than anything. He supposed the wilted flowers were recycled from earlier services, one more shot to brighten misery. A cold cut tray and pre-sliced rolls sat preserved and untouched beneath stretched plastic. He considered the significance of the knife's absence.

"Brimstone!"

"Drink," he'd answered, lifting the bottle and resolving to pick a bushel of flowers for his shitty room if he woke in the morning.

The camera zoomed in on the preacher, tongue moving across her bottom lip, specks of perspiration where tears might gather. She inhaled deeply then spoke directly to Dash. "Three words to know, to write down and copy a hundred times, and to share with everyone you touch …."

He looked around his room, but his notebook was zipped away in a backpack.

The preacher stepped in front of the blackboard and pulled down on its wood frame. It rotated to display the other side, where three words were written in the same script: *suicide hurts, amen.*

"Words from our Lord and Savior," said the preacher, turning back to the camera, hair swishing back over thickly padded shoulders. She righted her glasses then lifted the Bible over her head with two hands, head down, shirt pulled taut across full breasts. "Suicide hurts," she said.

"Amen," Dash whispered, putting down the imaginary knife he'd been holding to his wrist.

"Amen," Willy repeated from behind, the rumbles and

lightning waning as the sun began its rise from the hidden sea.

"Amen," said Tiki, who was smiling, watching the storm recede.

One less morning remained in Dash's life. He considered the active volcano might draw attention from the outside world, but there must be dozens if not hundreds of similar events, many within easier reach. And they were likely beyond the time when scientists would have evacuated, instruments left to record and transmit data, as well as providing the fate of recalcitrant villagers refusing to leave.

A new mist descended over the compound, and Dash held out a palm to discover it was a fine, gray powder. *More snow,* he thought, weighed down with despair. *Soon it will shower rocks, and then it will rain lava. But I'll be long dead, and won't get to see any of the real fireworks. Manu was right about the volcano keeping the soldiers away once and for all. They'll have no reason to come to a barren atoll populated only by charred skeletons half buried in cooling lava. No more pretty little girls.*

He touched Tiki's lopsided hair as they watched the four guards convene in the morning light, adjusting their underpants, the one back from Manu's hut talking fast, pointing up at the volcano. Their hair had turned white, as if they'd suddenly grown old.

"I wish I could have a kitten for one day," she whispered, right hand stroking his forearm. He could feel her sharp fingernails, could see how ragged they'd become from her new bad habit of chewing and spitting the tiny pieces.

He wondered how far the little amber disk had floated.

Chapter 32

———

COOKING FIRES WERE kept burning to light the afternoon when the sun was nearly snuffed out. Dash and Tiki sat over untouched food bowls left on the hut's front steps. Their last supper was the same as every other meal, except that this one was coated with ash from the persistent flurry.

A line of young men formed in front of the stage curtain after someone got the idea to use the ceremonial paints. Bright red triangles were drawn on cheeks and foreheads to represent the volcano. It was the same color that had been used on the women's nipples to entice Dash's libido. The demeanors of the decorated men changed once the paint was applied. Each one stalked away from the woman doing the artwork energized, ready for a fight.

"They look dumb," said Tiki. "I draw better volcanoes."

"The island is turning into a snow globe." Dash watched the smoky dome and wafting ash. "My father's store had glass balls with winter scenes inside, and loose plastic shavings for snow. The balls were filled with water and some kind of clear oil that made it thicker, so the snow fell slower. You turned it upside down and shook, and the scene became a winter wonderland. People collect them."

She held out a hand to catch a flake of ash. "I think the Volcano turned us upside down."

"And she's still shaking," he said. "I guess we'll be going in a few hours. Did Manu say how long?"

She ignored the question. "Is Sarah pretty?"

"Pretty on the outside. The kind of pretty that made me wonder why she fell in love with me."

"But she wasn't pretty inside?"

"She hurt me."

He pictured the disheveled bed. The sheet was an escaping ghost half on the floor, blanket pushed across his nightstand. They'd broken the shade of a hundred-year-old lamp, a gift from his mother. Maybe it was a Hong Kong knockoff. Tommy Chamber's hairy ass fully visible as they humped away directly on the dimpled mattress skin. Sarah's fingers were claws, nails pressing deep enough to puncture flesh, touch bone.

"You were going to marry her."

"Love does messed-up things. I hated what she did to me, but I lost control of my life. Her power over me was humiliating."

"Like when someone opens the outhouse door when you're not done?"

"Sure," he said. "It was just like that. But I convinced myself she'd change. I wanted to believe."

"Manu says I can't be loved because of what the soldier did, and no man will ever want me. The Volcano God is the only thing left for me because the soldier made me dirty and spoiled."

"Manu is wrong." His voice made her flinch. "What happened didn't change you. It was nothing but violence, something a weak man does to feel powerful. But even if you're small and have tiny muscles, you can still be stronger than the man who hurt you."

"I'm more valuable to the Volcano than the village."

"Manu is shit for saying that. He's giving the soldier power, and that's the opposite of what anyone should do."

"He's my father."

"Fathers are wrong all the time. My father was a coward for leaving us. He did the weakest thing possible," Dash said, then added, "except for what Manu is doing to you."

"You think Manu is a coward?"

"It's a cowardly thing for sure," he said. "A wise friend taught me where gods are born. You know how to see gods, how to get close to them. But do you know where they are made?"

She thought for a minute, and then shrugged.

He spoke slowly. "People create them from nothing. They are invented to fix broken lives, when a god is needed the most. A god becomes real when people believe he is real. You told me I needed faith, to welcome the gods into my heart. Maybe I was too broken, or maybe I was just too broken before I met you. You taught me belief is everything, the most powerful thing in the world."

"Like how magic works."

He nodded. "And you have to understand that the soldier is a coward, driven by his own fears of what he really is. He has no power to change who you are, unless you believe in him. It's entirely up to you."

"He was strong," she whispered. "I fought, but he was too strong."

"Shitter bugs move balls of poop that would be mountains to us."

"He's a shitter bug, right?"

Dash reached out, put fingers under her chin to lift her face. "Maybe someone with a heart like Sarah's never gets better, but cuts and bruises heal. Chopped off hair grows back. I believe you are the same beautiful girl as always."

She smiled.

"And bee stings heal," he said, and also smiled. "Do you know what a princess is?"

"I think so. There was a story in one of the burned books. A princess is a girl who marries a prince to get her glass shoe back."

"Okay, yes, and a princess is also a girl who will one day become queen of a village filled with people who love her."

"I want to be a princess."

"You already are a princess. You have a beautiful heart everyone loves. Manu learned things in another time, when people didn't know any better."

She fidgeted with one of the bowls, flattening the rice and then making indentations to form a face. She looked up at him. "Nobody will have a chance to love me, because I'll be dead."

⤝⤟

THE DRINKING CIRCLE grew louder as the painted men took their places. They laughed and elbowed each other, full of bluster as the cup made the rounds. The sounds were raw—backs being slapped, slurred curses, loud spitting. Dash guessed the young men were boasting in their language about girls they claimed to have kissed, fish they supposedly caught. Dash was an insider when it came to those lies, had joined right in at the beer pong table a hundred times.

When the ash fell thicker, Dash and Tiki moved back under cover and shared a mat. The air grew more humid, and thunder rolled back heavier than ever as their final afternoon passed into night. Everything was cast in the color of unhealthy skin. The sky's energy competed with the volcano to shake the buildings, knocking dead bugs and dry leaf slivers from the walls and ceilings to litter floors. A new wind mixed up the trash, carried some out to where the fog swirled like a wizard's hands. Great gusts occasionally pushed aside the haze to provide a fleeting glimpse of a moon nearly in balance, half black and half bright. Then darkness would fold back over, dirt shoveled onto a coffin.

"Maybe it'll rain," Tiki said in a hopeful voice. "I miss rain."

There'd only been a few brief showers since he'd woken after the plane crash. The drought was longer than most, judging by recent grumbling over how low the cistern level had dropped. The water tasted like poison, even worse when Manu ordered it boiled. There was no escaping the ash.

Lightning crashed close enough to share its heat, and Tiki cried out, covering both ears, cringing from the explosion that didn't come. Dash rose from his knees with old man grunts, ducked through the entryway. The four guards had turned gray in the gloom; only their eye sockets and where they'd dribbled clap-clap proof they weren't ghosts. The men parted from a huddle, Dash catching sight of the jug one had hidden behind his back. Not even the churning sulfur mist hid the smell of gasoline mixed with rotten fruit.

"Bottoms up, shitheads."

Dash stepped down into the night and then pushed his way through. Tiki's footsteps slapped against the wood floor to catch up. Off to his right, the elders continued drinking in their uneven circle, oblivious to Dash or the growing tempest. The women still tended the fires, darting in and out of huts to feed the coals. All the candles had blown out or suffocated.

Dash walked to the center of the playing field, left tracks past the crude soccer ball that might have been a decapitated head. The ball sat abandoned, with a stretched and deeply tanned layer of skin. He guessed it was made of pig and stuffed with grass or ferns.

Something struck Dash's forehead, and then his right shoulder. His chest was hit twice, his stomach and cheeks. When he was nearly convinced he was being pummeled with small rocks, the rain made itself known to the entire village and jungle beyond. The night creatures went silent, pausing from their quest for food, territorial claims, and romantic lures to find shelter.

He glanced back. The drinking circle was now brown men

with shiny vertical streaks stumbling to their feet, and Tiki was a few steps in front of two guards who followed. All were cast in silhouette by fires still hot enough to boil away the heavy drops.

The rain was glorious. Dash turned from the villagers, slipped his underpants down and stepped free. He shut his eyes and lifted his face to let the cold drops beat down and run over his skin in rivers of cascading fresh water. Like the moon and stars, it was the same rain as back home. But this was better than celestial objects thousands and millions of miles away because the rain enveloped him, touched every part of his lonely body. It ran across his lips, across blue veins carrying blood from his broken heart. The rain splashed down over his ruined privates now dangling free.

"I can feel the rain," Dash said, opening his eyes and looking back to where Tiki and the guards stood. They too were naked, discarded underpants in lumps. Beyond them was an approaching crowd, perhaps the entire population. In the now faltering flames, it took Dash a moment to comprehend their strange dance, each person stopping to hop from foot to foot, then continuing forward. He realized they were all removing their underpants, kicking them away, allowing the rain the touch them everywhere.

He smiled and could see a flash of white where Tiki's mouth was in shadow. He raised both arms, hands reaching toward the source of the rain. She also raised her arms, as did the guards. Beyond them, the field was crowded with glistening naked bodies also lifting their hands to the heavens, heads tilted up with parted lips.

"Simon says," he whispered, closing his eyes.

"Simon says," Tiki repeated.

The lightning returned close and bright, finding the tops of nearby trees, but nobody left the field until the last raindrop had fallen.

Chapter 33

━━

THE MIST CONTINUED its dance as they climbed the volcano. Thicker in places, it trapped and echoed their raspy breath and shuffling feet. Other spots were black holes, crevasses that might contain creatures worse than any spider. The sulfur stink had gotten inside Dash's body, was in his mouth, burned his tongue and soured his spit. It was in his tears and dripping nose, and probably in his blood and heart. He breathed it in and coughed stained yellow puffs.

He craned his neck to see the chiseled stones rise in the constant flashes and glow from the orange dome. Hundreds of steps to go, a staircase from base to summit of the trembling mountain. It was the view from the front roller coaster car that faced its first terrifying tower. What went up would go down real fast, and he knew they'd be going faster than any mere fun park ride. Their free fall would be the real deal.

Even the fishermen, accustomed to unstable footing in rough seas, were struggling for balance. People held hands, turned themselves into four-legged creatures as they continued the precarious ascent. There was no easy way to stand on the shaking ground, the steps changing height and the treacherous loose gravel either slick or sharp underfoot. Tiki held his hand, a set of guards in front and behind. Manu led every member of the village, including the very old and the women about to give birth. A few clutched dripping candles that weren't necessary and wouldn't stay lit.

Another hundred steps and Dash's lungs forced him to stop. He guessed they were ten times higher than the tallest tree, and was glad he could not see. He let go of Tiki's hand to grab his knees and wait for his breath to return. The air had gone less foul, as though some of the poison cooked away as they got closer. Falling ash was hotter, some pieces on fire, blinking fireflies on the swirling wind. He pictured the final clash of fire and water, when the volcano had consumed everything, had incinerated the last morsel of fragile life to come face to face with a battle that might not be winnable. Dash couldn't choose a side, not after drifting in the ocean's empty expanse that had also wanted him dead.

"Come." Tiki put her hand in his again, urging him on. Her fingers were cold, but only his were trembling as they climbed higher.

He counted steps—fifty since their last break—as the mostly double-wide line of villagers spread thinner. Now the birds were landing all around. The ones trying for flat purchase on the steps were unceremoniously kicked away. Those alighting on the steep rock face scrambled for hold in miniature landslides. Still more than a hundred steps from the summit, he could see the mass of birds on the ground above. They were agitated and fighting, pecking at one another, sooty feathers set free to dance on the increasing wind. The birds had been cornered; the ocean was never safe at night, and fire now rained on the treetops. The sky might be the least safe, electricity rushing among the clouds.

He counted sixty steps, eyes focused above. Heat from the rising magma set off mini-tornadoes that sucked in and swallowed some of the smaller birds, made them disappear.

She squeezed his hand. "Closer," he heard her say.

Closer to what? To sitting down and resting my burning legs? Closer to death? He didn't have the breath to ask.

As Manu's lead group reached the summit, a severe jolt sent most to their knees. The stairs fractured directly up the middle, the mountain pushing outward to open a vertical crack a few inches wide. Some people fell backwards and were caught, while others rolled and tumbled down the steep rocky face. In a series of bright flashes, he saw another much larger fissure open lower down, off to one side. Smoke or steam billowed from the wound, and at least a dozen villagers slid or bounded into the glowing space and were gone forever.

There was a renewed sense of urgency to continue, a brown tide surging from the gash and perilous steps toward the level summit. Those who had already arrived were urging climbers on with words and waving arms, were silhouetted against the fire reflecting off low clouds. Dash saw them not as people, but as demons welcoming them to hell. Tiki might have had a similar impression, her upward motion hesitating at the image. Birds had spread their black wings at the feet of demons, beaks open to scream territorial claims.

"I can't," she said.

He looked behind to where the frantic villagers were closing the gap they'd somehow managed, then realized their trailing guards were gone. He supposed the cocksure young men hadn't gone to their knees when the big jolt hit, had fallen down the mountain because they refused to look cowardly. Dash was elated by their misfortune, hoped they'd made it all the way to the new hole while still alive and fully aware. It served them right for their part in this, and too damn bad they were going to miss out on the chance to give him his final shove. What a great honor to bestow on young men normally in charge of cutting back jungle paths or weaving fish nets. But then he was miserable that anyone was dead. What grade would the boys have been in if they were all back in Vermont? Juniors in high school? Sophomores? They would be riding dirt bikes on their grandpa's back forty, and begging for the keys to the pickup to take girls parking at the closed drive-in. Stolen beer and French kisses instead of gods erupting with hate.

The crowd took the decision away from Dash and Tiki. With only a few dozen remaining, it was climb or be pushed off the steps.

"Here!" It was Manu's majestic voice, still the chief and very much in charge. Dash found the old man's face flanked by the two remaining guards, all with outstretched arms. He and Tiki were whisked up and onto flat earth by the strong young men, Dash's heart pounding, sweat pouring from his emaciated body. Tiki fell to her side, landing on small birds that complained but begrudged her the space. Dash tried going to her, but the anxious voices and groping hands of people consumed by fear and panic held him back.

They were led through the sea of birds toward an oven of impossible heat, and Dash had his first look inside its belly. The crater seemed perfectly round, maybe a hundred feet across. A huge stone slab had been set at the very edge, the rock's color out of place. It was a thousand pound behemoth probably hauled from the shoreline to serve as a ceremonial diving board. Wood wouldn't do up here with this heat, overlooking a pool of bubbling lava. Not a single bird dared set foot on the sacred launch pad; there were no droppings and no feathers. The rock was barren, waiting to bear the weight of the next human victim.

They were ushered by the survivors of the climb, pushed and pulled out onto the rock's hot surface, and Tiki again clambered for his hand. Her fingers were tiny, almost nothing, and perhaps her bones were as hollow as the protesting birds. He could hear her misery, pulled her against his stomach and put his free hand across her crinkly hair. Manu barked orders that caused reaching fingers to pry them apart, maybe to be sure the Volcano God knew they were two separate gifts. They stood touching as best they could.

The volcano's noise was vaguely familiar. Dash had experienced the same rush of air, of something enormous and unstoppable approaching when he took Sarah into New York City. He'd watched locals step back from the subway platform when this same noise began its approach from down the dark tunnel. And just as he'd seen in the black subway tube, there was a glowing orb at the bottom of the volcano's pulsating throat. It was orange and yellow, and blinked like the eye of a dragon.

The ground pitched again and the rim changed shape to the right of where Dash held Tiki, shuffling for balance. Dirt and rock broke free under the feet of people who'd managed to find a better view of the ceremony. He caught a glimpse of two women bounding head to feet, outstretched arms left behind, hands reaching but empty. The women gained speed, hair whipping, naked rag dolls that tumbled to a stop in the shadows. Had he known them? Had they cooked his meals or made the candles that held off the dark? One might have been the young woman he'd failed in the love hut, who'd touched him so wonderfully, had volunteered or been chosen to carry the baby meant to save them all.

Manu's voice made Dash turn his back to the awful blinking eye. Tiki still moaned, eyes shut, rubbing her face against his arm, catlike. Dash supposed this was what shock did to a child. If only his mind could shut down, take him away from this place. He tried summoning the icy brook behind his parents house where he fished alone as a kid. In the shade of trees that gave sweet syrup and home to peaceful birds, he figured out how to thread the worm onto a hook without a father's help. But Dash was too weak for the safe images to make any real difference. The heat on his shoulders might have been less intense, the sea of strutting birds reduced to a blur of smudged beaks. But Dash knew where he was, had a clear vision of the agony to come.

Manu stood with a sentry at each scrawny shoulder. The old chief's eyes betrayed an ocean of fear he had for his people.

"It is the way," Manu said, his tone nearly apologetic for the first time, as if he meant to say he was sorry, but had no choice.

"Let her live," Dash said, but had no energy to beg. "Let your daughter go."

Manu reached up to touch her face. "Listen to me, girl. Can you hear?"

Dash felt her head nod against his stomach.

"There is nothing to fear. You will see your mama very soon. Her loving arms will catch you." The chief's voice was meant to be soothing, perhaps even fatherly. "I have a message for you to deliver, and I need your promise. Do you understand?"

Again she nodded.

"Tell her that I love her, and that I did my best. Tell her I will come soon, once our people are safe. Do you hear me, girl? Do you understand my words? "

"Yes, Papa."

Manu stepped back, motioned the sentries up onto the rock, and then faced the mass of crowding people. He raised his leathery chin to the clouds and began reciting words in rapid bursts of his own language. A prayer. An appeal for mercy? Dash searched his mind to see if any prayer-like words might be hidden among the mounds of clutter and trash. There were none.

Tiki's hand was wrenched from his grasp, and they were turned to face the ledge. Both were shoved to the very edge of the precipice, Tiki waving her arms to keep from falling. Dash thought he heard gasps from behind. The heat wanted to lift his hair, and he imagined the greatest balloon ever rising up and carrying them away, along with the entire island.

Tiki found his hand again and he squeezed, but not too hard. He looked down at dirty toes curled over the front of the giant stone. He was hanging ten in what would have to be a surfer's absolute worst nightmare. "Cowabunga, dude," he said, then took a deep breath and laughed.

Manu shouted his final order.

Tiki looked up at Dash, who must have still had the amused look on his face because her beautiful smile was the last thing he saw before they were pushed.

Chapter 34

———

DASH DIDN'T DIE. His body never reached the burning cauldron, or even the scorched rocks. Something with superhuman strength snatched his shaggy hair, snapping his head back so hard that every joint in his body popped. The air was knocked from his lungs, and he reached for his throat, expecting an Old West noose, trapdoor sprung from under dangling feet after a two-foot plunge. Did those horse thieves and stagecoach bandits catch a glimpse of the ground before their necks were broken from the short fall? Dash thought it perfectly reasonable for a condemned outlaw to retain a final hopeful thought of hitting the ground boots first, spurs spinning, ready to hop into the saddle of the surprised sheriff's trusty mare for a gallop into the sunset. He'd be slapping reins to giddy the hell up before the posse reeled him back in, somewhere in the microsecond before the rope tightened.

"Giddy up," Dash tried saying, twisting at the waist but getting nowhere.

The sexy television preacher had devoted an entire episode to death, to a person's walk toward the guiding beacon of the Kingdom of Heaven. But she'd uttered the drinking game prompt too early and too often that night, rendered the entire party shit-faced before Dash had learned anything useful. The sermon's early parts made no mention of a celestial beam roasting your toes like marshmallows; there was nothing about a beacon singeing the hair from your legs, or a light staring up from the bottom of a pit like the eye of a hungry monster.

Dash smelled his burning hair, saw the violent creature below his feet blink. He didn't know what was gumming up the volcano's plan for swallowing him. He only knew his head was caught in a vise. And that he did not want to roast to death, sizzling and then bursting into flames fed by what oily fat remained in his skinny carcass. He tried wriggling free of his purgatory, but there was simply no give.

He shifted his dangling weight and was rewarded with a lung full of painfully hot air. He took a second breath, and then a third. It was a dance to remain conscious, the blackness coming close and then receding. His underpants slid off, fluttered down and out of sight.

Good riddance. You can have my dirty underwear. Enjoy.

In what he suspected was the boldest act of his entire existence, he used his newly extended life to roll his tongue and find the last bit of thick saliva. He gathered the ball of phlegm in the middle of his tongue and drew a breath. He used all his might to spit in the dragon's eye, a tiny glistening speck of defiance that evaporated almost instantly.

A small voice came from next to him. "It hurts."

He tried finding Tiki, but could only move his eyes. She was alive at the edge of his peripheral vision, and he realized she hadn't let go of his hand. Hidden by the pain in his head was the touch of her shaking fingers.

"Tiki."

"I wanted to see Mama."

"I know."

"I miss her."

Before he could console her, his neck was bent backward,

and there was a sudden rush of acceleration. Another light appeared, although this one much smaller—a gentle glow rather than a slice of blazing sun. It was familiar, as comforting as the lightning bugs he chased across his grandmother's manicured lawn as a child.

The good light blinked, and then he was dropped hard on his bare ass, Tiki uttering a sharp squeal next to him. There was enormous relief when his head was released. He looked up at the giant thighs, the bulging muscles of their savior.

He rubbed the back of his sore head where the former god's steel grip had seized him. "Hey, Willy."

Willy squatted to put a hand on Dash's bent knee. "You never believed I was real."

The touch seemed perfectly human, warm and caring. The villagers stepped back, as if to make room for something they weren't sure they were seeing.

"That's not true."

Willy cocked his head.

"Well, I always hoped you were real," he admitted, embarrassed because Willy knew better.

"You're a tough one to figure out, my friend. Most men would have knelt down and prayed for me to fix their broken wang."

"Would you have done it? Would you have fixed me?"

Willy made a scoffing noise. "You would have found another dangerous crack to stick it in."

Dash sighed. "You're probably right."

"I'll miss you, Cracker. It can't be the same after I take the big plunge."

"What if it kills you?"

Willy glanced over the edge, specs of orange fire reflecting from his black eyes. The light above his forehead pulsed. "She can't kill me. I'm pretty much indestructible as long as there are people who believe in me."

"What about our friendship? What about the airplane seats?"

"There will be too many voices. I'll have to stick to coming around once a month when the moon is black and humans can't see me." Willy looked down at Tiki. "Most humans, that is."

"You really want to take care of these people?"

Willy shrugged his mighty shoulders. "I will if they want me to. They aren't so bad. They just need their hope restored. That's second on my to-do list."

"What if it doesn't work?"

"Oh, it's gotta work. Who can resist a good resurrection?" said Willy, standing back up and taking a step toward the edge of the slab. He leaned out. "You know what I see down there? I see the light at the end of the tunnel."

"It's lava, Willy."

The enormous man turned and pointed at Tiki, who'd scrambled to bury her head against Dash. "That one's a real cutie. If you take her away, there's something you have to buy her."

Dash nodded. "A kitten."

"There are all kinds of good shots for allergies. You'll get used to having one around."

"I'll buy her two. I promise."

"I know you will, Cracker, I can read your mind."

Chapter 35

—

THE VILLAGE WAS busy in the sleeping volcano's shadow. There was plenty of bickering at first, everybody with an opinion over the design of their new totem. Manu wanted the fish heads up as soon as possible; he was anxious to keep their new god pleased. The hard part was the spiny dorsal fin arching over the carved face, and all those needle-like teeth meant raiding sticker bushes up and down the beach.

The haze and sulfur smell had lifted. Rain had scrubbed most of the ash, refilled the cistern. The taro crop was lost, but the fields had been turned and tubers planted. Fishing had never been better, skiffs returning with hulls heavy in the water and difficult to steer from all the whoppers that practically jumped into the boats. The drinking circle was unusually animated with tales of monsters that had gotten away, fish that dragged boats and chewed through the sturdiest lines.

Manu declared their island's new name was once again its old name, words that translated to 'No Hurry' in English.

"Long live the people of Moku Siga," said the old chief, lifting a full cup toward the volcano, his bloodshot eyes narrow and defiant.

As days passed under blue skies, time did seem to slow. The pace of life on Moku Siga began to live up to its name. Elders left the shade of their huts to sit cross-legged along the edge of the soccer field for the first time. They squinted at the mass of dirty children, crooked fingers pointing out grandsons and granddaughters. The old people hooted and cheered even though they didn't understand the game.

Dash decorated the former love hut with washed up treasures. His most recent score was a Mr. Potato Head with eyes, one pink ear, and a mustache. Like the stars, moon, and the rain, the toy was a link to home. Enough of one that Dash hadn't rebuilt the signal fire, at least not yet. His wang still failed him, but he was no longer fodder for the volcano. With the pressure off, maybe his wang would come around. Some of the new ceremonies had turned pretty spicy, and he'd felt a definite stir down there once or twice. He mostly steered clear of the drinking circle to keep the rest of him from going numb.

Willy accepted gifts. Villagers left a bounty of strung shells, woven vine wreaths, and lush bouquets of the sweetest smelling flowers. They switched to coconut milk when jugs of clap-clap were left untouched. Not a crumb of fresh octopus remained once the ink sacs were removed—that was Dash's suggestion. And the people knew their virgins were their own to defile, and that their mighty new god would never go for that human sacrifice malarkey. This god had seen enough death, had no interest in any more graves being dug.

Dash hadn't spoken to Willy since being reeled back in from the volcano. Willy had been right about things being different. Gods heard too many voices to be lounging around in washed-up airplane seats watching birds dive-bomb fish. Willy's big plunge had spoken volumes, had left no doubt where the real magic could be found. He'd put all those Acapulco cliff divers to shame with a quadruple twisting double backflip that elicited sounds of awe, delight in a place it didn't belong. No head-to-toe tumble down the rocky interior; those giant leg muscles easily propelled his mass out over the fiery pond. Villagers dropped to their knees when the dragon's eye went dark, the mountain's breath having been cut off. The earth stopped shifting and the clouds began rolling away. A child whispered, "Weeleekonawahulahoopa," and it was one of the loveliest sounds Dash ever heard.

"Weeleekonawahulahoopa," Dash had repeated. "My friend."

Not many people bothered looking up when a boy came charging out of the tunnel connecting the village to the lagoon. Dash did, because he'd been raised to expect unpleasant surprises, would probably never fully trust a higher being to watch over him, not even Willy. But he knew these people believed in their protector, had allowed peace to embrace them.

First the boy ran to the women at the main cooking fire, but was sent away with a slap to the bottom. Next he went to the women constructing the new fish head totems that were still missing spines and lures. They too scolded the boy, who was apparently told to knock off the tomfoolery and go play ball with the other children.

Dash stepped down from his love hut home when Manu emerged from his hut on wobbly legs. The chief looked a hundred years old, obviously suffering from another late night of hard drinking and long story telling, both shaky hands shielding the midday sun. When the old man strolled over to join him, Dash noticed Manu's underpants were on backwards.

Tiki's voice rose from the soccer scrum, firm and more confident since the night on the volcano. He watched her bend to pick up the ball, stopping the game around the frantic boy. The kids were all huffing, dripping sweat on the dusty field. "What's your fussing about?"

The boy, also winded, took a half-minute to catch his breath. He pointed to the tunnel, eyes wild, as if he'd seen the devil. "They're here," he finally said.

The children were quiet enough to hear laughter coming

from within the dark vegetation. Dash could make out English words spoken with an Australian accent, felt the hatred and revulsion surge, but didn't leave Manu's side. And none of the villagers stopped what they were doing. Not a single person moved to the center of the compound to kneel down for the white soldiers' arrival.

Tiki had the ball tucked under one arm, was fingering her new necklace, a small coral carving of a strange looking fish head hanging from a thin strip of vine. She spoke to the children, who nodded and then dropped to their butts one by one. She turned her back to them, and marched toward the sound of boastful alien voices.

It was the first time Dash had seen the soldiers, or whatever they were. They were dressed in identical tan khaki shirts and pants, each with a rifle strapped over one shoulder. The man in the lead wore a sweat-stained bush hat, its loose cord bouncing against his Adam's apple with each step of a heavy black boot.

Tiki intercepted the men halfway to Manu's hut, stopping with her feet planted wide, ball on her hip. The lead soldier towered over the girl as he stood looking her up and down, wide smirk settling across uneven whiskers. He spit into the dirt and pulled a green bandana from a back pocket, then removed his hat to wipe his brow. He unfurled the bandana with a jerk of the wrist and ran the tattered cloth through his red hair.

"His orange hair," Dash whispered, feeling a hand touch his arm and take hold of his bicep. Maybe it was there to hold him back, but more likely it was for support.

"Trust what you believe," said the old chief in a voice as numb and broken as Dash's private parts. "What will be, will be."

The soldier was still smiling when he replaced his hat and tucked away the bandana. Tiki's hands clenched into fists, and the ball dropped from her side. It rolled across the dark spot where the soldier had spit.

"I remember you, little one." The red-haired man squatted, rifle butt touching the ground by his heels. "We could use a few like you to come for a ride in our boat. How 'bout you introduce me to some of your pretty young friends?"

A breeze tumbled dead leaves, made soft rustling sounds that drifted across the sunbaked compound. The villagers whispered, perhaps a new prayer, their backs turned to an old god. The jungle paused, insects stopping mid-chore, snakes forgetting their hunger, birds leaning close.

"I have a brand new friend," Tiki said to the soldier, and Dash could tell from behind that her chin was tilted up, and he guessed that she was smiling. "His name is Willy."

A shadow fell over the soldiers.

COLE ALPAUGH is a former journalist, having worked at daily newspapers along the East Coast, as well as spending several years as a war correspondent in numerous hot spots around the world for Manhattan-based news agencies. His work has appeared in dozens of magazines, as well as most newspapers in America. He was nominated by Gannett News Service for a 1991 Pulitzer Prize. Cole is currently a freelance photographer and writer living in Northeast Pennsylvania, where he spends his afternoons watching his daughter hit fuzzy yellow balls and ski through slalom gates. You can find Cole online at ColeAlpaugh.com.

Made in the USA
Middletown, DE
01 May 2015